COUNTERSTRIKE

BOOK THREE
OF THE
BLACK FLEET TRILOGY

JOSHUA DALZELLE

Edited by Monique Happy Editorial Services
www.moniquehappy.com

Prologue:

Location: Unknown.

Time: Late twenty-third century.

"Hey!"

Colonel Robert Blake blinked against the bright light overhead and tried to move his arm up to shield his sensitive eyes again. Once again he was unable to do so. His mind felt like mush and he knew that he must have just recently been brought out of hibernation. He'd experienced the whole process during his mission training, but the side-effects this time seemed much more extreme.

"Come on, Siddell! Let me out of the restraints," he said again, calling out to the *Carl Sagan*'s medical officer and the woman who would have supervised their awakenings. He could hear the echo of his own voice and was relieved that at least his ears were working. "I promise I won't try to get up and walk yet... I just want to cover my eyes and scratch my nose."

"State your name," a deep, emotionless voice called out. It was an omnipresent sound, seeming to come from everywhere.

"Who is this?" Blake demanded.

"State your name," the voice said again.

"Blake."

"Blake," the voice repeated. "Colonel Robert, mission commander."

"Yes," Blake said. His mind was racing and the first twinges of panic were beginning to set in. "Who are you? Where am I? Please let me out of my restraints."

"Your body is not restrained," the voice informed him, now taking on a sympathetic tone. "I have simply not restored control of your voluntary musculature to your brain yet. Not until we have had a chance to discuss some matters."

"Who are you?"

"Let me ask you a question before I answer that," Voice said. "How long do you think you have been in space, Robert?"

"This is our first hibernation," Blake said, trying to kick his brain into gear. "No more than six months."

"Where do you think you are currently?"

"En route to the Proxima Centauri star system," Blake answered. "I'm not answering any more questions until I get a couple of answers myself."

"Very well, Robert," Voice said. "You have been in a form of suspended animation for just over two hundred and fifty of your years. Your species would understand the condition as death."

Death? My species? "Please," Blake whispered. "Please… who are you?"

"I am the lead researcher on a ship that encountered your craft, powerless and drifting through interstellar space," Voice said. "From what I've been able to deduce from my examination of your craft, you've not yet encountered an intelligent, space-faring species other than yourselves. Your isolation is as much for your protection as it is for mine. Your environment is sealed and sterile until we can acclimate your body to conditions aboard our vessel. The isolation serves a dual purpose, as my physical appearance could be somewhat distressful to you until you've had time to process events."

Crazily enough, there were actually protocols in one of his mission manuals for just such an occurrence. Tsuyo scientists had felt the risk of encountering alien life was low, but the U.S. military had decided that any risk was worth having contingency plans in place for. Blake had read through the manual during their flight out of the Solar System and found it to be utterly, utterly absurd. Now, face to face with just such a scenario, he found it to be even more so.

Blake drifted in and out of consciousness a few times, vaguely aware that there was movement around him but unable to fully wake himself and focus. When he was finally able to shake away the lethargy he found that his body responded when he tried to move. He slowly swung his legs over the side of the hard, unforgiving table he'd been lying upon and looked around the room.

It was stark white, circular, and apparently seamless. In fact, the table, walls, floor, and ceiling appeared to be constructed from one continuous piece of what felt like some sort of ceramic. He looked down at his skin and saw that it was grey, mottled, and sagging. Maybe he really had been dead. For some reason his previous conversation with the Voice seemed like a dream. No matter... it was time to see if there was a way out of the small room he found himself in.

When he tried to shift his weight from the table to his legs he discovered that they weren't quite yet up to the task. His knees buckled and he hit the floor with a clatter of bony joints striking the hard floor. There was a soft hissing sound from somewhere in the room and he felt warm hands—human hands—lifting him up and putting him back on the table. He looked up into the face of his rescuer and saw that it wasn't quite human, but close.

"Do not be alarmed," Voice said, the sound still emanating from somewhere in the room. "This is an artificial construct that will be assisting you until you are able to fully function on your own again. We built it to resemble your species in order to minimize the shock."

"Very considerate of you," Blake said, leaning back and breathing hard.

"You've obviously discovered that I've restored your voluntary motor functions, but it will be some time before your atrophied body will be fully repaired," Voice said. "In the meantime, there are some things I'd like to discuss with you. Things I'd like clarified before we begin trying to revive the rest of your crew." The mention of his crew swept away the rest of the cobwebs and Blake was now focused like a laser on what Voice said.

"Sure," he said. "I'll answer anything you'd like."

"We have been able to access the computers aboard the ship you were traveling on," Voice said, now sounding a bit hesitant. "It took us some time to differentiate between your factual records and your entertainment, but we feel that we've been able to begin seeing certain patterns within your species' behavior."

"Such as?" Blake asked, a bit terrified that all of humanity was to be judged by whatever bad movies happened to be on the crew's personal tablets.

"Your capacity for violence, even towards each other, is truly remarkable," Voice said, its tone indicating that wasn't an indictment, merely an observation. "Yet underneath this there seems to be a tendency to act along very well-defined standards of right and wrong."

"I'm not sure what you're asking," Blake admitted. "I'm actually not sure you're even asking me anything."

"I am just seeking simple affirmation and possibly some clarification," Voice said.

Over the next three hours they talked at length about the application of violent force as a means to solve problems, the ethical and philosophical consequences, and even walked through a series of scenarios in which Blake was made to describe how he'd handle the encounters. Some of the scenarios involved only him, some involved small groups like a family, and some were on a grand scale like an entire planet. In the end he was left exhausted and confused. The conversation tapered off to an uncomfortable silence as Blake wondered if the answers he'd given meant his crew would remain "dead" or if they'd be revived as he had. Since he didn't know what Voice wanted, he just answered everything as honestly as he could and let the chips fall as they may.

"I will admit to being far more intrigued about your species than I was when we conducted our initial evaluation of your ship," Voice said after a few minutes. "We have made our decision."

"Will my crew be revived?" Blake asked.

"Yes," Voice said simply. "As many as can be. There were a few members who are beyond even our help. We also have a proposition for you."

"A proposition?" Blake almost laughed. "What could we possibly offer to someone like you?"

"The one thing that we are fundamentally unable to comprehend," Voice said. "A concept so foreign to us that we have all but given up trying."

"And that is?"

"The thing you call 'war,'" Voice said. "We would very much like for you to instruct us in its intricacies, its implementations, and possibly even demonstrate its execution. Would you do this for us, Robert?"

Blake thought about what he was being asked for a few minutes and about the bizarre, unimaginable situation he now found himself in. In the end he still had one primary responsibility, and that was the well-being of his crew. That had to come before any philosophical debates he may have with himself later about what he was being asked to do.

"I will show you."

Chapter 1

Earth

Year: 2433

"You've been keeping secrets from us," Fleet Admiral Marcum said as he gazed out from the balcony at Lake Geneva. "This planet is not the polluted slum we were led to believe it was."

"It was when all of you left us here," Senior Captain Jackson Wolfe said. "It's taken us centuries to repair the damage and we didn't feel like inviting everyone back for a repeat."

"Feeling a bit peevish this morning, are we, Captain?" Marcum asked with an arched eyebrow.

"Not especially," Jackson said, still not addressing his superior with either rank or the honorific 'sir.' It was not lost on Marcum.

"Tell me what's on your mind, Captain," he said. "We're going to have to get past whatever this is if we're going to continue to work together. I was following orders. Just like you *mostly* do when asked. What is it you want of me?"

"Tell me about the Ark," Jackson said. "Who initiated it? How long was it out there? When did you know what it was? Make me believe in you like I did when I was pulled out almost dead from the wreckage of a *Raptor*-class destroyer."

Marcum stared at him a long moment before sighing heavily and turning back to the lake. "It was never called the 'Ark,'" the admiral said. "That was also not its original purpose. The planet was the next phase in the Board's plan to detach Tsuyo Corporation from the Confederate government and operate as a sovereign entity.

"It was found by one of their top secret automated exploration drones, and when they saw how perfect the existing ecology was for a colony, they began building immediately. That was nearly twenty-seven years ago, well before the Phage showed up on our doorstep. They even had a fully functional shipyard, albeit on a very small scale. That's where the new boomers came from... built one at a time in that system, hidden from prying eyes."

"That explains the existence of the colony and an entirely new and unknown class of battleship," Jackson said slowly. "But not any of the important things."

"As you guessed, there was great concern on Haven that we simply weren't up to the task of repelling the Phage," Marcum nodded. "A concern that was well-founded, I might add. Your blind idealism aside, the fleet had little chance of winning at Nuovo Patria against just the forces the Phage brought with them, to say nothing of the fact it wasn't even their main objective.

"Anyway… when talk became serious about how to save the species if we had to begin accepting the loss of entire systems, Tsuyo began coming to individual senators and lobbying them to channel resources and our best and brightest to the new planet." Jackson's humorless laugh interrupted the admiral, causing the senior fleet officer to frown at the inappropriate outburst.

"So even with the species facing extinction the corporation was still looking to play any angle it could," Jackson said, still laughing.

"I don't get it," Marcum admitted.

"You said that they were looking to declare themselves sovereign, separate from the Confederacy," Jackson said. "So what would happen if the Senate authorized our most brilliant people to accompany most of the resources to this new little empire and then we *didn't* get wiped out by the Phage?"

"I hadn't even considered that," Marcum admitted, still frowning. "The new enclave would have a monopoly on science, art, technology… you name it, and the Confederacy would have to crawl to Tsuyo and beg for anything and everything. Do you really think that was the root of what they were doing?"

"Of what *you* were helping them do," Jackson corrected. "And yes, I think that the Board and the Senate are one and the same: rats crawling on top of each other trying to gain some advantage regardless of the fact the ship is sinking out from under them." When Marcum didn't answer him, the beleaguered captain turned back to the view of his home planet.

After the horrific attack by the Phage that had completely destroyed the Confederate capital, Haven, the shell-shocked survivors of the government had eventually found their way back to the birthplace of humanity: Earth. They were not treated to a warm welcome as ships trickled into the Solar System. The citizens of the blue planet had not forgotten the insults heaped upon them by most of the Confederate worlds, nor were they overly anxious to have the Phage follow those fleeing the Alpha Centauri System.

For Jackson Wolfe, the return to Earth was viewed through the numbed, glazed stare of a man who had been pushed far beyond his breaking point. He still bore the guilt of Haven's destruction despite the fact that little could have actually been done to prevent it. He still felt that if he hadn't bucked the chain of command yet again and drawn most of the Seventh Fleet's combat recourses to the Frontier then maybe there would have been a force there strong enough to repel the assault.

"I wonder how long they'll keep him in there," Marcum said.

"I wouldn't even begin to guess," Jackson shrugged. "I'd imagine they're having some difficulty believing his story."

"I'm not even sure I do either," Marcum said. "But as long as he sticks around with those ships of his, he could say he's the Queen of Sheba and I'd vouch for him." Before Jackson could ask Marcum if he even knew what he was referencing the double doors to the reception area they'd been cooling their heels in banged open.

"Captain Wolfe, Admiral Marcum… sorry to keep you waiting," the officious little man in an absurd-looking, albeit trendy, suit said in a tone of voice that made it quite clear he wasn't actually all that sorry.

"And?" Marcum said irritably.

"And if you'd follow me I'll escort you to the main conference room," the man said, still trying to puff himself up in the presence of the two famous Fleet officers.

"After you." Marcum rolled his eyes at Jackson as he followed the man out of the room that Jackson had begun to suspect was more of a holding cell than a reception area.

Jackson had been somewhat surprised at how they'd been treated once they had landed. The *Ares* had made orbit and had been brusquely ordered to not get in the way of Earth's normal orbital traffic and then, nearly four days later, a summons was sent for Jackson, and only him, to arrive via shuttle at Geneva with no deviations. He'd wanted very much to set foot on the North American continent again while he was home, but all requests for a course change or an explanation for the apparent urgency were met with the repeated order to land in Geneva. Even as ships began to trickle into the system it was becoming more than clear that Earth was not too keen on receiving the displaced citizens of the Confederacy.

The hall they were led down was long and curving, with an unbroken floor to ceiling window on the wall facing the picturesque landscape provided by the Alps reflected in the calm lake. The building they were in was one of the few new built along the shores of the lake, as most others dated back several hundred years. Even during the most tumultuous times in Earth's past, Geneva, and actually most of Switzerland, seemed to avoid being touched by the devastation wrought in the late twenty-first century.

"Right in here, if you please," the man leading the procession said, standing aside and gesturing them past. Neither Jackson nor Admiral Marcum favored the cretin with as much as a nod as they walked into a dimly lit, lavishly appointed room that was dominated by an enormous oval table in the middle that was made of a type of wood only found on Earth. It was these tiny observations that had begun to add up and tug on the strings of Jackson's heart. Despite living almost all of his adult life aboard a starship, this was home. This was where he belonged.

"Senior Captain Wolfe," a middle-aged woman with long, silver hair near the table head spoke up. "It is an honor to have you join us. Please take a seat."

"The honor is mine, Madam Minister," Jackson said, dipping his head respectfully. Even though he'd never seen her in person, the serious, almost stern countenance of Minister Adavail Nelson was well-known even to those not familiar with Earth politics. She was the fair but relentless overseer of the Council of Nations, the organization that had once tried to negotiate between the fractious nation states of Earth and in recent times, under the leadership of Nelson and her predecessor, had smoothly transitioned into the planet's first worldwide governing body. At least the first effective one and certainly the first in which all participants entered the agreement willingly.

"Madam Minister—"

"Do sit down, Admiral Marcum," Nelson said with a dismissive wave. "You were invited to this meeting as the ranking representative of the Confederacy's remaining military and as a courtesy, but you hold no sway here. There is no political power you can bring to bear nor are you entirely welcome. I apologize for my bluntness, but I wish there to be no misunderstandings before we begin."

"Of course, Madam Minister," Marcum said smoothly, appearing completely unruffled.

"We're holding this informal briefing with the key players in the events that led up to the complete loss of Haven before a full session of the Council convenes to determine what, if anything, Earth will do about these unprecedented events," Nelson continued. "Feel free to ask questions if there are points you're unclear on… it's imperative that everyone is up to speed in case you're called up to give testimony."

Jackson sighed inwardly at that last part. He was certain there was no way he would avoid being called up before the Council if for no other reason than he was the most notorious "Earther" serving in Starfleet. His role in the Phage War, as it was now being called, had been wildly exaggerated by Earth's media outlets to the point that he was portrayed as a hero, a bungling fool, or a bloodthirsty lunatic willing to let millions die to satisfy his desire for all-out war with the first space-faring species encountered by humans. Unfortunately, he wasn't all that sure where he actually fell on that spectrum.

"We've questioned the alleged Colonel Robert Blake extensively and have even been able to analyze his DNA, comparing it to samples that were miraculously preserved in what used to be the United States." Nelson grimaced slightly as she eased herself down into the plush chair at the head of the ovoid table. "By any measure we would use to determine such things, Colonel Blake is who he claims to be. That doesn't preclude the fact that our investigative means just aren't up to the task, but given his intervention on the Frontier I'm willing to take his story on faith. The real question now becomes what do we do about it?"

"Madam Minister, might it not be useful to have Colonel Blake present for this meeting?" Jackson said, ignoring protocol and speaking to Minister Nelson directly.

"Possibly," Nelson's careworn face gave no indication that she either agreed or disagreed. "However, Captain, there are certain mitigating factors that might make it easier if Blake is kept in the dark about these proceedings."

"Such as?" Jackson asked.

"Not that it's any concern of the Confederate Fleet," an older man whose uniform identified him as an admiral in Sol Defense Forces said contentiously. "But the man you've so blithely led back to Earth is in possession of eighteen ships that could easily destroy everything in this system, or just as easily repel a Phage advance should they have tracked you here. Either way, if he is who he claims to be we're not so sure he should be the one left in command of such weapons."

Jackson was suddenly alarmed at the line of thought and was about to voice as much when he felt Marcum kick his ankle and shake his head almost imperceptibly.

"This is just an informal meeting prior to the full Council Session," Nelson reminded them forcefully while glaring at the outspoken SDF admiral. "Speculation such as this is not needed or especially helpful. Now… let's begin with a rough overview of the Battle of Nuovo Patria and work back from there."

For the next three and half agonizing hours, Jackson was forced to sit and listen as his previous mission was dissected and argued over by people of questionable pedigree to judge such things. It wasn't long before he quit interjecting or correcting the record, as it became clear the politicians and bureaucrats in the meeting weren't actually on a fact-finding mission and were, in fact, carefully constructing a narrative that would be fed to the full session of the Council and, in turn, the citizenry of Earth.

Once the torturous meeting was concluded, Jackson escaped the room, Marcum right on his heels, before he could be cornered by any of the half-dozen attendees who looked like they wanted to speak to him privately. As much as he loved breathing the air on Earth after such a long time away, he was now wondering how difficult it would be to sneak off and catch a shuttle back up to the *Ares*.

****

"How was the meeting, Captain?" Robert Blake said, taking another long pull of his beer and not bothering to get up from the lounge.

"What meeting would that be?" Jackson asked, helping himself to one of the local brews before flouncing down on the couch across from the former Air Force officer.

"The one where you all sat around and tried to make up a plausible tale to feed the Council later this week," Blake said.

"Ah, that one," Jackson shrugged. "About like you'd expect, I imagine."

"Just between you and me, the ships my crew and I arrived in do not actually belong to us," Blake said casually. "I couldn't hand them over, even if I was inclined to."

"I see," Jackson said carefully. "Any particular reason you're offering up this random fact?"

"I'm serious, Captain," Blake said. "I know what's being whispered about in this building. Understand that those ships, the seventh generation since we began our work, entrusted to us, are not simply tools to be wielded by whoever is in possession. I cannot even begin to explain the complexities of the Vruahn's artificial intelligence that each carries."

"Why such rigid safeguards?" Jackson asked, dropping the pretense of ignorance.

"We're useful to the Vruahn," Blake said after a few moments of silence. "But they don't entirely trust us, and for the very reason that we're useful. Our violent and unpredictable nature has made them leery of simply handing over the keys to ships capable of sterilizing planets."

"I suppose that's understandable, but it doesn't bode well for our species having any sort of relationship with them," Jackson said.

"Would you simply hand over an armed tactical nuke to a playground bully?" Blake said. "No matter what they've said before, I have no doubt that's how they see us. As absurd as it sounds, I'm not sure we're much different than the Phage in their eyes."

"That's... distressing," Jackson said. "What happens if you defeat the Phage? They hire a new bully to deal with us?"

"They're not genocidal lunatics if that's what you're asking, but I will admit that I'm never fully certain of their motivations or intentions," Blake said. "But that's neither here nor there. I asked you here for a different reason."

"Oh?"

"I need to talk to you, privately," Blake said. "I've found and disabled much of the surveillance equipment in this suite, but I need to be absolutely sure we won't be overheard. Can you arrange that in a way that doesn't arouse suspicion?"

"I believe I can," Jackson said. "But definitely not here. Not in the Council's seat of power."

"Then where?"

"How would you like to visit what used to be America, Colonel?" Jackson asked.

"I thought you'd never ask," Blake said with a wide smile.

Chapter 2

As one of the shuttles assigned to the *Ares* banked gently over the coast of Florida, the first twinges of anxious excitement crept up from Jackson's gut. He'd been twenty years old when he had left and now, twenty-two years later, it would be the first time he'd been back to North America. He looked around the cabin of the small tactical shuttle and saw Robert Blake squirming in his seat as he looked out over the Florida coast. Gillian Davis, a citizen of New America, looked on with polite interest.

Jackson had lobbied one of the lower-level bureaucrats at the facility in Geneva to allow members of the *Ares'* crew to visit the areas of Earth that held significant cultural importance to their respective enclaves. It had been a ruse, of course, and one that the administrator couldn't resist. Despite all their protests to the contrary, many of the policy makers of Earth were desperate for approval from the powerful Confederacy, and the chance to show off the planet was readily agreed to. Then, as if an afterthought, Jackson had mentioned that it would only be right to take Colonel

Blake back to Florida as well. Since the colonel wasn't a prisoner, the official had little grounds to deny the request and, after failing to seek higher approval, allowed it so long as strict schedules and regular check-ins were adhered to.

It seemed pathetically transparent, but Jackson knew he had him when the man bristled at the suggestion that he contact someone with the authority to let them leave the compound. Not wanting to be seen as inconsequential, the administrator put in word with the dockmaster that two shuttles would be departing the *Ares* and landing at the airfield near the outskirts of the small city, with passengers cleared for travel within Earth's atmosphere.

"While I'm thrilled to be back home, I fail to see how this will be any more secure than finding a dark broom closet in Geneva." Blake stared out the window as the shuttle banked gently into a descending turn over the Florida coast.

"You might be surprised," Jackson said. "The Council's influence wanes greatly once you cross the Atlantic. There may be a lot of lip service paid to a unified Earth, but there are many that still recognize the old borders even if they no longer officially exist. You'll even meet quite a few people here in the NAU that identify as 'American.' Besides that, it was a good excuse to get out from under CN security and visit North America again."

"Wouldn't everyone in the North American Union be *American?*" Jillian Davis asked. She was seated across the aisle from Jackson and watching the approaching coastline with interest.

"People who lived in the United States were universally called Americans," Jackson explained. He wasn't entirely certain why Davis had come down from the *Ares,* nor why she'd asked to accompany him and Colonel Blake. She'd never before expressed any real interest in Earth or the original nation that founded her native enclave.

The air shuttle's engines whined as the pilot flared the craft into a gentle landing, rolling off the pad and up to the waiting ground car. As Jackson unbuckled his restraints and stood to leave, the woman he'd assumed to be the crew chief grabbed his arm and placed a device into his palm.

"CN Security, Captain Wolfe," she said respectfully. "This device can be triggered by you, or anyone in your party, and we'll be anywhere on the continent in a few minutes." Jackson felt her words could be taken a few ways, and he was getting the distinct feeling that they were meant more as a warning than any helpful advice.

"I appreciate that," Jackson said, palming the device. "We'll not be long. I just wanted to see home again and show the colonel the monument that was built in honor of his mission."

"Just press the button on top twice," she brushed off his explanation. "Twice and we'll come charging in.

We can also come to your position should the device lose contact with the satellite."

"Good to know," Jackson said. "Now… if you'll excuse me." He reached past her and palmed the control to pop and lower the hatch so they could all disembark. There was no doubt that the rest of his crew that had come down from the *Ares* were being followed just as closely, nor was there any doubt that the driver of his waiting ground car was also a member of CN Security. He wasn't especially worried. While he was sure the CN Security forces were good, he knew the CIS was likely better. With a slight smile he slipped the device he'd been given into his right pocket while discreetly patting a similarly sized device that was resting in his left.

****

The trio made a slow, solemn walk through the grounds of the former Cape Canaveral Launch Facility, looking at the plaques and ancient fixtures that held no meaning to any of them save for one. Colonel Blake's face remained fixed in a grim stare as he looked over the ruins of one of the marvels of the twentieth century. Jackson felt for him. The last time he had stood there the Cape had been a hub of activity and a beacon of hope for a bright future. Now it was just a collection of rusting, decrepit structures with some plaques scattered haphazardly around to drive the point home. The starship captain began to wonder if the Air Force colonel had truly come to terms with his situation before being confronted, literally, with the ruins of his previous life.

"I wonder if I have any relatives alive. Or descendants, to be more precise," Blake said softly as he looked out over where the two most famous launch pads had stood for over a century, now just overgrown marsh with chunks of concrete stabbing obscenely into the bright Florida sky.

"Not a lot is known about you or your past, Colonel Blake," a new voice said from behind them. "Tsuyo made sure to allow your name to slip through the cracks, but I'm sure I can dig something up if you're really interested."

"Who are you?" Blake asked.

"Colonel Blake, allow me to introduce… who are you supposed to be at this moment?" Jackson asked.

"Agent Pike, Confederate Intelligence Service, at your service, Colonel," Pike said with a sarcastic bow. "That sounded oddly redundant. Anyway… thanks for sending the signal that you'd broken away, Captain. May I?" Wordlessly, Jackson handed over the small device that the CN Security agent had given him and watched as Pike scanned it and then dropped it into a small cylinder before pocketing it.

"The bug will keep pinging the satellite but won't be able to transmit any clear audio," Pike continued. "Actually, I've been jamming it since you got out of the car. So what can I do for you?"

"You summoned him here?" Blake asked.

"I did," Jackson confirmed. "I think any conversation we have that you don't want the CN overhearing is likely something Pike needs to know about. Not to mention he'd just find out anyway."

"More than likely," Pike shrugged. "I've recently learned that my work is much easier if I just loiter in the area around Wolfe and wait for the shit to hit the fan. So, here we are. The area is clear of long-range surveillance and there won't be any satellite coverage that will be able to tell you've gained a member of your party for another fifty minutes. So... what's going on?"

"You were saying that the Vruahn had a pretty tight grip on the ships your crew is flying," Jackson prompted when Blake looked as if he was confused and unsure where to start.

"Yes," Blake nodded. "The reason I bring that up first and foremost is that I have reason to believe that there are at least two separate factions that intend to either persuade me to turn them over or try and take them by force."

"Interesting." Pike narrowed his eyes. "And just how did you come by such information?"

Blake coughed uncomfortably before answering. "The Vruahn are quite familiar with human languages and engineering methodology thanks to the examination of my crew and I as well as the *Carl Sagan*," he said. "My ship has been monitoring communications here on Earth since we arrived and forwarding me the pertinent information."

"It's so easily able to defeat the encryption routines?" Pike asked.

"Almost in real-time," Blake nodded. "The more chatter there is about obtaining my squadron, the more... concerned, for lack of a better word, the AI aboard becomes. I can't overstate how dangerous it would be to try and coerce the ships from someone the Vruahn designated."

"The most obvious answer is to remove the temptation," Jackson said. "More ships are arriving every day now that the news of Haven is becoming widespread. The skies are filled with panicky, irrational representatives from all the enclaves that may do something foolish before too long."

"Not only them. The government here on Earth likely wouldn't mind leap-frogging over the Confederacy in terms of firepower and technology," Pike said.

"There's something else I needed to talk to you about I didn't want to be general knowledge just yet," Blake said. "That warning you got, Captain... the transmission from the Alpha. That's never happened to the best of our knowledge. I've passed it on to my Vruahn contacts, but the initial response is that this is something new."

"While that's interesting—"

"You're not seeing the full picture," Blake ran over top of Pike. "We have access to very specific predictive models of the Phage based on centuries of observation and interaction by multiple species that have encountered them. The fact they've decided to communicate with you, with Wolfe specifically, throws all of that out the window. I can no longer tell you with certainty that you have any time before they swarm through human space in force and wipe you out. Equally, I can't tell you if the message was meant to tell you that you'd be left alone. The shift in behavior swings the needle so far off the norm that I'm basically as much of a bystander now as all of you."

"If this species has been wreaking havoc across the galaxy for as long as you say, I somehow doubt that we're the first ones they've decided to talk to," Jackson said. "Hell, we didn't even really put up that much of a fight."

"You did better than you give yourself credit for," Blake said. "But the facts stand. In all the recorded encounters known to the Vruahn, which are a lot, there has been no attempt of communication from the Phage."

"Well... this puts an interesting spin on things." Pike looked as his watch, a stainless steel timepiece that was meant to resemble an ancient chronometer. "But we need to wrap this up. You continue on with your sightseeing expedition and I'll start putting this information in the ears of the people that need it. I'll be in touch soon." The agent tossed the small CN device back to Wolfe and headed off into the scrub behind one of the squat launch support structures.

Chapter 3

"So what is this area called?" Jillian Davis asked as Jackson piloted the borrowed aircraft down to their designating landing spot.

"Lexington," he said. "It's a city in an area called Kentucky. From what I understand, it used to be a nation state within the old United States of America." Blake, having had his conversation with Jackson, had decided to go back to Geneva. Jackson decided to press on and visit his former home since he was certain this would be the last time he would ever set foot on Earth again. Davis had decided to come with him and now that it was just the two of them, out of uniform, she'd adopted an alarmingly casual manner when talking to her captain. "It'll be just a short train ride from here up to Louisville. I grew up on the outskirts there."

Jackson breathed in slowly and deeply, enjoying the almost sickly sweet smell of Kentucky in early summer. It had taken the humans that had remained behind on Earth centuries to rethink their stewardship of the planet and make a concerted effort to employ the new technologies available to not only live with less impact but to reverse much of the damage caused by the carelessness of the early industrial era.

Unlike the planet that people fled in droves during the first great exodus to the colony planets, the Earth of the mid-twenty-fifth century had become a model of sustainability. Most notable were the powerful seawater fusion reactors that provided clean, safe, and cheap power to every corner of the globe. With the abundance of clean electricity, they'd been able to not only clean up the first world but bring sanitation and technology to the third world.

In many ways Jackson was still awed at how quickly the planet and her people were able to right the ship. By the time the third great world war was winding down, things looked quite grim for humanity. The world's mighty superpowers were on the brink of ruin, there was widespread economic depression, and an increasingly toxic environment was having an alarming impact on birthrates. Many academics felt that humanity was in its twilight, as no obvious answers presented themselves and a war-weary population seemed to have little will left to try and salvage what was left of their civilization.

The Tsuyo Corporation had tried to spark the world's imagination with the announced discovery of an alien spacecraft and the subsequent adaptation of its propulsion system onto a manned, human vessel, but it was to no avail. Shockingly, people reacted to the news of the alien ship, the first firm proof of extraterrestrial life, with the same apathy they applied to every other aspect of their lives. The launch of the *Carl Sagan* came and went to the disinterest of billions. Years later, when the mission had been deemed an expensive and embarrassing failure, Tsuyo quietly began making plans to explore and colonize the handful of suitable planets their automated probes had discovered.

For generations anyone with any education, skill, or even just hope for a better future fled a broken and battered Earth for the promise of a new start for themselves and their families. Those that remained behind watched the lifters haul away their fellow humans with a collective sigh and a shrug as if to say, "What's the point?"

"It's so green and vibrant," Davis said. "Don't take this the wrong way, but every image or vid I've seen of Earth depicted a post-apocalyptic wasteland."

"I've seen those same images," Jackson shrugged. "Honestly, by the time I was born we were already on the trailing end of what we call the Resurgence. The air and water were clean and society had mostly picked itself up and was moving forward again."

"So why stay so isolated?" she asked as they walked towards the terminal. "Why didn't Earth petition the Confederacy for membership?"

"Pride," Jackson said, unsure why he felt so defensive about the question. "This planet is the birthplace of humanity. To go crawling to the Confederacy and beg membership of the very people who had abandoned us in the first place was never a popular proposal. Earthers aren't necessarily cheerful isolationists, but most of us just aren't willing to let go of the old resentments."

"And you?"

"I'm a bit more pragmatic," Jackson said. "I understand the motivations of those first waves of colonists. I also had only wanted one thing for my life and that was to go to space and travel between the stars. Since the Sol Defense Force never ventures out past Saturn, the obvious answer was to try and snag one of the slots to the Academy that Fleet set aside each year for Earthers."

"But it's always been a struggle, being from here," she said.

"Nothing worthwhile comes without sacrifice," Jackson said with a forced smile. "I don't regret my decision to leave."

They walked the rest of the way to the transit hub in silence. Jackson wasn't sure if it was the casual way in which she now addressed him, the stylish civilian attire, or the fact that she insisted on walking so close to him that their hands would sometimes brush together, but he was becoming suddenly aware that Jillian Davis was a very beautiful young woman. He was also quite aware at how inappropriate things had become between them in the short time since leaving Geneva, but he wasn't sure how to address it without embarrassing her. As her proximity wasn't especially unpleasant, nor was he in uniform, he decided to let it slide for the time being.

****

Admiral Joseph Marcum replayed the message one more time before leaning back in his plush leather seat and rubbing his temples with the heels of his hands. He'd always considered himself a good officer. The kind that was willing to do what was right even if it meant sacrificing everything he'd worked for. But after watching Jackson Wolfe practically single-handedly usurp half the fleet in order to make a stand for what was right, he had to concede that he'd become the very thing he'd always hated: a politician masquerading as a military officer. The sad part was that it had happened without him even noticing it.

He was sitting in his well-appointed office aboard the TCS *Amsterdam*, a *Dreadnought*-class battleship, the biggest and baddest thing to ever come out of a Terran shipyard. The mammoth warship was sitting in between the Earth and the Moon while the rest of her squadron had taken up a high orbit over Mars in order to keep the traffic over the blue planet to a minimum.

The latest com drone to buzz through the Solar System had delivered a lengthy message for him from Confederate President McKellar, who was still safely in a bunker on a planet they were calling the Ark. The President was typically pompous, absurdly out of touch, and managed to display a lack of understanding about their current situation that was simply breathtaking. Marcum had to assume that McKellar wasn't actually a stupid man, he did manage to get himself elected to the highest office in the Confederacy after all, but the fact that he still considered himself to be "in charge" was laughable.

Haven was gone. A smoldering, irregularly shaped ruin spinning through space without enough mass left to even stay in its original orbit. With its loss went any remaining stability within the Terran Confederacy. The more powerful enclaves like New America and Britannia were now declaring their independence, while envoys from the smaller enclaves were now filtering into the Solar System like lost sheep just looking for some sort of direction.

"The man is a complete fucking moron," Marcum muttered to himself. McKellar had sent a directive that he marshal any forces remaining from Wolfe's "ill-conceived" effort in Nuovo Patria, take the senior captain into custody, and return to the Ark where they would regroup and discuss their strategy going forward. Marcum was still technically serving as CENTCOM Chief of Staff, but with no Haven, no Jericho Station, and no CENTCOM to speak of he had to wonder what power that title even commanded anymore. What he did know, however, was that any effort to arrest Jackson Wolfe would not only result in further harming a completely demoralized force but may well serve as the spark for a compete mutiny within the ranks. He wasn't even all that confident that his own captain aboard the *Amsterdam* wouldn't shoot him in the head if he tried to order an intercept of the *Ares*.

"Orderly! Have our JAG rep haul ass to my office," he stabbed at the intercom button on his desk.

"At once, Admiral!"

He'd been on the wrong side of every major decision since the Phage had first appeared in the Xi'an System. It was a trend that he very much would like to correct.

****

"So you don't remember anything leading up to the evacuation of the *Blue Jacket*?" Davis asked.

"Just some fragmented imagery," Jackson said, sitting down next to her on a bench that overlooked the Ohio River. "The neurologists tell me that anything I remember is likely something my brain is fabricating to try and fill in the gaps, since the head trauma would have made it virtually impossible for my short term memory to transfer to long term. To be honest, maybe it's best I don't remember."

"Why do you say that?" she asked, sounding oddly hurt.

"The decision to ram the ship into that Alpha was one I made out of utter desperation," he said, eyeing her sidelong, confused by her reaction. "I think that if I vividly remembered everything leading up to the impact it could adversely affect my ability to command now, cause me to second guess every decision."

"I see," she said, now looking uncomfortable.

"You seem like you have something on your mind that wants to get out, Lieutenant," Jacksons said, intentionally addressing her by rank to remind himself that there was a line that could not be crossed.

"Perhaps now isn't the best time to—" the strident alert tone of Jackson's comlink interrupted her.

"This is Wolfe," Jackson said, slipping the earpiece in. "Understood, we'll be at the pickup location in approximately ninety minutes. Wolfe out."

"Bad news?" Davis asked, standing and composing herself.

"Fleet-wide emergency recall," Jackson nodded. "A shuttle will pick us up at the airport here in Louisville and take us directly to the *Ares*. The order came in from Admiral Marcum. What was it you were saying?"

"It will wait, Captain," she said crisply.

"Then let's get moving," he stood. "The shuttle is already on its way."

Chapter 4

"Report."

"We've been told to stand by for a command-level briefing from the *Amsterdam*, sir." Lieutenant Commander Barrett stood and vacated the command seat as Jackson walked onto the bridge of the *Ares*.

"Any word on what it's all about, official or otherwise?" Jackson asked as he walked around the bridge to take a quick look at all the stations.

"Negative, sir," Barrett said. "I reached out to see if anyone knew anything on the back channels, but the rumor mill is shockingly quiet on this one."

"That fact alone is terrifying beyond all fucking measure," Master Chief Green said from the hatchway. The salty chief's massive arms were crossed over his chest and he wore his usual scowl as spacers scurried about to prepare the *Ares* for any potential orders that came down during the briefing.

"I don't suppose the enlisted intel network was any more successful than Lieutenant Commander Barrett's friends?"

"Not a peep, Captain," Chief Green said. "Whatever this is about, the admiral is keeping a tight lid on it. I *might* have heard from an unsubstantiated source that he had the entire legal section aboard the *Amsterdam* working for twenty hours straight on something before ordering the recall."

"Interesting," Jackson said, not bothering to ask how the hell the master chief had contacts aboard a warship whose very existence was a highly classified secret until very recently.

"Captain, word from the *Amsterdam* is that Admiral Marcum will address the fleet within the next hour," Lieutenant Keller said from the com station. "I'm being told to have all hands standing by."

"Very good, Lieutenant." Jackson sat in his seat, cringing inwardly at the residual warmth left by Barrett. "Send out the word to all sections: keep working but be ready to get in front of a monitor within a moment's notice."

"Aye, sir."

****

"I will keep this brief as we all have a lot of work to do," Fleet Admiral Joseph Marcum said to the camera lens sitting in front of his desk. "I am recording and broadcasting this command level briefing from the *TCS Amsterdam* and it will be distributed to every corner of Terran space via the com drone network.

"As per the charter that the Terran Starfleet and all of CENTCOM operates under, I am exercising my right as Chief of Staff to declare a state of dire emergency and supersede all previous postings, orders, and assignments until said emergency is reduced in threat or eliminated." He leaned back and slid the paper he'd been reading from aside.

"All of you know what's been happening on the Frontier and that the Phage have gone on the offensive and destroyed Haven and Jericho Station. It is now obvious that this enemy is not content to harass our borders and intends to hit us, hard, wherever it can. It is also obvious, at least to me, that with our elected leadership in tatters it falls on us to mount any sort of meaningful defense.

"We've been given a real chance in the form of an ally with extensive intelligence on the enemy that has allowed us to begin forming a plan that will take the fight to them. Greater details will be forthcoming in later technical briefs and specific orders. For right now, all you need to know is that, in following within the letter of the law, I am temporarily restructuring Starfleet in order to provide our command and control greater agility. In short: all Terran warships are now on detached duty to Seventh Fleet and will operate within those parameters. You heard me correctly. We are *all* Black Fleet now.

"Specific orders are attached to this message, but they all say more or less the same thing. Every CO needs to get his or her ship prepped and steaming for New Sierra at best possible speed. I will forego the motivational speech at the end of this brief because you all have a *lot* of work to do. Marcum out."

****

"The admiral isn't fucking around with this one," Chief Green said, the first one on the bridge of the *Ares* to find his voice.

"Does he really have the authority to do that?" Barrett asked.

"Yes," Davis said even as she read from the CENTCOM operational charter. "He's stretched the meaning a bit, but he's exercising a clause that's never been used since the restructuring of Starfleet over a century ago."

"Captain, there's a private com channel request coming in for you from the *Amsterdam*," Keller said.

"I more or less expected this, Lieutenant," Jackson stood up. "Send it to my office."

"Aye, sir."

****

"That was quite a surprise, Admiral," Jackson said once the channel had been established and the encryption routine was stabilized.

"I'm taking a page out of your book, Wolfe," Marcum growled. "I figured I'd see if taking direct, shocking action will garner me the same sort of luck you've enjoyed."

"I see," Jackson said noncommittally.

"Now here's where it gets serious," Marcum went on. "I don't expect every ship to follow their new order. Most COs were put in place due to political connections within the individual enclaves, and their loyalties likely will remain there. I also don't expect President McKellar to take this lying down. He still thinks that he's in control of the Confederacy despite the fact everyone is running down whatever rabbit hole they can find to hide, and he may issue some countermanding order as Commander in Chief."

"Doesn't your order supersede his authority for the time being?" Jackson asked.

"Technically," Marcum shrugged, an odd-looking gesture when combined with the video interference of the encryption. "But we both know I'm working with a legal loophole that was never closed all those years ago. Realistically, the best I can expect is that the ships that survived the Battle of Nuovo Patria may be all that will show up to the rally point."

"I'm also assuming we can add Colonel Blake's strike force to that mix," Jackson said.

"I'm counting on it," Marcum nodded. "We're breaking orbit and heading for the jump point now. I'd like the *Ares* to stay and make sure the colonel doesn't get detained by CN Security."

"Understood," Jackson said. "The rest of the Ninth is loitering in the outer system. I'll send Captain Wright orders and get them moving to New Sierra immediately."

"Good, good," Marcum said distractedly as he looked off screen. "This feels like the endgame, Captain. Whatever we do next... we better get it right."

"Agreed, Admiral," Jackson said. The channel closed and he typed out his orders to the rest of his squadron while reflecting on what had just happened. He could only shake his head in disbelief. Against all odds, Admiral Marcum *had* restored Jackson's faith in him.

Chapter 5

"**I** need to see the colonel, please."

"And you are?" the CN Security trooper sneered.

"Aston Lynch. Personal aide to Senator Augustus Wellington." Lynch flashed his ID. "Senator Wellington is one of the surviving members of the Confederate Senate and, so far, is most pleased at how the Council of Nations here on Earth has treated his friend and guest. Now please step aside."

"I'll need to run this up—"

"I've been as accommodating as I can be, given the circumstances," Lynch said. "Is the colonel a prisoner?"

"No."

"Has he committed some crime here on Earth you intend to charge him with?"

"No."

"You do realize there are six *Dreadnought*-class battleships in the Solar System right now, each of their captains sworn to carry out the political will of the Confederate government?" Lynch asked, smiling indulgently.

"You can't possibly mean to threaten us—"

"Step aside. *Now!*" Lynch barked. The outburst had the desired effect and Lynch was able to shoulder between the two guards and get to the door of Colonel Blake's quarters. He knocked twice and was ushered in before either guard could try to physically restrain him or call up to their superiors.

"Agent Pike," Colonel Blake said calmly. "I take it there have been some developments since last we spoke?"

"You could say that," Pike said. "While I'm sure your slick Vruahn hardware has already decrypted the transmission, it will take CN Security just a bit longer to figure out what's going on. I'm afraid they might get desperate and do something foolish."

"You're referring to the transmission from the TCS *Amsterdam*?" Blake asked.

"You're going to have to tell me what sort of bug they put in you that is able to evade every scanner we have," Pike said in disgust. "But yes, Admiral Marcum has essentially declared the civilian authority over the Terran Confederate Armed Forces null and void and is massing the fleet near one of our largest depots. The aftershocks from his creative interpretation of the Charter are likely to send politicians into fits, both on Earth and in the enclaves."

"So the admiral has decided to act on my initial proposal," Blake mumbled. "I have to admit that I'm surprised."

"Surprised doesn't even begin to cover it," Pike rolled his eyes. "Either way, we need to get you safely out of here."

"Couldn't I have just asked to leave?"

"Can't chance it," Pike shook his head. "The Council has already made noises about wanting to lay claim to your ships and I don't trust any decision that comes out of the full session to be the right one."

"How are we even getting off the planet if the Fleet is already pulling chocks?" Blake asked. "My ship can't come within the atmosphere."

"I've got that covered," Pike said. "Now get your shoes on and fall in behind me. It may be a bit of a fight to get off the compound."

Once Blake slipped on the generic-looking civilian shoes he'd been supplied with, Pike opened the door and swung a vicious elbow directly into the temple of the guard on the right, dropping him where he stood. The CIS agent was turning before the first body hit the ground and smashed the heel of his palm into the other guard's throat. When the guard dropped to his knees and began clawing at his throat, Pike drove a knee into the man's face, splattering the door frame with blood. He took a quick look around before relieving the two badly injured guards of their weapons and comlinks.

"It looks like they didn't bother to call in my arrival," he said as he thumbed through the menu on one of the comlinks. "This should buy us some more time. Let's go."

Colonel Blake's quarters were in guest billeting, not a secure facility. This worked greatly in Pike's favor since the only real security presence was the two guards they'd posted ostensibly for the colonel's protection. He'd disabled all the surveillance systems on his way in, but he couldn't discount the possibility that there were failsafes somewhere that he'd been unable to detect. He also knew better than to underestimate Earth's security forces. Despite his familiarity with the area, this was still their home turf.

They made it all the way to the lifts without encountering any further resistance save for a startled woman who yelped at the appearance of two grown men sprinting towards her down a deserted corridor. Once in the lift car, Pike was able to override the security locks and descend all the way down into the subbasement two stories under street level.

"This isn't going to be the cleanest you've ever been, but we need to get out of the compound without being spotted," Pike said as he pulled the heavy cover off one of the enormous ducts that was lined with power and data cables, just barely large enough for them to walk through slightly hunched over.

"Is all of this really necessary?" Blake asked.

"Honestly? Probably not," Pike admitted. "But if I'm wrong, would you rather do this or allow Admiral Marcum to move his battleships into orbit and begin making threats in order to secure your release?"

"Got it," Blake nodded. "Let's move."

They quickly moved down the access tunnel and came out into a darkened building that was just on the other side of the compound's security wall.

"This looks freshly cut." Blake ran a finger over the shiny stubs of metal that used to be part of a heavy security grate.

"How do you think I got in here?" Pike smiled. "Aston Lynch's credentials may have given a couple of bored embassy troopers pause, but they wouldn't have allowed me to move about the compound freely had I walked in through the main gate." He carefully opened the steel exterior door a crack and listened. He could just make out the sirens wailing near the main gate as the compound initiated lockdown procedures.

"We're clear," he said after a moment. "But we don't have much time before they expand their search. I have a ground car a few streets over. We need to be as far away from the compound as we can get in a short amount of time."

"I'm ready," Blake said. "Let's just make a run for it."

"It's as good a plan as any," Pike shrugged.

****

"Incoming channel request, Captain," Lieutenant Keller said. "No specific identifier, but it's routed through a military com satellite."

"Put it through here," Jackson said. He had ordered the *Ares* into a descending orbit towards Earth, stabilizing their descent just before reaching the outer holding orbit controlled by the SDF. From there he'd waited patiently for some sign that Pike had been able to get Blake off the surface without sparking off an incident between Earth and the shambles that used to be the mighty Terran Confederacy.

"Captain Wolfe," an elderly man with a pinched face wheezed once the video had stabilized. "Minister Nelson would like to have a word with you." Before Jackson could reply the man's face disappeared and the face of an obviously angry Adavail Nelson replaced it.

"Senior Captain," she said with a cold glare. "I see you have returned to your ship and look to be making preparations to leave without so much as a notice sent to SDF Orbital Authority. Is there some reason in particular the Fleet is leaving the Solar System just prior to the scheduled full session?"

"My apologies for breaking protocol, Madam Minister," Jackson said with genuine respect. "I've been ordered away by my commanding officer and, in spite of recent occurrences, this is still a Confederate warship and I am still a Fleet officer so I have little choice in the matter."

"I see," she said. "I suppose since Admiral Marcum's ship was the first out of the system there's no point in asking him what is going on." Nelson continued, "What is of great concern to us, however, is that Colonel Robert Blake appears to have been abducted. Many of our guards were injured during the operation and I'd like to know if you are harboring a citizen of

Earth on your ship. It's the last one left in the system, after all, and I'm told you've been in a decaying orbit dropping back towards the surface."

"I can say with certainty that Colonel Blake is not aboard the *Ares* nor did any of my crew have anything to do with his disappearance," Jackson said.

"How carefully worded," Nelson deadpanned. "Captain Wolfe… if you know anything about the bizarre events that have taken place in the last few hours I would appreciate you sharing. We accepted the remnants of your tattered government to our planet, your homeworld, without question. We certainly never anticipated this sort of blatant disrespect in response to our hospitality."

"I am truly sorry, Madam Minister," Jackson sighed. "I can tell you no more than I already have."

"Very well, Captain," Nelson said. The channel closed, and before Jackson could ask if it had been unintentionally dropped he had his answer.

"Captain, two SDF cruisers are coming over the horizon on a direct intercept course," Barrett said. "No targeting radars yet."

"They won't actually bring weapons to bear on us," Jackson said confidently. "This is a face-saving maneuver by the SDF. They'll make a big show of chasing us out of the system to avoid looking completely impotent when the full session convenes later."

"I'm getting a coded burst transmission, unknown source," Keller said. "Running decryption now."

"If I was to guess I'd say our elusive CIS spook is calling in to let us know they're off the surface," Jackson said. "Nav! Plot a course to the outer system and send it to the helm. Make sure we avoid those cruisers but try not to make it look like we're running. A Fleet destroyer does not flee from a pair of antique cruisers, after all."

"Understood, Captain," Specialist Accari said from the Nav station. "Course plotted and transferred to the helm."

"Helm, come about onto the new course. All ahead one-third."

"Ahead one-third, aye." The helmsman began swinging the nose of the *Ares* onto their new course and advanced the throttles.

"Transmission confirmed, Captain," Keller said. "Pike and Blake are aboard the *Broadhead* in low-orbit. He's asking for a bit of a distraction so he can climb out and make his way to the jump point unnoticed."

"Of course he is," Jackson muttered before pulling up a chart of the system. "Helm, come starboard forty-two degrees, thirteen degrees inclination."

"Helm answering new course."

"Engines ahead flank," Jackson said. "OPS, inform Engineering that we'll be running at full power out into the outer system."

"Ahead flank, aye!"

"This course doubles us back towards those SDF cruisers, sir," Davis said quietly.

"Yes it does, Lieutenant," Jackson nodded. "But not so direct a route that they'll think we're turning in on them to open fire. We have the advantage of a higher orbit. Even at such a close range those cruisers won't have the power to come about and climb up out of the well before we're already by and appearing to be on a direct course for a Martian intercept."

"I see now." She looked over her own display. "This is your distraction?"

"Just a bit of theatrics," Jackson said. "They won't know why we've suddenly slammed into full acceleration away from Earth and towards Mars. There will be a bit of hesitation that should allow Pike to slink off and we'll have not wasted any propellant as we'll achieve our transition velocity well before we hit the jump point. It's a relatively transparent ploy, as the cruiser COs know we won't actually be attacking them, but for the sake of their own performance they'll have to respect our move and respond by either slowing or turning in."

As he'd predicted, the two cruisers began braking to keep the destroyer out in front of them for as long as they could. Both sides knew it was inevitable that the *Ares* would blow by and be out of range in a matter of hours, just as they all knew that nobody was actually going to make an overt threat towards the other. All it did was allow the SDF commanders to report back to the Council that they'd tried to apprehend the *Starwolf*-class destroyer but were simply outmatched.

"Coms, any further word from our CIS asset?"

"Negative, Captain," Keller said. "No chatter on the open bands that would indicate they've been spotted either."

"Very well," Jackson said. "Nav, set a course for the Alpha Centauri jump point, maintain acceleration for now. I want to be out of this system ASAP."

"Aye, sir," Accari said. "Sending course adjustments to the helm now."

"Lieutenant Davis, you have the bridge," Jackson stood up. "You're clear to prepare the *Ares* for warp transition. Alert me when we're two hours from our jump point."

"Aye, sir."

Chapter 6

The bridge of the *Ares* was practically silent as they drifted through the Alpha Centauri System. Since there was only one known jump point from Earth they had no choice but to pass through the system and look at the horrific aftermath of the attack on Haven through the sensors while flying along to the New Sierra jump point.

As per the final request from the Council of Nations that came in just prior to the *Ares* transitioning out of the Solar System, they launched a com drone with a message from Earth meant for general dissemination: Confederate ships were not welcome in the Solar System nor would they be given safe passage. Jackson was dismayed by the message, but he understood it. The Haven-Earth jump point was rarely used and there was legitimate concern that if more and more ships were using the warp lane between the two systems that the Phage might more easily detect the presence of a lightly defended human planet.

There was no real agreement on how the Phage were finding planets, but a popular theory was that well-used warp lanes were somehow detectable. It was possible that the passing ships in warp were somehow affecting space in a way that wasn't detectible to humans, or it was possible the Phage were able to detect ships in warp with a degree of accuracy that allowed them to backtrack a flightpath. It was all fairly academic to Jackson. His job was to fight the Phage wherever they showed up, but now it seemed that he'd been given a chance to really settle the score. If Colonel Blake was being honest, and there was no reason to believe that he wasn't, then it was possible to deliver a crushing blow to their enemy that they likely wouldn't recover from. Either way, it was something they had to try. If the Battle of Nuovo Patria taught them anything it was that even a combined Terran fleet couldn't expect to stand toe to toe with the Phage and slug it out in a conventional fight.

"How long until we hit the New Sierra jump point?" Jackson asked.

"Fourteen hours, sir," Specialist Accari said without a moment's hesitation.

"Lieutenant Davis, when we make our closest pass to Haven I want a general announcement to render honors to starboard." Jackson consulted his display to see where their flightpath would orient them in the system.

"I'll handle it, Captain," Davis said quietly. Jackson nodded and turned back to his display. He was in the middle of drafting a request to CENTCOM to get

Davis officially promoted up to lieutenant commander in order to continue allowing her to serve as XO on the *Ares*. Her time in grade was a bit on the short side, but he figured her actions during the last battle should grease the wheels and get it through quickly even as scattered as CENTCOM was at the moment. It felt like an odd time to be concentrating on the mundane parts of command like getting his people promoted and recognized, but maybe it was better to try and shift back to some sort of normalcy given what the crew would likely be facing in the near future.

"Do you think the other numbered fleets will answer the admiral's call, sir?" Davis asked after a few moments.

"I'm not really sure, Lieutenant," Jackson admitted. "These are unprecedented times. I would hope that the commanders and crews of any Terran warship understand what's at stake, but many of them were appointed as political favors so I wouldn't want to make any bets as to where their loyalties actually lie."

"I hope you're wrong about that, Captain," she said.

"As do I, Lieutenant," Jackson nodded.

****

"Transition complete, position verified: we're in the DeLonges System," Accari said. "Plotting course for the New Sierra Shipyards."

"Picking up a lot of com traffic in this system, Captain," Lieutenant Keller said. "Forty-six separate transponders verified so far, with more coming in every minute."

"That's heartening," Jackson said. "Go ahead and announce our arrival, Mr. Keller. OPS, find out where Ninth Squadron is down there and send the coordinates to Nav."

"At once, sir," Ensign Hayashi said. The young officer had settled into his role as first watch OPS Officer so well that Davis rarely had to offer any assistance, which in turn allowed her to concentrate more fully on learning the ins and outs of being second in command on a starship.

"Helm, take us down, ahead one-half once you get your updated course," Jackson said.

"Ahead one-half, aye."

"Sir, most of these ships are Fourth Fleet," Keller said, still reading off the transponder codes as they were resolved.

"That makes sense," Jackson said. "In the immediate aftermath New America likely recalled their forces to a strategic chokepoint in order to think over their next move. Let's just keep this as simple as possible... has Admiral Marcum's squadron of *Dreadnought*-class ships arrived yet?"

"Yes, sir," Keller said.

"Send a direct message to the *Amsterdam* letting him know we've arrived in-system and will be forming up with the rest of the Ninth," Jackson said. "OPS, try to see if our friends in the Vruahn ships have managed to make it here yet."

"Aye, sir."

It was another three hours before responses and direct messages began filtering in from the chaos of the inner system. Jackson had ordered the *Ares* into a leisurely descent down from the jump point near the edge of the system to let his OPS and Tactical officers gather as much intel as they could about the huge, haphazard formation that was buzzing about in orbit over New Sierra.

"Sir, we're being given new orders," Keller said as he tried to sift through the incoming com traffic. "Admiral Marcum is moving his squadron in orbit around the sixth planet and is ordering the Ninth to form up on him. The Vruahn squadron is already there."

"Was there anything else in the message?" Jackson asked.

"No, sir."

"Very good. Send the new rendezvous coordinates to Nav," Jackson stood. "Helm, engage on new course when you get it. Ahead two-thirds."

"Ahead two-thirds, aye."

The long flight down the well from the outer system was filled with a seemingly never-ending list of administrative tasks that, inexplicably, CENTCOM was still able to generate despite having lost nearly three-quarters of its command and control apparatus with the loss of Jericho Station. By the time the enormous

Dreadnought-class battleships were appearing at the periphery of the *Ares'* navigation radar's detection range Jackson had managed to complete all his paperwork, submit the reports that the brass on New Sierra were squawking about, and even managed to sneak in six hours of uninterrupted sleep.

It didn't take long once the *Ares* slipped into formation for Admiral Marcum to send word that he wanted Jackson to shuttle over to the *Amsterdam* for a classified briefing with Colonel Blake. Jackson had more or less been expecting this, so he had already turned the ship over to Lieutenant Davis and had Commander Juarez prep a shuttle and crew to ferry him over. With one last wary look at the tactical display that was showing all the Fourth Fleet firepower orbiting New Sierra, he walked off the bridge on his way to the hangar bay.

****

"Captain Wolfe, thank you for coming," Admiral Marcum said as Jackson was escorted through a security checkpoint and into a secure briefing room. Jackson just nodded and quickly moved to the indicated seat. A quick look around showed that it would be a small group, but there was no shortage of clout. Senator Augustus Wellington was in attendance, as were Colonel Blake and Agent Pike. There were a handful of other flag officers that Jackson didn't recognize by sight and a few more people in civilian clothes. At least this wasn't likely to be more of the same. With a gathering like this Jackson assumed that they were there to begin finalizing their strategy.

"If everyone would take their seats, we'll get started," Marcum said. "We have a lot to do and, like always, we're already far behind. We're not going to do much rehashing, so for those who weren't present during recent events I hope you've read the prepared briefs I transmitted.

"After we learned of Colonel Robert Blake and his crew's extraordinary journey since leaving Earth hundreds of years ago we've been trying to find the best way to exploit the situation given our limited resources and current state of political upheaval. So without wasting any more time… Colonel Robert Blake, Commander of the *Carl Sagan* and an officer in one of Ancient Earth's most powerful militaries."

"Thank you, Admiral." Blake stood and nodded to the room, seeming completely comfortable now that he was running the briefing. "As the admiral alluded to, since our return to human space and to Earth we've been working on a strategy that will allow us to defeat the alien species you've been calling the Phage. I would like to say that despite your horrific losses, you've done far better than most species when it comes to defending yourselves against them. The relentlessness and sheer numbers they can bring to bear more often than not overwhelm a species before they can mount any sort of defense.

"Your affinity for kinetic weapons has slowed them down and confused them somewhat, but that won't last. These are not mindless beasts, and even though a comparison could be made between them and locusts, they are frighteningly intelligent and will have adapted the next time they come into human space."

"Do you have any idea when that might be?" Wellington asked.

"I do not, Senator," Blake shook his head. "It could be decades from now, or centuries, or they could already be moving across the Frontier en masse. Which leads me to the next unpleasant point: the Vruahn strike force that my crew and I pilot will not be able to stay in human space indefinitely. We're tasked with providing emergency relief for species that seem about to be overrun by the Phage, but our orders and mandate are non-negotiable. Even if we decide to stay, the ships will leave without us."

"Is there no way you can entreat the Vruahn on our behalf?" a woman with vice admiral stars on her uniform asked. "Possibly either for the ships themselves or the specs of—"

"They will not share their weaponry," Blake apologized. "But to answer your question, Admiral, I have already asked. Multiple times, in fact, once we found out that humanity was in the crosshairs. For reasons that are entirely their own, they will not allow their ships or weapons to be transferred to any other species. It might be better if you looked at them as more than just machines. They're coded specifically to their pilots and work almost symbiotically, but they have their own hardwired protocols and can be recalled by their owners in spite of any orders given by us."

"I will admit to some confusion on that point," Marcum admitted.

"The Vruahn are leaps and bounds ahead of you in technology, but they lack any will or instinct to fight," Blake seemed to struggle with the explanation. "They can build machines with incredible destructive power, but when it comes to developing even the most rudimentary strategies for fighting a war they fall flat. They discovered that by enlisting the help of more aggressive species they can accomplish the goal of keeping the Phage at bay while still maintaining their pacifist natures. We were the first, but I know there have since been other species brought into the fold as the threat of the Phage in this part of the galaxy grows."

"Just how large is the Phage threat?" Jackson asked. "Big picture."

"They're quickly becoming the largest power in this region of space," Blake said. "Their lack of any apparent motivation other than to devour all life unlike their own makes it impossible to communicate or negotiate with them."

Jackson saw an obvious flaw in the colonel's statement but let it pass for the time being.

"So other than to scare the shit out of us and tell us that you might not be here the next time they attack, what is the point of this meeting?" Wellington asked.

"The Phage do have a fatal weakness," Blake said. "Ironically, it's this weakness that makes them so difficult to fight. Their 'group minds' are not independent structures that just pop up when enough of them get together. Everything they do, everything they are… it all leads back to one single entity that drives them."

"So?" Wellington said belligerently. "How does that help us?"

"I know where it is," Blake said, causing the room to erupt into half a dozen shouted conversations.

Chapter 7

After the briefing devolved into a shouting match in which several of the attendees felt they could make their ideas more valid through sheer volume, Marcum angrily dismissed them all, holding Jackson and Blake back.

"Hell of a bomb you dropped there, Colonel," Marcum said when the hatch slid shut. "You could have given me some sort of warning."

"I was worried had I divulged that information too early it may have led to some rash decisions, especially when emotions were running high after the destruction of Haven," Blake said. "I apologize. There are a few other things that you'll need to be aware of before you decide how best to use the information I have."

"Oh?"

"The core mind, for lack of a better term, will not be easy to get to," Blake said. "It may actually be impossible if you were to just fire up the fleet you have sitting here and go tearing across space."

"Is that why you've not made a move on it yourself?" Jackson asked.

"Not exactly," Blake squirmed in his seat a bit. "The main reason we haven't tried is because the Vruahn won't allow it."

"What?" Marcum shouted, slamming a palm down on the table.

"We don't know for sure what eliminating the core mind would do," Blake said. "But the Vruahn are concerned that the probability is high it would begin a cascade effect that would lead to the extinction of the Phage."

"I'm still not seeing a fucking problem." Marcum's nostrils flared.

"You don't, but they do," Blake said firmly. "The Vruahn will not willingly exterminate an entire species, even one as brutal and destructive as the Phage."

"What are they willing to do should the Phage become powerful enough to threaten their existence, or even just strong enough to nullify your efforts, Colonel?" Jackson asked.

"An interesting philosophical question, Captain, and one that ties into my next item," Blake said. "They want to meet you."

"They want to meet me specifically?" Jackson asked.

"Yes," Blake said. "My liaison asked that I bring you to them for a face to face meeting. I reported back about the message the Alpha had transmitted to you and they are highly curious, if somewhat dubious, that after so many years the Phage decided to reach out to a species they'd marked for consumption."

"I don't think it was to me specifically," Jackson argued, shuddering inwardly at the colonel's casual term for what the Phage did to conquered planets. "It was just to the 'leader.'"

"Our analysis indicates otherwise," Blake shrugged. "Either way, I get the feeling any continued assistance from them hinges on this meeting with you."

"Oh isn't that just fucking great," Marcum rolled his eyes. "The fate of the species yet again hinges on what one wildcard captain may or may not do. I have to say that I'm not entirely comfortable with you speaking for all of humanity, Wolfe."

"And I would agree with you," Jackson said. "But I get the impression we're not being asked."

"That's correct," Blake said. "You can refuse, of course, but the invitation is to you only. As I said... with the immediate threat gone I can't guarantee that we'll be allowed to remain in the area unless we terminate our agreement with the Vruahn. If that happens— if we leave our posts—and the Phage return... I think you get the picture."

"Yeah, I get it," Marcum said sourly. "Captain, make sure you leave the *Ares* in good order and then get your ass to Vruahn space and see what they want. Hopefully you come back with good news."

****

"*Ares* departing!"

Jackson saluted the Marine stationed by the airlock hatchway before stepping through with some trepidation. The lead Vruahn ship had docked a few hours prior, but Colonel Blake had made no move to disembark onto the *Ares* as he waited for Jackson to get things in order so they could leave.

Blake had said they would be gone no longer than a week, but with no idea how fast his ship was capable of travelling he couldn't even fathom a guess as to how far away from Terran space they would be going. Suffice it to say that, other than Blake and his crew, he would be going further than any other human in history. The fact he was taking such a trip when the end result was meeting another unknown alien race face to face made him reconsider how much he really trusted the man who claimed he was from twenty-first century Earth.

"Colonel?" he called out as he approached the end of the flexible gangway. As the word left his mouth the flat white material of the Vruahn ship rippled and irised open into a hatchway.

"Welcome aboard, Captain," Blake's voice called out from somewhere within the interior. "If you'll step onboard we'll get underway. We have a long way to go."

"If you say so," Jackson muttered as he stepped over the threshold and onto the alien ship.

The interior wasn't what he had expected at all. In his mind he had envisioned exotic materials, indecipherable text on the walls, and strange, curving shapes. Instead, the ship looked oddly like something human engineers would design. There were even the requisite warning placards on the walls and hatchways cautioning people to duck or watch their steps.

"This was done entirely for our benefit, of course." Blake appeared from around one of the corners ahead, seeming to read his mind. "The first ships they built for us mimicked many of the design cues from the *Carl Sagan* and we've never seen any reason to deviate from that, although I wouldn't mind a bit more in the way of creature comforts here and there. Let me show you to your quarters and then we can shove off."

"I see you're becoming more comfortable with Fleet vernacular," Jackson observed.

"Just trying to fit in," Blake smiled. "To be honest, there are more similarities between your Fleet and our old Navy than there is with the Air Force."

"I suppose it makes sense in a way," Jackson said, following Blake until they came out of the narrow corridor and into a sprawling, wide passage that was at least as large as one of the main access tubes on the *Ares*. "And you're the only person on this ship?"

"Correct," Blake said. "This main corridor runs down the centerline of the entire ship. It's more for moving components and machinery than for people. She can carry up to one hundred and fifty crew members comfortably, while the two cargo bays can be reconfigured to haul up to a thousand in a pinch."

"That just raises more questions than it answers," Jackson said. "I thought these ships were always designed just for you."

"They were," Blake confirmed. "The first generation ships were actually little bigger than your cargo shuttles, but when we discovered we were being redeployed to defend human planets we asked for this iteration to be built with a larger crew in mind."

"Wait... each mission you deploy on you completely redesign your ships?" Jackson was utterly shocked.

"Have to," Blake said, leading him off another side corridor. "The Phage adapt each of their sub groups to target a specific threat. That's why we were so easily able to defeat that many Alphas at Nuovo Patria. While these ships *are* extremely powerful, the fact those Alphas were built to counter your specific types of armaments and strategies made them completely incapable of standing up to the heavy energy weapons we employ on these ships."

"I see," Jackson said. He let the conversation drop as he was led into a small suite that would have looked completely natural on a Terran starship from two hundred years ago. The casual comments from the colonel were new information and might be important when it came to how they were to move forward in allying with them. What troubled him was that he couldn't tell if these little gems were being deliberately withheld during the previous meetings.

"Go ahead and toss your pack here and then I'll take you up to the flight deck," Blake said from the hatchway. Jackson did just that and turned to continue following the colonel forward.

The bridge, or flight deck, was nowhere near as spacious as what he had on the *Ares*. In fact, it was rather on the cramped side. There appeared to be two identical stations facing forward with an array of monitors and panels for each and two more seats behind those, offset slightly outboard, that seemed to be more specialized in function.

"Sorry for the lack of space," Blake said as he slid into the left seat and motioned Jackson to take the right. "Since I'm usually a one-man-band I never bothered to try and make the flight deck as expansive as the bridges of your starships. To be honest, the ship does most of the work so this is more of a glorified monitoring station with a few rough inputs from me along the way."

"So is this ship... sentient?"

"Not exactly," Blake said as he began activating his control panels. "Stand by to detach. No, the AI aboard is extremely intuitive and has been working with me for a long, long time, but it isn't really a freethinking being. Not in the sense that you're talking about anyway."

"How do you communicate with it?" Jackson asked.

"Drifting away from the *Ares* now. We'll engage the main engine when we have more separation," Blake said. "You can either use these input panes that you'll see throughout the ship, or you can simply speak to it."

"How will it know I'm addressing it? Does it have a name?" Jackson asked.

"Not really," Blake said. "I just call it 'Computer.' Strange since it's my only companion sometimes for months on end. Anyway… Computer, go ahead and introduce yourself."

"Hello, Senior Captain Jackson Wolfe," a disembodied, decidedly female voice spoke to him. "It's a pleasure to make your acquaintance. I have been analyzing all the data from your previous engagements and look forward to speaking to you about them at length."

"Is that right?" Jackson asked.

"Yes, Captain," the ship answered him.

"We're now clear of the formation," Blake said. "Building power now for our first hop."

"Hop?" Jackson was fascinated. He'd felt no sensation whatsoever, not even the subtle change in lighting or hiss from the air vents, that the ship had been accelerating.

"The Vruahn ships don't try to play games by distorting spacetime like your warp drives," Blake explained. "They circumvent it completely and fold space so that we'll just pop out at a different point, the distance being dependent on the power we apply to the drive."

"How much power is available?"

"The correct way to ask that question is how much power can this ship handle?" Blake smiled. "Power generation happens on planets scattered throughout Vruahn space and is transmitted to this ship through manipulation of quantum vacuum states. I can barely understand the computer's stripped-down explanation of this, so don't ask me any details on how it works. Apparently the entire Vruahn power system is based on this."

"That would have a lot of advantages." Jackson was awed. "But it also seems to inject a lot of vulnerability depending on how centralized the power generators are."

"I couldn't even hazard a guess," Blake shrugged. "My contact with the Vruahn doesn't include conversations about any of their vulnerabilities."

Jackson said nothing, but he was beginning to form a picture of the relationship his living ancestors shared with this enigmatic alien species, and it wasn't a pleasant picture. He understood the Vruahn not wanting to divulge too much to a comparatively primitive and violent species, but that wasn't what he was seeing so far. Rather than question Colonel Blake about it he decided to wait and get his answers directly from the source.

"You may as well go and try to get some rest, Captain," Blake said after a moment. "We're not permitted to hop directly into Vruahn-controlled space and the negotiation process can be a bit lengthy, even for one of their own ships. We won't get there for at least another day."

"Very well," Jackson said. "I could use a bit of sleep. I'm assuming the computer can tell me where the mess deck is?"

"Confirmed, Captain," the computer answered.

"Then I'm all set," Jackson stood up. "You know where to find me if you need me."

"Sweet dreams, Captain," Blake said.

"Not likely," Jackson muttered once he was off the flight deck.

Chapter 8

The "flight" out of Terran space was short and uneventful, as there was no discernible sense of travel while in the Vruahn ship. As Jackson explored the bit that the computer allowed him to see it became obvious to him that very little of the interior, meant to imitate a human ship, was actually functional. It was just a veneer that seemed to have little effect on the ship itself. The more he thought about it, the more confused and disturbed he became by what he was finding. In turn, this led him to be more guarded and cautious about what he said around Colonel Blake.

"We just arrived in one of the Boundary Systems," Blake said as he read off his displays. "This is where we've always come to make direct contact with our Vruahn liaisons. The second planet in this system even has a settlement where we can go to relax and interact between deployments."

"Interesting," Jackson said neutrally. "Is that where I'll meet with whomever requested this get together?"

"Most likely," Blake nodded. "Just to give you some warning, you'll be talking to a surrogate, not an actual Vruahn. To be honest, we don't even know what they really look like. They appear to us in a form that is an attempt to look 'human' but it can be a bit… unsettling."

"It can't be any more unsettling than some of the Phage forms we've seen," Jackson shrugged. "Why do they bother using a remote form like that?"

"I assume they feel we'd be too disturbed by their appearance," Blake said. "Or it could be as simple as they're unable to exist in an environment suited to us. I've never received a direct answer to the question, really."

The pair fell into an uncomfortable silence as the ship drifted further into the system. Jackson tried to manipulate one of his own terminals to display how far away they'd traveled from New Sierra, but the computer seemed unwilling to give him the information. Just as he was about to ask Colonel Blake for the distance they'd 'hopped,' a short alert sounded and data began scrolling quickly across the displays. The colonel was visibly shocked.

"What?"

"This is highly unusual, but it looks like the Vruahn came in person to talk to you," Blake said. "One of their cruisers just appeared in the system and I'm being ordered to dock with it directly."

"Do they come here often?" Jackson asked.

"This is the first time I've seen one of their ships in this system other than the ones we pilot ourselves,"

Blake shook his head. "I'm sorry, Captain, but I have nothing to offer you as far as what to expect. This is a bit beyond any interaction I've ever had with them."

"Aren't I always the lucky one?" Jackson sighed.

****

The docking procedure was as anticlimactic as everything else aboard Colonel Blake's ship. One minute they were drifting in space, the next the computer piped up and told them they'd achieved hard dock with the Vruahn cruiser. Not even a bump like you'd get on a Terran fleet carrier when a cargo shuttle slammed into an airlock.

"Captain Wolfe is requested at the port, aft airlock," the computer said.

"Will the colonel be joining me?" Jackson climbed out of his seat.

"No, Captain," the computer intoned. "You are the only human requested at this time."

****

Jackson found himself in a white, sterile room that had no discernible angles, corners or even light source. Even the form-fitting chair he sat in was made of that same nondescript material and seemed to meld seamlessly into the floor. He'd been sitting there for what seemed like hours, but the lack of any sensory input could have been playing games with his internal clock. For all he knew he'd only been there for ten minutes.

After what could have been another few minutes, or another hour, a second chair flowed up out of the floor facing across from him, hardening into a shape nearly identical to the one he sat in. While mildly impressed at the casual implementation of what would have been an incredibly exotic and expensive material in the Confederacy, Jackson was beginning to feel the first twinges of real annoyance at how he was being treated. Just when he felt he could take no more the wall across from him slid apart slightly and a bipedal... something... slipped in through the seam before it rescaled itself. Not sure what the protocol was, Jackson stood and waited respectfully while the being walked further into the room.

"Senior Captain Jackson Wolfe of Earth," the androgynous face said without a trace of emotion. "Thank you for coming at our request."

"Thank you for making it sound like I had a choice," Jackson said, sitting only when the other being in the room did. Since no physical greeting was offered, Jackson kept his hands at his side and tried to calm himself down.

"There is always a choice, Captain," the being said. "In everything we do, or don't do, even the most mundane choices we make cause ripples that affect everything around us."

"So you're a construct meant to communicate with me on behalf of the Vruahn?" Jackson said. "Why such an elaborate system?"

"You are correct in a way," the being said. "This body is an artificial construct, but you are interacting directly with me in real-time. You may call me Setsi."

"And my second question?"

"These protocols were established when we began encountering fledgling species taking their first tentative steps into the vastness of the universe," Setsi said. "Unpredictable reactions from both the species being contacted as well as the various microbes we all invariably carry led us to develop ways to minimize the physical and psychological impacts on those we may chance upon."

"Sensible, if a bit inexplicable once communications have been normalized," Jackson said. "So... why am I here?"

"There's no single answer to your question," Setsi said.

"I was led to believe you were interested in me because of a possibility the Phage had directly contacted me," Jackson said. "Am I incorrect in that?"

"That is indeed the reason why we asked to see you, but it is not the only reason you are here."

"Whose reasons are we referring to?" Jackson asked.

"Very good, Captain," Setsi's mouth turned up at the corners in a fair imitation of a smile. "What is it you hope to accomplish by this meeting? Would you really risk such a long trip just to provide a bit of information to someone you'd never met?"

"I want a way to stop the Phage." Jackson put all his cards on the table.

"Have we not already provided that?" Setsi asked. "Colonel Blake's force arrived just in time to save one of your planets, did they not?"

"And they also arrived far too late for a handful of others," Jackson countered. "Millions of lives lost. There's also nothing to prevent them from returning with a force so large that even Blake's squadron would be overwhelmed."

"A fair point," Setsi said. "But let me divert the conversation for a bit. When you say you wish to 'stop' the *Phage,* as you call them, what is it you're really saying?"

"Ideally I'd like a weapon of such scope and power that it would keep the Phage from attacking another human planet ever again, but we both know that's impossible," Jackson said. "So that leaves me with one alternative… I want to eradicate the Phage presence from our surrounding space and hit back so hard that they never venture near us again."

"You would declare a war of genocide on an entire species as recompense for the loss of less than five percent of your species' total population?" Setsi asked coldly, the previously dead eyes now glimmering.

"I will do what I must to keep the other ninety-five percent safe," Jackson said hotly. "As a matter of philosophy I see no difference in the loss of one life or millions. An unprovoked attack on our species cannot stand without a response."

"So what if I offered to assist you in eliminating an equal number of Phage lives, or even a proportionate number?" Setsi asked calmly.

Jackson could tell he was being prodded, tested for specific responses. He had no doubt that the Vruahn had built a fairly accurate predictive model on human behavior given their long interactions with an observation group as large as Blake's crew.

"Allow me to deviate slightly at this point," Jackson said, wanting to exert some control over the conversation. "Why bother with the human crews at all? I find it difficult to believe that they offer anything that a well-designed piece of software can't duplicate after some trial and error. The fact the ships in Colonel Blake's squadron are crewed is a bit of a mystery to me."

"We certainly tried," Setsi said. "In the future we may do exactly as you say, but it was Colonel Blake and his group that taught us the fundamentals of warfare. For now we're content to keep a working system in place."

"I doubt that's it," Jackson said.

"You doubt?" Setsi actually frowned. Jackson wondered if the human analog was so complete even facial expressions were translated as he doubted the Vruahn themselves actually frowned.

"I do," Jackson pressed. "Colonel Blake is from a time where wars were fought within the atmosphere of a single planet against opponents of the same species. He has zero frame of reference when it comes to fighting in space with starships, much less going up against something as utterly alien as the Phage. I refuse to believe that he's been able to develop such effective strategies in a vacuum and apply them so successfully."

"So then, Captain," Setsi said, the mouth a hard, thin line. "Why do *you* think we've allowed Colonel Blake the opportunity to serve as he has?"

"You have me at a disadvantage, I'll admit," Jackson said. "I've only had this one interaction with your species, and it's not even direct communication, so my assumptions are skewed by a certain bias... but I think you've left your rescued humans in those ships as a firewall. You develop weapons of incredible power, but in the end it's the human who decides to press the button. It's the morality of the human that decides if a living, intelligent being dies. I beg your forgiveness if I'm wrong, but from where I sit... Blake's crew allows you to keep a clear conscience while still getting a job done that, despite your revulsion, needs to be done."

"You've dared to come here and accuse us of... using... your primitive race as some sort of attack animal?" Setsi's expression was again unreadable.

"I'm simply offering an outlook based on my limited observations and experience," Jackson said. He'd not actually meant to come all this way and insult the Vruahn. "But if I'm so out of line answer me this one question: when you discovered that ship full of dead humans and decided to revive the ones you could, why did you keep them here? Why didn't you simply take them back home if your intentions were as magnanimous as you claim?"

"The usefulness of this conversation has run its course, I believe," Setsi stood. "You will be escorted back to Colonel Blake's ship and we will call upon you if needed."

"I understand," Jackson said with a nod. "I sincerely apologize if I've given any offense."

Setsi simply stared at him with its cold, dead eyes before turning and exiting the way it came.

"I feel like that could have gone better," Jackson mumbled.

****

"How did it go, Captain?" Colonel Blake asked as Jackson walked into the ship's small officer's mess.

"I think very badly," Jackson said honestly.

"How so?" Blake seemed very concerned. "Were they unhappy with your explanation about the Phage message?"

"We never actually got to that," Jackson admitted. "Tell me, Colonel… why did you never bother to return to Earth once you were revived?"

"Like I said, so much time had passed none of us felt like we'd really recognize the place anyway," Blake frowned. "It was better to stay out here and help those that needed it than try to piece together a life that no longer existed back home. Why are you asking about this, Captain?"

"Idle curiosity," Jackson lied. "Setsi and I had talked briefly about your initial revival."

"I see," Blake turned back to his meal. "There were a few of us that wanted to just head back home. Well, most of us did, if I'm honest. But in the end we decided to remain a crew and they left the choice up to me. When I saw how much destruction the Phage were causing, I decided we'd be of better use staying with the Vruahn and trying to help."

"What did you guys call them back then?" Jackson changed the subject after seeing Blake's obvious discomfort.

"The Vruahn never gave us a term for them that we could ever hope to pronounce," Blake said. "We actually were calling them 'cockroaches' for the longest time since one of the original forms we faced had an uncanny resemblance to the bug. Imagine a cockroach two-thirds the size of an Alpha."

"No thanks," Jackson shuddered. "But it does make me wish CENTCOM Science and Research had come up with more clever names than just going down the alphabet."

They ate a rushed meal before going their separate ways. Blake was heading back to the flight deck to try and make contact with the rest of his squadron and Jackson, although fascinated by the possibility of real time coms over a distance of lightyears, was just too exhausted after his conversation with Setsi. He was asleep before the lights had even fully dimmed and as such was a bit shocked and disoriented when the computer woke him up after what seemed like only a few minutes of rest.

"Captain Wolfe, your presence is once again requested."

"Shit."

Chapter 9

"Welcome back, Captain Wolfe." Setsi was already seated in the same sterile room when Jackson walked in.

"Setsi," he said with a polite nod. "Thank you for having me back."

"I will admit to finding you quite fascinating," Setsi said. "When Colonel Blake's ship was in proximity to your own vessels we were able to access most of your computer records. I've been reviewing those that your own people keep pertaining to you and your exploits." Jackson decided not to mention that forcibly hacking into a secure computer network was considered rude, to say the least.

"Tell me this, Captain… why fight so hard for a people that seem to feel your life is of a lesser value than their own simply by virtue of where you were born?"

"This sort of shortsightedness and bigotry has been part of the human experience, in one form or another, since we crawled out of our caves and discovered fire," Jackson leaned back with an explosive exhale. "If the Phage win, Earth won't be spared, so there will be little satisfaction for me by knowing I stood aside while those who participated in that foolishness burned. Had I allowed myself to be held back by what others assumed to be a handicap I would have never made it to space, never commanded my own ship… why should I let their unqualified opinions of me limit my dreams?"

"But you must still hate them on some level," Setsi dug a little deeper.

"Yes," Jackson admitted. "And on that same level I always will. But that doesn't mean that I'm willing to stand by and let the entire species die for it."

"Fascinating," Setsi repeated. "Let's move back to the present. What would you do if we gave you what you wanted? Would you show the Phage the same sort of compassion you're willing to show your fellow humans?"

"I'm not going to lie to you and I think you already know the answer to your question," Jackson stared into the other's eyes. "If you give me the means, I will destroy the Phage. I will do the thing that you cannot bring yourself to do. Instead of skirmishes and meaningless holding actions I will take the fight to them and make sure that there isn't another species that falls before them."

"Your directness is shocking, Captain," Setsi said. "Would you feel no remorse for your actions?"

"More than you'd ever know," Jackson said. "But this is what I do, Setsi. My goal is not to return to a peaceful life without the Phage, I don't even expect to survive the coming fight. My goal is to make sure that nobody else has to come after me and make the hard decisions that I wouldn't."

Setsi just stared at him, motionless, for several moments.

"We have decided to grant you your wish," it said finally. "But it will not be easy and it may turn out to actually be impossible by this point."

"I can't imagine that," Jackson said. "A whole fleet of those ships you have and—"

"We will not be providing direct military support," Setsi raised its hand. "Your instincts regarding our motivations have been more accurate than you likely realize, but we are still not able to make that leap, give up all that we are, and actively participate in what amounts to extermination."

"I see," Jackson said, waiting to see just what the Vruahn were offering.

"What we can give you is knowledge," Setsi said. "Colonel Blake believes he knows the location of the Phage core, the main neural center that controls them all, but this is imprecise. We are willing to turn over all the exact data we have on the core as well as how to defeat it. As I said, Captain… it will not be easy."

"If there's any possibility then we have to try," Jackson said. "Will Colonel Blake and his squadron at least be permitted to aid us?"

"I will speak to Colonel Blake shortly," Setsi evaded the question. "I must be honest, Captain... this was not a unanimous decision. There are many who do not wish for your success. We will need to act quickly before those voices are able to gain too many allies."

"So why are you helping us?" Jackson asked.

"Trillions upon trillions of beings have suffered and died because of our arrogance," Setsi said after another long pause. "While we justified our inaction we failed to see that it was also our responsibility to address the Phage simply because we were the only ones able to do so. Farewell, Captain. I do hope that you find some measure of peace in your own life before your task is concluded."

Jackson left the chamber confused and contemplating what in the hell Setsi had meant about their 'responsibility' when he passed Colonel Blake by the airlock.

"Here to escort me the rest of the way, Colonel?" Jackson asked.

"Not exactly, Captain," Blake fidgeted. "I've been ordered to speak face to face with Setsi."

"I take it this is an unusual request?"

"It is," Blake said.

"Interesting." Jackson wasn't sure why Blake seemed so apprehensive.

He continued to be troubled by the relationship the crew of the *Carl Sagan* had with the Vruahn. Setsi had more or less admitted that they'd been using humans as their personal attack dogs and Blake, despite having served in his current role for damn near a century, seemed to be almost fearful of his Vruahn handlers. Again... the attack dog analogy was becoming more and more apt.

The more he thought about it, the more Jackson was pretty sure he didn't like the Vruahn. There was an arrogance and smugness he'd detected in Setsi about the arrangement they had with Blake and his crew that didn't sit well with him. It certainly wasn't a partnership born out of mutual need, and from what he could see the crew of human explorers were being tricked into doing the dirty work the Vruahn felt was far beneath them.

Jackson's ruminations were harshly interrupted by a klaxon alarm accompanied by a flashing light. He knew that on any human vessel that meant trouble of some sort, so he turned back the way he'd come and raced for the flight deck. He'd only taken three steps before the lights in the corridor cut out and he felt the gut-wrenching sensation of freefall as artificial gravity failed.

"Computer!" Jackson barked as he caromed off the bulkhead, still trying to arrest his forward momentum. "Report!"

"Main power failure," the computer intoned. "Backup systems initializing."

"No shit," Jackson muttered as he got a good grip on the edge of a hatchway. "Is Colonel Blake on his way back to this ship?"

"Affirmative, Captain Wolfe."

Jackson only grunted a response, now able to get his bearings and begin moving up the corridor again. A soft glow of emergency lighting came up along the edges of the deck to at least let him see where the hell he was going. He was still heading to the flight deck, but he had absolutely zero working knowledge of the exotic energy transmission system employed by the Vruahn. He'd at least be moral support for the colonel once he made his way back over.

It was only a few minutes after Jackson had gotten himself settled down into what he now internally referred to as the copilot's seat when Colonel Blake, executing a precise flip to orient his feet towards the front of the flight deck, shot in and quickly took his seat.

"Impressive," Jackson nodded his appreciation of Blake's zero g aerobatics. "So do you know what's happened?"

"I do," Blake said grimly. "The Phage executed a three-pronged, simultaneous strike on three Vruahn power production facilities, one of which provides power to our ships. I don't know the extent of the damage, but from what I can infer the planets them-selves may have been lost."

"Damn," Jackson let out a low whistle. "So how long before our backup power takes over?"

"I'm not sure," Blake admitted. "I've never had to switch over to it. In the meantime the computer will begin negotiating with other feeder sites to get main power back online as soon as possible. The cruiser has just detached from us so we're free floating right now."

"Not a pleasant proposition," Jackson frowned. "Why would they cut us loose and leave this ship adrift with no engines or maneuvering?"

"Four Phage ships just entered the system," Blake said tightly. "They look to be generally Alpha-like in configuration but with completely different power signatures."

"So they're not the variety built to kill humans," Jackson nodded. "Have the Phage ever made such an overt move against the Vruahn before?"

"Not since they were discovered over three hundred years ago," Blake shook his head. "Setsi seemed genuinely shocked at the news."

For the next thirty minutes the pair tensely watched the monitors, while the computer displayed data from the two other Vruahn ships in the system of the Phage ships deploying out from the point where they emerged into the system.

"What are the combat capabilities of the two Vruahn ships that still have power?" Jackson asked.

"Zero," Blake said. "I told you, they're completely pacifist. We're the only thing in this system that isn't Phage that has a chance of fighting back."

Jackson bit back the retort he had about how high and mighty ideals were fine… until you were staring down the barrel of a gun with nothing to defend yourself but sanctimony and self-righteousness.

The Phage ships seemed intent on trying to cut off the two Vruahn cruisers, deploying into a picket line that was moving to cut off their retreat. Jackson wasn't entirely sure of the scale he was seeing on the display, but it looked like the Vruahn ships, though mobile, weren't at full power themselves. They were struggling to stay ahead of their tormenters and he surmised their FTL drives must have also been offline since they hadn't hopped out yet.

"One of the Vruahn ships is flagging," Jackson pointed out. "Do you know which one that is?"

"I know it isn't Setsi's ship, but nothing more precise than that. We don't have too much interaction with their regular fleet," Blake said. "The Phage see it too." Sure enough, two of the Phage ships peeled off from the formation and went to pounce on the stricken cruiser that was now trying to turn in and catch a gravity assist from the sixth planet in the system, a Class I gas giant with striations similar to Jupiter.

It was a desperate move that was destined to fail. The two Phage ships put on a burst of acceleration that put them directly behind the fleeing ship in less than an hour. On the rudimentary telemetry link all they could decipher was that the Vruahn ship was no more. Jackson could make out from the accompanying data that the Phage had utilized a more intense form of the directed plasma weapon he'd been up against when they encountered that first Alpha.

"That second cruiser is in deep shit if we can't get this ship up and running," Jackson said.

"You want to pit us against four Phage heavies?" Blake cocked an eyebrow at him.

"*Want* might be too strong a term," Jackson said. "But we're the only warship here and apparently the only beings with any compunction to fight."

"True," Blake said quietly.

What Jackson didn't tell the colonel was that they'd yet to receive the promised help from Setsi. If the cruiser was destroyed with the alien still aboard, Jackson feared that their agreement might not be honored without another protracted negotiation with some other Vruahn. Or not at all. The Terran fleet was massing near New Sierra and they were waiting on him to bring back something that would allow them to kick the Phage right in the teeth. He wouldn't go back empty-handed.

After another hour of watching the Phage formation redeploy to try and box in the last cruiser, there were some promising flickers from the other terminals on the flight deck. With one last *thump* that could be felt through the deck plates the lights came back up fully and Jackson could literally feel the power course through the ship. All of the other displays flashed to life and the thrum of the engine coming back online vibrated the backs of their seats.

"We're in business," Blake said. "We're receiving power from a secondary generation site. We'll be at full capacity in another twenty minutes. Propulsion and weapons energizing now. How do you want to do this?"

"This is your ship." Jackson was taken aback by the question. "I haven't the first clue as to her capabilities."

"You're far more qualified at long odds like this," Blake argued. "I can pilot the ship, but I'd feel more comfortable with you handling tactics."

"Fair enough," Jackson acquiesced, more interested in getting moving than in arguing the point further. "Target the closest Phage ship. Hit it with a full power active scan to get its attention. We need to break up that formation. From what I saw at Nuovo Patria I think we have the speed advantage. That's going to be important."

"Active scans coming up now," Blake said.

"Phage fleet is already responding," Jackson said in awe. "Even your sensors are instantaneous?"

"For all practical purposes, yes," Blake said. "At least at distances as short as within a star system."

"This advantage alone would be a game changer for us," Jackson shook his head. "Too bad the Vruahn aren't interested in a technological exchange. Keep focusing on that closest target and leave the engine in standby. Let's wait to see what the rest do before we tip our hand that we have teeth and legs again."

"Yes, sir," Blake said without a trace of irony. "Switching weapons back to standby as well."

"What's the response time if we need offensive systems?"

"Eight seconds."

"I could get used to this," Jackson muttered. "Look! Both the trailing ships in that formation are braking and turning in."

"One is still pursuing the cruiser, though," Blake said.

"But it's not closing anymore," Jackson said. "It's just going to maintain position to keep us honest, but we're now the focus—"

The chirping from a panel on Blake's side interrupted him.

"Colonel, Captain," a likeness of Setsi appeared on most of the monitors. "What is it you're still doing in this system? Our data shows your ship has had power completely restored."

"We're pulling the Phage off your ship so you can extend and escape," Jackson answered. "That last one will likely hang back near you, but we'll try to at least keep these other three occupied."

"I see," Setsi said. "Is there any particular action you'd like us to take?"

"Given your lack of offensive or defensive systems, I'd advise you to continue your retreat," Jackson said. "Try not to give any overt indications that your main flight systems are coming back online until you're ready to hop completely out of here."

"A sound strategy," Setsi said, its face as impassive as ever. "I shall leave you to your task."

"Not very chatty," Jackson observed as the monitors switched back to their previous display modes.

"Never is," Blake said. "So what's your next move? We can't just sit here drifting forever running the sensors at full power."

"I want to lure in the closest one to us a bit more," Jackson said. "He's already taken the bait and is now accelerating towards us enough to know that he's committed. Now we just have to hope your primary weapons are still as effective as the last time I saw them."

"You think these particular Phage are adapted to our ships?" Blake asked.

"It's a fair assumption," Jackson said. "They're obviously part of the larger, incredibly well-coordinated attack on the Vruahn, so I would think they'd have been adapted to the known threats. Stand by... the other two have stopped braking and are coming onto a direct intercept course."

They continued to watch as the three ships approaching formed up into a loose phalanx, their reactionless drives making it possible for them to come at them in a relatively shallow arc, paying little respect to neither the gas giant they were passing nor the primary star. Jackson noted a distinct difference in how these Phage were operating even with the little amount of observation he'd been afforded. Rather than behaving like a pack or a swarm they were flying in distinct formations, coordinating against targets... they were fighting like humans. While he wasn't sure exactly what it meant, he knew it couldn't possibly be a coincidence.

The two trailing Phage ships in the formation continued to widen out from the lead ship that was bearing down on the seemingly helpless Vruahn warship. Jackson watched for a moment longer, unable to tell if they were trying to goad him into a rash move or if their tactics were really so simplistic that they'd given no thought about trying to disguise their flanking maneuver.

"Okay," Jackson said after a few more moments of silent observation. "Give me a crash course on your weaponry: types, ranges, and any limiting factors like charge times or guidance."

"Main weapon is a pulse laser battery, primary and redundant projectors with a maximum output of four hundred kilojoules," Blake said. "There's also two racks of guided fusion warhead missiles, eight missiles per rack, per side. Defensive systems include full coverage point-defense batteries and an EM diffusion screen that can take the sting out of their plasma bursts, but won't completely deflect them."

"Impressive," Jackson nodded. "Computer, give me a display of concentric rings with this ship as the epicenter. Label and adjust each ring to correspond with nominal and maximum effective range for all weapons."

"You are unauthorized—"

"Override!" Blake shouted. "Captain Wolfe is to be accepted as command personnel with his authority to be superseded only by myself for the duration of the engagement."

"Acknowledged," the computer said after a long pause and began populating one of Jackson's displays to comply with his request.

"Very good," he said. "Now, superimpose the sensor data from local space onto this. Include all threats and scale accordingly to make sure I can still make out the details of the ranging rings."

"Acknowledged."

"Colonel, if you would, bring the primary flight systems online and stabilize our drift," Jackson said. "Leave the weapons on standby for now."

"Yes, sir," Blake said, his hands dancing over the holographic displays. "What reaction are you hoping to get?"

"If they see that we're regaining propulsion and attitude control they may decide on a reckless charge before the weapons come up as well," Jackson said.

The response from the Phage wasn't exactly what Jackson was hoping for, but it was something he could work with. Instead of abandoning their methodical approach and coming at them in a blind rush they became even more cautious. The flanking ships turned in so they were paralleling the lead ship even as it began braking slightly, slowing enough so that it could closely observe the Vruahn ship while not risking flying into weapons range at speed.

Again, Jackson was intrigued, and horrified, at how these Phage seemed able to reason out basic tactics beyond the usual swarm and destroy he'd observed from all but a single Alpha since the war began. He made a mental note to ask Blake for all the sensor logs of the encounter for Fleet Research and Science Division. Maybe the Phage employed a more careful strategy with a technologically advanced foe like the Vruahn, while a less capable species like humans were just bludgeoned with the less-capable units. Bruised ego aside, it was certainly something to consider.

"Now what, Captain?" Blake asked, clearly becoming agitated that Jackson was letting three massive Phage ships continue to close with complete impunity.

"Now, Colonel, we spring our trap," Jackson grinned at his companion. "Put our nose on the lead Phage. Activate all offensive and defensive systems and accelerate to flank speed at your discretion."

"Coming about," Blake dialed in the new course. "Guns coming up… here we go!" There was no sensation of acceleration inside the advanced warship, but Jackson was so accustomed to interpreting his universe through the passionless numbers on a navigation display that he felt an electric thrill as he watched the ship scream towards their target at over six hundred g's.

"Computer, I want a firing solution for an automatic full salvo from our main guns the moment the target crosses our maximum range threshold," Jackson said.

"At that range there is no guarantee the target will be disabled or destroyed," the computer said.

"I asked for a firing solution, not a lecture," Jackson said. "Make it happen."

"Acknowledged," the computer responded. "Firing solution calculated and verified. Please confirm order to auto-fire main battery." Jackson looked over to Blake and made an 'after you' gesture with his hand.

"Confirmed," Blake said. "You are clear to automatically fire the main battery as per Captain Wolfe's instructions."

"Acknowledged."

Jackson watched the acceleration taper off as the ship quickly approached its maximum real-space velocity and was already travelling an order of magnitude faster than any thrust powered Terran vessel could achieve. He tamped down the resentment and jealousy of the Vruahn's technical prowess and concentrated on the matter at hand. Their closure rate was now over .65c and was actually decreasing despite their acceleration, since the Phage were now braking hard in the face of Jackson's charge. He ruefully acknowledged that due to the difficulties of precisely timing the shot of a laser, a speed of light weapon, at relativistic speeds the two humans had no choice but to turn the operation over to the computer.

"Full salvo standing by... firing," the computer said.

"Fire at will," Jackson ordered. "Maintain continuous fire on the target."

"Acknowledged."

They didn't have long to wait and Jackson thrilled at a battle unfolding in the span of hours instead of days. He had to temper himself as the compressed time scale certainly upped the adrenaline factor, but it also took away the extended periods of time he was accustomed to when devising strategy and reacting to his opponent.

The powerful laser battery continued to fire even as the first salvo ripped into the prow of the target. Unable to evade the blasts or absorb that much energy, the Phage ship mushroomed out and gave the next few blasts unimpeded access to its internals. The organic hull material stretched and cracked as the laser energy superheated the internal workings of the ship, sublimating them to a fast-expanding gas and exerting inexorable pressure against the hull, stretching it to its limit.

"Cease fire!" Jackson barked as the Phage ship began to spin out of control, thousands of cracks in the hull acting as tiny gas jets and pushing the now-lifeless hulk into an erratic tumble. "Colonel, angle us away from the debris and keep us on a trajectory towards the outer system."

"The other two ships are turning in and pursuing," Blake pointed out. Jackson checked again on the sensor data coming in on their other two targets.

"Ignore them for now," Jackson said. "Look at their acceleration profile. They're coming about to pursue, but I don't think they actually are trying to catch us. Set course for a direct intercept of the Phage ship pursuing Setsi's cruiser."

"Course set and engaged," Blake said. "We're now at maximum velocity. Time to intercept... four hours and eight minutes." Jackson saw that the target was nearly half a system away and could only shake his head again. He amended his earlier thoughts slightly as he realized that if the Vruahn would simply give them ships like this stripped of their weaponry that Starfleet could still mount an effective defense along the Frontier.

"We're going to leave those two behind us, Captain?"

"For now," Jackson said. "I know leaving an enemy in your wake flies in the face of most warfighting doctrines, but we have one objective here: keep the Phage from taking out that last cruiser. We could amuse ourselves with those other two ships, but we'd risk losing Setsi and thus failing in our mission despite destroying three-quarters of their force."

"So what's the strategy for this next encounter?" Blake asked. "We'll be coming at them head on again."

"And we're not going to have a good angle on the enemy ship without firing past the cruiser at a range I'm not entirely comfortable with," Jackson frowned. "If we shallow out our angle we risk having too short of a firing window before we'd need to reverse course and try to catch them. I'm open to suggestions."

"Computer, message the cruiser and request that they alter course to angle out further towards the outer system," Blake said. Jackson nodded his silent approval of the officer reasserting control over his ship and the engagement.

"This could work," Jackson said. "Hopefully they can get a little more speed and then we'll be in position to slide past them with plenty of room for a shot." Apparently the Phage realized what would happen as well once the cruiser began to alter course. At first it tried to follow the ship to keep continue using it as a shield, but it was trailing too far behind and Blake's ship was coming underneath too fast.

"Computer, begin calculating a trajectory for optimal firing range—"

"Don't bother," Jackson interrupted. "Look." The Phage ship had decided that a suicidal blaze of glory wasn't a viable option and had altered course to head even further out of the system, obviously looking to put some distance between it and the incoming warship.

"The two ships we left behind are following suit," Blake said, confusing Jackson with the expression. He understood what the colonel meant when he saw that both other Phage ships, instead of continuing their half-hearted pursuit, had split and were also flying hard for the system boundary in opposite directions. There was a subtle intelligence in even a move as simple as that.

With only one combat capable ship in the system the fact the three had split up meant that they could only pursue one target. While not a stroke of tactical genius, it yet again flew in the face of the observed Phage tendency to bunch up while traversing through space. Then again... retreat wasn't normally an option they used either, especially when they had a three to one numerical advantage.

"Let's form up on that cruiser and make sure they're okay." Jackson left out that he wanted to make sure Setsi honored his side of their agreement before bugging out of the system.

Chapter 10

"You and Colonel Blake have my gratitude, Captain," Setsi said. Jackson was staring at the human-like face on a monitor that had coalesced before him in his quarters. The warship was in a trailing formation behind the cruiser at a range of two hundred thousand kilometers.

"I take it the Phage ship never fired on you?" he asked.

"A few low-intensity bursts that our anti-navigation hazard screens were able to diffuse. There was no loss of life in the attack and thankfully our power generators are not staffed, so there were no deaths or injuries in those attacks either," Setsi said. "The reason I've asked to speak with you again, Captain, is that our leadership is quite shaken by the brazen assault carried out on our power generation facilities. It has caused immediate and profound economic damage as the three stations hit were vital to much of our heavy production."

"That is quite an opening salvo," Jackson nodded.

"You think this will not be an isolated attack?"

"With the Phage? I'd have to assume it's not," Jackson said. "However, the behavior of this group is quite different than the one we've been fighting. Even their choice of a simultaneous attack on three strategically important targets shows a more advanced command and control apparatus than we're used to dealing with."

"Yes," Setsi said. "Well, there are some logical reasons for that. But the point of this communication is to inform you that our position on the Phage situation has shifted."

"How so?"

"We will provide you a more comprehensive form of support in your fight." Setsi didn't elaborate.

"In exchange for what?" Jackson asked. "I can understand you're shaken and probably quite angry after this attack, but that hardly seems a reason to come about and provide support us."

"In exchange for you doing what you're planning... for doing what we will not." Setsi's face morphed into an unreadable, alien expression for a moment. "We want you to... eliminate... the Phage."

Jackson was stunned into silence for a moment. This was a profound shift in the very core principles the Vruahn professed to hold so dear. They tossed out their morality over an attack that only hurt their economy? Maybe they weren't so different from humans after all.

"What's in it for us?" Jackson narrowed his eyes. "Let's not dance around this: we're going to do this for our own reasons, for the protection of humanity, but any victory will come at great cost. We're sure to lose tens of thousands of men and women before this is all over, not to mention the devastation to our fleet and infrastructure."

"The difficulties of your task and the sacrifices your people will make are not unnoticed," Setsi said. "In addition to our martial support we will also provide assistance in rebuilding and advancing your people in the wake of the Phage attacks."

"Very well," Jackson nodded. "One more thing... when this is done, and the Phage are eliminated, will you release Blake and his crew from service so they may return to Earth?"

"We will release them from service," Setsi agreed. "There will no longer be any task for them, but there is something you should know before you welcome them back among your people."

****

"Everything okay, Captain?"

"Yes, Colonel," Jackson slid back into the copilot's seat. "Why do you ask?"

"You were staring at me pretty hard there for a moment." Blake turned back to his displays.

"My apologies," Jackson said. "Are we about ready to depart?"

"The last of the technical data has been download-ed from the cruiser and we've been given coordinates to rendezvous with the freighter that will be coming out of Vruahn space so we can escort it the rest of the way to New Sierra," Blake said. "So yeah, we're as ready as we're going to get."

"Then let's get to it," Jackson leaned back. "We've got a lot of work ahead of us."

"We do," Blake nodded, "but it's almost over. I'm not sure how you convinced Setsi to let us completely take out the Phage, but for the first time in longer than I can remember I feel like there's some hope."

"Hang on to that, Colonel," Jackson said, his eyes closed. "I have a feeling hope will be in short supply before this is all over."

"For someone who's come out on top in half a dozen no-win situations you sure are a pessimist," Blake groused as he brought the drive fully online and began to slide out of formation.

"I prefer the term 'realist.'" Jackson didn't open his eyes.

****

The flight back to Terran space was just as uneventful as the trip out had been, and before Jackson knew it they were sliding into formation beside a hulking Vruahn freighter. He was struck at how ugly the vessel was compared to the graceful lines of the warship he was sitting on and the cruisers he'd seen before the Phage destroyed one of them.

"They must have had this gear just lying around," he remarked as he watched the ship through the optical sensors. "I can't believe they could manufacture it that quickly and get it out here."

"Believe it," Blake said. "This ship was built in about forty-eight hours. The Vruahn fabrication process is entirely automated and utilizes nano technology and energy-to-matter conversion and it makes building even the most complex structures look like child's play."

"I wonder if we can have some of that tech tossed in on this deal," Jackson mused.

Blake didn't answer as he talked to the freighter with the help of his ship's computer translating everything. Jackson tried to keep up with the conversation for a bit, but the cultural specific content and unfamiliar terminology left him lost and quickly bored with the whole thing. He went back to reading his tile that he'd managed to convince the computer to load with some of the overview files provided by Setsi.

Despite the Vruahn being far more technologically advanced than humans, there was no magic bullet or ultra-powerful standoff weapon that would allow Jackson to kill the Phage with the press of a button. Though they'd been given a huge advantage with the help Setsi was sending their way, the fight would be won the old-fashioned way: down in the trenches slugging it out until either their enemy faltered or they did. It wasn't something he was looking forward to.

"We're ready to make the final hop into the DeLonges System," Blake said. "We'll arrive first, make contact with Admiral Marcum, and then the freighter will hop in two hours behind us."

"That works," Jackson nodded. "Hopefully things are more or less in the same state of fucked up as they were when we left."

"See… I knew there was an optimist in there somewhere," Blake smiled and engaged the ship's FTL drive.

Chapter 11

"I gotta tell you, Wolfe... I'm not entirely sure how comfortable everyone is going to be with all the alliances you've taken upon yourself to build." Admiral Marcum leaned back in his seat.

"I wouldn't exactly call this an alliance, Admiral," Jackson said. "The Vruahn are offering some material and logistical support, but any military cooperation is still being limited to Colonel Blake's squadron." They were aboard the *Amsterdam* and waiting for the Vruahn freighter, which was now overdue by twenty minutes. Marcum had insisted they dock with his flagship despite Jackson's protests that he wanted to return to the *Ares*.

"How have things been here? Any new political upheaval?"

"Nothing much more than when you left a week ago," Marcum shrugged. "We don't have instantaneous communications like your new friends, so a lot of planets will have gotten the news from the com drones not too long ago. I'm sure we'll start getting some movement one way or another within the next few days."

"I'd imagine President McKellar will have to reassert his authority somehow," Jackson said. "And soon."

"You're not wrong there," Marcum nodded. "It's been quiet on that front since you left. That's not necessarily a good thing. McKellar isn't one to give up power so easily and certainly not for something as petty as the survival of the species."

Jackson resisted the urge to roll his eyes at his superior's joke and instead looked over at the wall display that was currently showing the DeLonges System and updated data on all the ships in it. He quickly found the Ninth Squadron and the *Ares*, his spirits buoyed by the little blue dot representing his ship flying in formation with her sister ships. He was also impressed by the order Marcum had asserted on the chaos he'd left behind. All the ships were now flying in formations and organized by type, all ready to be quickly redeployed into strike packages once they finalized their plans.

"Has Fourth Fleet come over yet or are they still staying loyal to New America?" Jackson asked as he noticed a lot of the dots around New Sierra and DeLonges were red.

"About half and half," Marcum said. "But the commander of the shipyards has turned over control to us, as well as the superintendent of the weapons depot. Both gave up without us having to deploy any NOVA teams. Those were the two assets we absolutely needed to secure. I'm not going to lose any stomach lining over a few captains that feel more loyalty to their political connections than to their oaths as officers. Yes?"

Jackson turned and saw a junior enlisted spacer had just walked into the room and snapped to attention.

"The alien freighter has arrived in the system, sir."

"Very good. You're dismissed," Marcum stood up. "Come on, Wolfe. Let's go greet our guests and then you can quit dancing around and get back to your ship."

"Yes, sir."

As it turned out, the freighter crew didn't think much of their hospitality. After completely ignoring their overtures to speak directly, a plain text message came in saying the cargo had been deposited in orbit over the eighth planet before the ship vanished from their sensors.

"Don't take it too personally, Admiral," Blake said. "I've worked with them for decades and they barely talk to me."

"Whatever," Marcum growled. "Have your squadron get out there and grab the package, Colonel. Bring it back to the shipyards before any of the COs out here gets stupid and decides to go poking around on something that doesn't concern them. Wolfe, you're dismissed. Have one of our shuttles take you back to the *Ares* and then I want the Ninth to make way for the shipyards as well."

"Aye aye, sir," Jackson said enthusiastically before walking off the bridge on Colonel Blake's heels.

****

"*Ares* arriving!" The sound of dozens of boot heels slamming together as the large gathering of crew came to attention greeted Jackson as he walked in through the airlock hatch. He took a moment to look around and sucked in a deep breath of the familiar and unique brand of recycled air that was pumped through his ship.

"At ease!" he called before walking over to where his XO and a surprise visitor were standing. "Captain Wright... to what do we owe the pleasure?"

"I wanted to be here to greet you in person, sir," Celesta Wright smiled. "I was also hoping you'd have time for a face-to-face debrief before the Ninth is called to action."

"No time like the present," Jackson nodded. "Lieutenant Davis, please ask Commander Singh and Major Ortiz to join us in the command deck conference room. Captain Wright, if you'd please come with me."

"Aye, sir." Davis turned on her heel and walked back towards where the large gathering of spacers was beginning to break up.

"How are things aboard the *Icarus*, Captain?" Jackson asked as Celesta fell in step behind and to his right.

"Very good, sir," she said. "After the Battle of Nuovo Patria the crew has become more cohesive and is starting to trust in themselves and each other. Since then we've been running readiness drills around the clock to sharpen response times."

"And you took time away from your training regimen just to fly over and see me walk out of a shuttle?" Jackson arched an eyebrow at her.

"Well—"

"I'm not asking you to sell out a superior, Captain," Jackson almost laughed. "As the person who has spent the most time serving closely with me I'm sure Admiral Marcum felt you'd be uniquely qualified to determine my mental state after returning from direct contact with an unknown alien species."

"There may have been some conversations to that effect," Celesta admitted. "Just so you know, sir, I wasn't entirely comfortable with the idea."

"But orders are orders," Jackson nodded. "I'm not upset, Captain. It's a prudent step taken by a man who has a lot on his shoulders. I'd have been disappointed had he not taken some sort of steps, although I'm a bit insulted by his lack of subtly."

"Yes, sir," Celesta floundered.

"We'll begin serious mission prep within the next few days once the Fleet tech crews get the package opened and inspected," Jackson went on. "But I'll be honest… this is *not* going to be an easy task even with the help of Colonel Blake and his squadron."

"How not easy is it going to be, sir?"

"It's going to make the first Battle of Xi'an seem like a training flight," Jackson grimaced as he walked into his office. "And that's before the hard part begins."

****

"Is everyone online?" Jackson asked, standing at the head of the table.

"Yes, sir," Ensign Hayashi said from the seat to Jackson's left. "All participants have linked in and are live."

"Very well then," Jackson spoke up, addressing the camera near the back of the room. "Thank you all for joining in on this meeting on such short notice. Originally I planned to have us all meet face to face on the New Sierra Shipyards platform, but time is short and we all have a lot of work to do.

"By now you've all received the technical overview of our mission—"

"About that, Captain," Admiral Marcum spoke up. Jackson nodded politely for the admiral to continue. "The most glaring issue we have here could end this mission before it starts. The primary objective is thought to be just over eight thousand lightyears away. As you know, that is *far* beyond the effective range of even our scout ships, let alone our heavy warships with comparatively short legs."

"Part of the Vruahn assistance includes a way to navigate large formations at least two-thirds of the way there using precise navigational data of local spatial anomalies that can work in conjunction with your own warp drives," Colonel Blake spoke up from the flight deck of his own ship. "But that still leaves a distance to cover that is beyond the range of most of your ships."

"Which is why we're compressing our schedule so aggressively," Jackson reasserted control over the meeting. "Even with the Vruahn help, the Fleet will need to make preparations for the extended voyage…

one that ends with a battle that will be like nothing we've ever seen before.

"While the technical teams at New Sierra prep the fleet for its extended voyage, the Ninth will deploy with Colonel Blake's squadron for a task that will be the critical first step in completing the overall mission that ensures the Phage are never able to threaten another populated world. Colonel…"

"Thank you, Captain," Blake said. "I'll keep this brief since this is just a general overview. Mission details are available in the technical package each ship received. In a nutshell, to make this work we will be required to capture an Alpha intact… and not just any Alpha. We'll need the same type that first ventured into Terran space: one of the Super Alphas, as we've come to call them." The shared conference channel erupted into simultaneous conversations that caused the video perspective to flicker wildly before Hayashi locked it back to focus on the *Ares*.

"Let's all settle down and focus," Jackson said loudly. "You heard the colonel correctly, we're going to try and catch one of the bigger Alphas alive. We've been given some specific equipment to that end, but it won't be an especially easy task. Ninth Squadron will depart the system almost immediately and head for the Frontier, while the rest of the Fleet is reorganized into two separate task forces and prep *Ares* for departure should we be successful."

"We'll now begin hearing from individual team leaders and begin receiving specific assignments," Marcum said. "Godspeed to the crews of the Ninth Squadron in their unenviable task, but don't think for a moment that they have the most dangerous assignment in this mission. Before this is all done we'll have all bled."

"Colonel Blake, for organizational purposes I'm rolling your strike force into the Ninth Squadron even though you obviously don't fully report to CENTCOM."

"Understood, sir," Blake nodded. "It will be an honor to fly with the Ninth."

"If nobody has anything else to add we'll now switch everyone over to their respective sub groups," Jackson said. "Good luck, everyone."

For the next three hours the COs and their respective staffs quibbled back and forth over the details even as the Ninth broke orbit and began pushing for the outer system. Colonel Blake's group formed up behind the five *Starwolf*-class ships and easily kept pace.

What hadn't been included in the briefing was that the five Terran destroyers were on their own in the task of capturing one of the more advanced Alphas. Colonel Blake's potent group of warships had a different job. It had come to light during the initial planning stages of the mission that the Vruahn didn't actually know precisely where the main core mind was, only a general area, because the Phage had wised up to that particular vulnerability and began moving it at random times and to random places.

So instead of coming with Jackson to try and wrangle an Alpha and capture it intact, all eighteen of Blake's ships, with their superior range, ability to quickly scan a system and get out unseen, and then report back instantaneously over vast distances, would split up and begin searching the area where Setsi said the "big brain" was most likely moved to.

Admiral Marcum had convinced Jackson to keep the details of Blake's mission murky. While he wasn't exactly trying to deceive his captains, he was trying to minimize the losses through defection that might occur if they began to catch wind of how shaky the plan really was. The extended trip alone would likely lead to the loss of more than a few ships and crews.

Jackson suppressed a shudder as the *Ares* accelerated to transition velocity ahead of the rest of the squadron. They were betting it all on one roll of the dice. Even if they were right, the losses were sure to be horrific and it would take the Fleet decades to recover. If they were wrong, however, then humanity would be left defenseless and stripped bare before the retaliatory onslaught of the Phage.

Chapter 12

"Report!" Jackson ordered once the *Ares* shuddered back into real space.

"Passive scans already started, sir," Barrett said.

"We're getting a status ping from the CIS drone still in the system, Captain," Lieutenant Keller said.

"If that's still here we can assume there aren't any Phage assets in the system," Jackson said. "Stand down from general quarters, normal watch schedule. Tactical, begin high-power active scans of the entire system."

"Aye, sir."

"Coms, let the rest of the squadron know we're clear as soon as they transition in," Jackson stood. "OPS, let Engineering know I want to be under power immediately. Nav... set your course for the X-Ray jump point."

"Aye aye, sir!" Specialist Accari said smartly.

"Warp drive is secured and stowed, sir," Ensign Hayashi said. "Main engines and maneuvering thrusters are online."

"Helm, come onto your new course and get us moving," Jackson began pacing around the bridge. "All ahead full."

"Helm answering new course," the helmsman said. "Ahead full aye!"

The squadron had made the flight from the DeLonges System where the New Sierra Shipyards were to the Xi'an System, the place where the Phage War had officially begun. Jackson figured it was as good a place as any to start their hunt given that the Phage seemed to have a strong compulsion to keep the Xi'an System under their control. It had been well over a year since the last time Fleet ships had chased away or destroyed their rearguard, just after the Battle of Nuovo Patria. To everyone's relief they had yet to make another appearance, but Jackson was hopeful there might be another Alpha hiding in one of the two systems that the Asianic Union had secretly colonized. Some even accused the AU of ignoring colonization protocols and attracting the attention of the Phage in the first place. After receiving a personal message from the Phage and meeting with the Vruahn, Jackson was no longer sure that was the case.

The argument was academic at this point. They were already engaged with the Phage and no matter who started it there was only one way it was going to end. Jackson didn't like the fact that the most critical parts of the mission relied on Vruahn technology that was currently sitting in the cargo holds of the *Ares* and the *Icarus*, but he also had no alternative readily available.

The Vruahn had provided a few sets of self-contained sensor units that the Fleet Science geeks were calling "sniffers." Essentially, they had the ability to detect a Phage presence by sensing the apparatus they used to build their group consciousness. It couldn't decipher what was on the mind of the Phage nor could it tell what type of Phage specifically it was detecting with much accuracy, but the fact that it could operate nearly instantaneously within the sphere of a star system meant Jackson had a theoretical advantage he'd not had before. But his lack of experience with the equipment and his instinctual distrust of the Vruahn made him take it slow rather than blundering into a situation that he couldn't get out of.

"It's too bad we can't interface all the loaner gear the Vruahn sent with our own systems," Davis said softly. "Having to prop up crews to sit in the cargo bay and watch the terminals down there isn't all that efficient."

"The help came under duress," Jackson said. "I don't think they're all that wild about us having any of their tech at all so they made sure there was no way we could do anything but watch the displays. To be honest, I'm perfectly happy to not let them have direct access to our systems."

"I see," she nodded. "Was there any talk of maybe upgrading our systems with some of the gear we've seen on Colonel Blake's ships?"

"I floated the idea out there, but it was quickly shot down," Jackson snorted. "It would be wildly impractical with the time table we're working with. Our ships can't produce one-tenth of the power needed to fire just one of their primary weapons, and their power systems are completely incompatible with our technology. It would be faster and easier for them to build us a whole new fleet... but that wasn't going to happen."

"Is their distrust of us so complete?" she asked.

"Probably more arrogance than distrust," Jackson corrected her. "They seem to view us as little more than jabbering primates, and they sure as hell weren't going to give us the hardware we could use to threaten our neighbors." He fell silent as he felt he may have said too much. They all had a lot to worry about; there was no point in filling his XO's head with the same doubts he carried.

"Initial scan complete, Captain," Lieutenant Commander Barrett announced after five hours of constant scanning. "Nothing of note that we weren't already aware of."

"Has the rest of the squadron checked in?" Jackson stood and stretched his lower back out.

"Still waiting for the *Artemis* to appear, sir," Ensign Hayashi reported. "The rest of the squadron has come through and is reporting normal operations across the board."

"Very good," Jackson said. "We keep steaming for the X-Ray jump point. Lieutenant Davis, you have the bridge."

"Aye aye, sir, I have the bridge," she said and moved over into the command chair he'd just vacated.

Jackson took the opportunity of relative calm they were having while crossing the Xi'an System to walk through his ship and do a more detailed inspection while also, and most importantly, gauging the crew and how they were feeling. He snuck off the command deck without Master Chief Green taking notice, not because he didn't enjoy the salty senior spacer's company but because the crew was almost more intimidated by him than they were of their captain.

He watched them go about their tasks with an almost enthusiastic efficiency and again marveled at how they'd matured in the short time since the war had begun. A lot of them had served on the *Blue Jacket* and were typical of Black Fleet spacers: young, bored, and mostly with some sort of disciplinary issues in their past. After the initial encounter with the Phage Alpha, despite the many casualties, they'd adopted an undeserved swagger and irrational eagerness to go to battle again.

Jackson chalked that up to the fact that they'd been the only combat-tested crew in the Fleet at the time. Now, over five years later, enough blood had been spilled and enough lives snuffed out by an enemy that still none of them really understood that the reality of war had sunk in. Now they were warriors, trained professionals that went about their job with a grim competency while knowing that the next engagement could be their last just as easily as another victory. They still had unwavering faith in their captain, and he in them, but they'd all witnessed how quickly things could go so badly.

"Captain," Commander Daya Singh greeted him as he walked in through the main hatchway to Engineering. "What brings you down here?"

"Just a walkthrough," Jackson said. "Don't let me interrupt anything you have going on."

"Just routine operations, sir," Singh said. "She's running like a top."

"That's good to hear," Jackson nodded. "Have you had a chance to go down and take a peek at our cargo?"

"I have," Singh scrunched up his nose. "I'm not thrilled at having so many closed systems aboard without even really understanding how they work or what they're supposed to do, but so far they don't seem to be interfering with ship functions so I've put it in the back of my mind."

"I'm not much happier about it than you are," Jackson said quietly. "But I do know that we're not equipped to capture an Alpha without the help."

"So why all the added difficulty?" Daya motioned Jackson over to a monitoring station that wasn't currently in use. "Why can't Blake and his group handle this capture and the Vruahn employ other resources to do the recon for the Phage nerve center?"

"I think there is probably more than one reason as that would be the most logical strategy," Jackson shrugged. "But even this amount of help came with great struggle. From what I understand there are many in the Vruahn leadership that aren't happy we're being assisted at this level with the expressed goal of wiping out an intelligent species no matter how horrible they may be."

"Funny how they changed their tune after getting punched in the nose," Singh mused. "How much do you really trust these new 'allies' of ours, Jack?"

"I don't... at all." Jackson struggled with a way to sugarcoat what had been weighing his mind down since his original meeting with Setsi. "But 'the enemy of my enemy' and all that."

"That's terrifyingly shortsighted, even for you."

"I'm not sure what you want me to say, Daya," Jackson said. "I think the Vruahn have their own agenda, but I also don't see anyone else coming forward to help us. One crippling, existence-threatening crisis at a time is about all I'm able to handle."

"I'm not throwing stones," Singh raised his hands. "I'm just thinking aloud."

Jackson left Engineering feeling decidedly worse than when he'd left the bridge. There so many unknowns and things were happening so fast now and everyone still seemed to be looking to him for answers that he'd never felt qualified to give. He was a starship captain, and he hoped a decent one, but it seemed the more he tried to extricate himself from being the one making choices that could possibly have profound ramifications the more he could do nothing to avoid them.

The rest of his tour was happily devoid of any further existential conversations that called into question his judgment. His crew was rested, calm, and as ready as they would ever be for what was coming next.

****

"We're coming up on the X-Ray jump point," Lieutenant Davis reported as Jackson walked onto the bridge at the beginning of First Watch.

"And the rest of the squadron?" he asked.

"Already in position and maintaining intervals for a standard staggered transition," she said.

"Very good, Lieutenant," Jackson said. "OPS, deploy the warp drive and prepare to secure the main engines from standard flight mode."

"Aye, sir," Hayashi said. "Deploying warp emitters and prepping the drive for engagement."

"Coms, signal the rest of the squadron and tell them we're not pausing," Jackson ordered. "They're to hit the jump point at speed and maintain full combat readiness on the other side."

"Aye, sir," Keller slipped his headset back on fully.

The *Ares* disappeared from the Xi'an System as quietly as she'd come in. While it was strange to be actively wishing for an encounter with a Phage Alpha, Jackson didn't want to drag this mission out any longer than necessary.

****

"Captain! Monitor Team One reports their display just lit up," Hayashi called as the main display was just coming back up after the transition back to real space. "Confirmed Phage presence in this system; they're working on narrowing it down to a general direction now."

"Stow the warp drive and get the mains up," Jackson said calmly. "Tell the monitor team to keep at it. Tactical, begin passive scans but keep the active arrays off for now. Nav, get us a course to clear the jump point and put us in a shallow descent down into the system."

"Helm, engage on the new course when you get it," Davis said as Jackson picked up his comlink. "Thrusters only until the engines come online."

"Aye, ma'am," the helmsman said. "Thrusters only."

"Set engines for low-output mode until we know what we're dealing with," Jackson nodded to her. "Also, set up the laser beacon so the rest of the squadron knows what's going on."

"Yes, sir," Davis said quietly. She began relaying his orders as he talked on the comlink to the two monitor teams watching the Vruahn gear in the cargo hold.

The rest of the squadron emerged into real space over the next twenty hours and each was greeted with a low-power, wide-beam laser that was pulsing with a predesignated code that let each ship know there was potential danger in the system, to rig for quiet running, and begin forming up loosely behind the *Ares* while she began trying to sniff out what had triggered the Vruahn equipment.

During that time Barrett was able to clear their local space of any threats with the passive scanners, so Jackson rotated a full watch on and off duty while waiting for the rest of his ships. Even though the jump points were just conveniently chosen points in space and were actually a large area more than a "point" Jackson never felt comfortable loitering after a transition. Despite the odds being against it, having another starship pop out of warp just to ram his ship was always one of those "can never happen" scenarios that played through his head.

"The *Hyperion* just transitioned in, Captain," Davis said when Jackson walked on the bridge fifty minutes before First Watch. "All the squadron is stacking up behind us and running silent."

"Excellent," Jackson sipped his coffee and ignored the fact that it was still far too hot to drink. "Have the monitor teams had any luck pinpointing the direction of the Phage contacts?"

"Negative, sir," Barrett frowned. "If anything, the information displayed on the Vruahn machines has become even more vague. Monitor Team One is still insisting that there are strong Phage contacts in this system, but they're unable to confirm bearing or distance."

"I really thought the Vruahn help would be a little more… helpful," Jackson sighed as he sat down. "OPS, maintain stealth protocols for now. Any light or EM emissions are to be carefully controlled. Nav! Let's set a course that takes us on a more direct flightpath down the hill. We can waste a lot of time searching the outer system and sneaking around, but we all know that larger Phage formations prefer to be close to a system's primary star."

"Course plotted, Captain," Accari said. "I have a direct course and one that will swing the formation around the seventh planet for a grav assist without having to fire the mains for too long."

"What's the time differential between the two courses for crossing the orbit of the fourth planet?" Jackson studied the most recent diagram of the Zulu System.

"Approximately thirty-seven hours, sir," Accari said.

Jackson squinted his eyes at the display and ran the pros and cons of each through his head.

"Option two it is, Specialist," he said after half a moment's contemplation. "Helm, come onto the new course and program your burn as directed by Navigation. Coms, make sure the rest of the squadron knows the plan… tight-beam laser coms, no order confirmation, and keep them stacked single file between us… standard intervals."

"Aye, sir, sending the order now," Keller said and began programming the short laser burst from the aft of the *Ares* that would disseminate Jackson's orders to the other four ships in the formation.

"Helm answering new course, Captain," the helmsman said. "Seventeen percent burn on the mains for nine hours."

"Acknowledged," Jackson said. "Let's look alive! We have a long flight down the well, but make no mistake: we are now on the hunt. Tactical and OPS, I want six-hour rotations at your stations to keep fresh eyes on the passive arrays. We can't fully trust the Vruahn equipment just yet, so we will rely on our own eyes and ears and verify with the help of the two monitor teams."

"Aye aye, sir," Hayashi and Barrett said almost simultaneously.

"XO... make sure that they're rotating out." Jackson didn't bother to lower his voice to make sure Barrett heard him loud and clear. "You're authorized to man the OPS station for a rotation if any departments are short-staffed from propping up the monitoring crews in the hold."

"Yes, sir," Davis nodded.

The mission proceeded at a nice, boring clip for the majority of the flight. The *Ares* maintained the lead position in the formation the entire time and her passive sensors were unable to detect any of the Phage that the Vruahn equipment insisted were there. By the time the destroyer was swinging around a dull, brown/gray gas giant for their one and only gravity assist Jackson had become concerned that either the Vruahn gear was faulty or his own was, since they'd routinely been able to pick up Phage ships at a greater range with just the optical and thermal sensors. He'd debated deploying the laser interferometer network each ship carried to try and detect the presence of any anomalous masses large enough to be an Alpha, but the network broadcast on standard radio frequencies and would announce their presence like a carnival barker while they tried to sneak down into the system.

Just as he was coming back on the bridge prior to First Watch officially starting, an odd flicker, almost like interference, ran through the main display. He frowned and watched the enormous screen as a few more pixilated lines ran through. Before he could ask the Second Watch OPS officer if they were having trouble with the system, strange and alien icons began appearing all over the tactical overlay.

"Sir! I've lost control of our sensors!" the officer at Tactical cried shrilly. "Active array is coming online!"

"Shut it down!" Jackson roared, dropping his coffee mug and lunging for the station.

"It won't respond!"

"Captain! The helm is no longer answering commands! We're changing course and—"

"Engines are running up to full output!"

"Everyone quiet!" Jackson shouted. "Who has control of their equipment?"

"Coms is still fully operational, sir," Keller said as he relieved his Second Watch counterpart.

"Find out if the other ships are experiencing a similar failure and do it quickly," Jackson said. "No point trying to maintain radio silence at this point."

"What do these symbols mean?" Davis pointed at the strange symbols that were still dancing across the screen.

"I have no idea," Jackson said. "If we've picked up some malicious software it would at least help if it was in Standard." He stared in shock, mouth hanging open, as the symbols quickly rearranged themselves into Standard with Fleet familiar iconography.

"Sir?" Davis almost whispered.

"Captain, all other ships report no unusual malfunctions," Keller said. "Captain Wright wants to know if you want the rest of the formation to break stealth protocols and follow the *Ares*."

"No," Jackson said. "They're to maintain speed and course. We'll call if we need them, but for now they're to remain hidden."

"Aye, sir."

"Captain, these target brackets, along with our new course, are indicating there are three Alphas on the far edge of the system," Barrett stood next to Jackson and Davis while the lieutenant sitting at Tactical tried futilely to reassert control over his systems. "We're on an intercept course and the targeting data is being updated in real-time."

"That's impossible, Lieutenant," Jackson scoffed. "Our radar can't reach that far with that degree of accuracy in less than ten minutes."

"I know that, sir," Barrett said. "But *Ares* thinks there's something there and we're flying right at it."

"Okay! Enough of the fun," Jackson said. "Everyone get a hold of your backshops and get this ship back under control. You have five minutes."

Five minutes came and went and the only answer from the ship was to ignore the crew's every effort, run the engines up beyond accepted full power, and bring the weapons online. Jackson held his tongue as his crew frantically talked back and forth with their respective backshops trying to figure out how a dozen independent systems were all acting in an autonomous, coordinated fashion. It was a scenario that should have been impossible and was, in fact, a built-in design feature to prevent sabotaged or defective software from compromising the entire ship.

"Sir, I'm picking up some faint returns on the radar," Barrett said. "They're consistent with what's being displayed up on the main. We could actually be looking at three Alphas."

"Fuck," Jackson tried to mutter under his breath. "Start building track profiles; let me know if they're reliable returns and if they're reacting to our mad rush."

"Aye, sir," Barrett said, his brow already glistening with a sheen of sweat.

It was another hour of teeth-grinding tension when Jackson began to feel the onset of genuine fear. He was no idiot. He knew the Vruahn machinery he'd willingly brought aboard his ship had now exerted control over it in a way that apparently his crew couldn't understand or reverse. There were some extreme options available to him, but he had a lot of open space ahead of him and he'd rather give his crew the extra time to come through and salvage the mission before he intentionally began dismantling his ship.

"Tracks confirmed, Captain," Barrett spoke up, his voice tight. "Three Alphas and at least eleven Bravos, all turning toward us and arraying themselves into what appears to be a loose picket."

"They're going to let us come to them," Jackson said over Barrett's shoulder. "They're well aware of our limitations with RF-based detection systems. They may think we don't see them yet."

"I'll keep tracking them, sir," Barrett said.

"Coms! Send a general call out to the rest of the squadron," Jackson ordered. "Tell them I want all active sensors at full power and to begin accelerating at flank to our current position."

"Aye, sir."

"Tactical, let me know the moment there's a change from the Alphas sitting down there." Jackson sat back in his seat, forcing himself not to fidget in front of his already stressed crew.

The rest of the squadron blossoming into existence on multiple bands had the desired effect. Three Alphas had enough brain power between them to know that five Terran destroyers would be more than a match for them. Almost immediately they wheeled on the display and began pushing for the outer edge of the system, unsurprisingly near the Zulu jump point.

"Sir, the helm is correcting course to pursue and Engineering reports that the fuel lines to the auxiliary boosters are priming," Davis said.

"Lieutenant Davis, call Commander Singh and tell him to shut her down," Jackson sighed. "I want both reactors spooled down and the generators physically decoupled from Main Bus A and B."

"Captain—"

"I'm well aware of the risks, Lieutenant," Jackson cut her off. "We have no choice."

"Yes, sir."

The *Ares'* main propulsion and directional thrusters were all electrically fired. Prodigious amounts of current were routed from the main reactors and their associated generators to turn inert argon into a high-energy plasma that could then be directed out of magnetically constricted nozzles, another system that required enormous amounts of electrical power. The powerplant aboard the *Ares* would have been capable of powering at least half of mid-nineteenth century United States with a little bit of juice to spare, well over half a million kilowatts of sustained output, and without it they were reduced to their emergency backup systems, an array of chemical rocket motors and compressed gas jets that were not all that effective now that the ship was roaring down towards the primary star after accelerating at full power for hours.

Jackson was painfully aware that it had been wildly irresponsible to not cut the power when the backups would have had a chance to work or the other ships would have been able to render assistance, but playing the odds was part of the job. It was just too bad that this time he had lost.

"Stand by for main power shutdown," Davis called out while still talking into her headset. A moment later, Jackson could see their acceleration taper off as Singh vented the plasma from the main engines just before he disengaged the load contactors. These were manual devices, massive electrical conductors mounted to hydraulic rams, and he hoped whatever had taken control of the *Ares* wasn't able to somehow manipulate them and restore power.

"Coms are up on emergency backup power, Captain," Keller reported.

"Emergency attitude control is functional," the helmsman said.

"Tactical?" Jackson asked.

"No active sensors," Barrett said. "Backup fuel cells will take a few minutes to build enough power to bring the array back up."

"Monitor teams in the hold are reporting that both Vruahn devices have gone dark," Davis said.

"Tell them I'm on my way down there." Jackson stood up. "Do not restore main power until I give the word."

"Of course, sir," she said.

With main power being offline the lifts were disabled in order to keep more essential systems like life support and gravity running, so Jackson was forced to run down a series of steep ladders to get down off the command deck and into an access tube so he could sprint for the main cargo hold.

In the dim lighting he could see the frightened faces of his crew, most having nothing to do while the power was disabled. He rushed into the cargo hold and saw both monitor crews walking around both of the huge obsidian cubes that had been delivered to New Sierra by the Vruahn and loaded aboard the *Ares* per their instructions.

"Everyone out!" he ordered without preamble as he ran up to the startled crews. "Out! And close the hatch behind you."

"You heard the captain," a specialist third class said. "Let's move."

Once the hatch clanged shut Jackson walked around the smaller of the two cubes, the one with the single display embedded in the side, trying to gather his thoughts.

"This is the captain of this vessel," he said finally, feeling more than a little foolish. "I know you can hear and understand me… just like you did on the bridge. Why did you take control of my ship?"

All that answered him was silence and he began to question his initial instincts about what happened.

"Are you in contact with the Vruahn who created you? With Setsi? Am I able to talk to them through you?"

Silence.

"Last chance," he said with an exaggerated shrug. "Either we talk about what happened, about what happens next, or I will order my crew to jettison you and have another ship in my squadron hit you with a two-hundred megaton nuclear missile. Anything to say to that?"

"Was I not performing the function I was sent here for?" a voice seemed to emanate from everywhere in the hold and sounded eerily similar to Setsi's own voice.

"That's better," Jackson said "We'll begin with a few more questions before I answer any of yours. Are you an intelligence housed within this container? If so, why did you not make yourself known to my crew before now?"

"Yes. My processing matrix is entirely housed within the structure you are standing in front of. My task is very specific: assist a Terran vessel in the subduing and capture of a specific alien construct, referred to as a Phage Alpha by you. I was unaware direct communication was required to perform this task."

"Who authorized you to assume control of this vessel?" Jackson asked.

"The detection systems of this vessel are inadequate for proper targeting and deployment of weapons at ranges over five hundred thousand kilometers," the cube said.

"That doesn't answer the question. Who authorized you to assume control of my ship?" Jackson said firmly.

"The assumption was that authority was granted when an agreement was made with a Vruahn representative to the human species. Is that incorrect?"

"It is," Jackson said. "You are here to assist us. Not grab the helm and take us for a ride without warning. In this instance you are subordinate to me."

"This is not an optimal configuration," the cube said after a moment of hesitation. "This decreased the odds of a successful mission outcome by an order of magnitude."

"I think we might surprise you." Jackson flexed his shoulders to relive the tension that had been building there. "Are you willing to accept new mission parameters so long as they don't conflict with your primary task?"

"I am."

"If there is a conflict, will you let me know here, now... before it becomes an issue?" Jackson asked. "Like in the middle of stalking a fucking Alpha?"

"Yes."

"Good," Jackson sighed. "See? We're already becoming friends." His joking was wildly out of character and more than a little inappropriate given the circumstances, but he couldn't help it as relief flooded into him and replaced the dread he'd been feeling since he realized what had been influencing his ship. "Are you a sentient being?"

"That question has little bearing on my mission. I have the requisite abilities to fulfill my tasking," the cube said.

"So then I don't suppose you have a name?"

"I do not."

"Very well," Jackson smoothed out the front of his Fleet utilities. "To avoid any... confusion... you will report directly to whoever is in command on the bridge and *only* to that person. No direct communication with anyone else on the crew of this ship and no more unauthorized actions. You are cleared to use the ship's intercom system to contact the bridge, but all else will need to be approved. Agreed?"

"Agreed with protest," the cube said. "This is highly inefficient—"

"I heard you the first time," Jackson said. "Normally I would agree, but these are hardly normal circumstances. Now, since we're on speaking terms... what's in the other cube?"

****

"Captain! What the hell is going on?" Daya Singh shouted over the din in Engineering when he saw Jackson walk in.

"There were some interface issues with the Vruahn equipment we took on," Jackson shouted back. "Why is it so steamy in here?"

"One of the coolant jacket bypass lines blew," Singh waved his arm back to where a group of spacers were pulling out a portable welder. "Reactor One. No big deal, it's clean water."

"You're clear to bring main power back up." Jackson shielded his eyes as the group of technicians began welding a prefab angle onto a pipe in preparation for repairing the coolant line. "Try to move it along quickly if you can."

"I always do." Singh was already walking over to another console and began issuing orders to run Reactor Two back up to full power and to reengage all the load contactors for the main power busses.

Jackson slipped out of Engineering so he wasn't a distraction or in the way as his chief engineer brought everything back up after the emergency shutdown. He hustled back up the starboard access tube to the set of ladders that would take him all the way back up to the command deck. By the time he was walking up the corridor that led to the bridge he could feel the harsh thumps through the deck of load contactors being engaged for different areas and could feel his ears pop from the pressure change as the environmental systems came back online.

The bridge was still somewhat chaotic, but his people weren't panicking and he could see that they were working together to maintain what control they could before main power came back completely.

"Both reactors are coming back up, Captain," Davis said when she saw him. "Engineering is telling me it will be another thirty minutes after that before the turbines are fully reengaged and they can begin switching over to normal power modes."

"Did they happen to say how long before we'll have propulsion?" Jackson asked.

"From ninety minutes to two hours after Main Bus A is energized," she apologized. "They had to vent the plasma chambers completely on both main engines before de-energizing the power MUX."

"Understood," Jackson nodded. "It is what it is. Let's just make sure we're ready on our end once power is available again. Nav! What's our position?"

"We're in a stable ballistic trajectory towards the inner system, Captain," Accari said. "Without engines we're being affected by the star's gravity and we've been pulled off course by .013 degrees. No navigational hazards along our present course, and the nearest stellar body is two hundred and fifteen million kilometers and increasing."

"Very good, Specialist," Jackson nodded. "Keep tracking our position and let me know if anything changes. Coms! How long until the rest of the squadron rendezvous with us?"

"Just over six hours, sir," Keller said. "Captain Wright has already ordered a braking maneuver so they don't overshoot us if we don't have engines available within the next few hours."

"Tell Captain Wright I want the *Atlas* and the *Hyperion* to push ahead along the escape vector taken by the Phage," Jackson said. "We'll want as much early warning as we can get if they decide to come back."

"Aye, sir."

"OPS, make sure the two monitor teams are back on watch in the cargo hold and keeping close tabs on our guest," Jackson said.

"Uh, yes, sir," Hayashi said.

"Guest?" Davis asked quietly.

"I'll fill you in on that in a bit," Jackson said. "Apparently we got more than we bargained for from our new friends."

Chapter 13

"So in addition to the AI personality that inhabits the tracking cube, the Vruahn also sent a larger container full of specialized munitions that should help us get one of the big Alphas down and out." Jackson remembered to look at the camera on his terminal and not the screen itself that showed the other four Ninth Squadron captains.

"Is there any sort of failsafe in case things get out of hand once we begin the actual capture attempt?" Captain Oliva Forrest asked. "Something that we can blow the Alpha with if we feel like we're losing control over it?"

"Nothing from the Vruahn, but I've got my own chief engineer working on exactly that sort of device." Jackson shook his head. "We'll wire up a few high-yield warheads and put them in place to make sure we have a way to maintain ultimate control."

"So what's our next move?" Celesta Wright asked.

"Once the *Ares* is FMC we'll redeploy into a staggered column and continue on to the Zulu jump point," Jackson said. "I'm working with the Vruahn computer to develop what I hope will be an operational plan that will keep all five of our ships out of range of their plasma weapons while still accomplishing the mission.

"I decided to brief you like this since every time we use the main conference room the scuttlebutt on the ship spreads like wildfire, and it's usually distressingly accurate. Please brief your individual crewmembers that will ever be put in a position of commanding your respective vessels. I'm having my XO set up an encrypted data stream through the Link that will allow you access to everything I see and hear from the Vruahn cube. Are there any questions?"

"Not enough information to have any questions," Forrest quipped quietly. She and Jackson had been engaged in a long-running cold war that went all the way back to when he'd first assumed command of the *Blue Jacket*. He narrowed his eyes slightly, but let the comment go.

"That's all I have," he said slowly. "I'll give you one final update before we transition out and then it'll be com silence protocols again once we arrive in the Zulu System, at least until I get a feel for the local space. Any questions or requests you have will need to be addressed before we depart. Dismissed."

"I see Captain Forrest is still as pleasant as ever," Davis said once the terminal confirmed it was disconnected.

"I think it's almost done out of habit now," Jackson said. "She does have a point though. I'm not giving them much information to work with right now."

"Is there a particular reason for that, sir?" she asked, moving unnecessarily close to him to grab the auxiliary microphone she'd hooked up for the video conference.

"I want the time we have left before the transition to get a better feel for whatever the hell that thing is in my hold," he said as two sets of ingrained instincts fought each other over what reaction he should have to her proximity, one as a commanding officer and the other as a male that was too close to a beautiful woman. "I also don't want a lot of second-guessing or arguing when they get their assignments. I'm not fighting this battle by committee."

"Understood," she said, finally, mercifully, moving away and back around the desk. "We should be getting close to firing the mains."

"Hopefully." Jackson stood and smoothed out his utility top. "Go ahead and relieve Hayashi on the bridge. I'll be up shortly."

"Yes, sir."

****

"Magnetic constrictors are at full power," Ensign Hayashi reported from the OPS station. "Fields are stable. Engineering is asking for the go ahead to prime the injectors and start generating plasma."

"Tell Engineering to go ahead." Jackson sat in his seat. "They're clear to do whatever Commander Singh feels is necessary to get this ship underway without asking for specific permission."

"Aye, sir. I'll let them know."

It was only another thirty minutes before Jackson could see the plasma chambers on both main engines go hot, and the temperature and pressure began to rapidly climb into operational levels. He checked the status of his ship's navigation systems, including the attitude jets and thrusters, while his crew continued to get the destroyer ready to fly and fight after the power cutoff.

"Helm, you are clear to stabilize our flight with thrusters only," he ordered. "Nav! I want a heading that puts us back on course for the Zulu jump point."

"Sending new course to the helm now, sir," the petty officer at Nav said. Jackson had never seen her on the bridge before and idly wondered where Specialist Accari was. He checked her course and saw that it was a decent compromise between trying to make up lost time and not having to run the engines too hot just after a cold start.

"OPS, confirm with Engineering that we're cleared for normal flight," he said.

"Engineering has turned over control of the engines to the helm," Ensign Hayashi said. "They've cleared us for normal flight mode."

"Very good." Jackson spoke up, "Let's get this mission back on track. Helm, engage along your new course, all ahead two-thirds."

"All engines ahead two-thirds, aye."

Jackson grimaced as the loud bangs and pops of the engines smoothing out jolted the deck. The *Ares* was significantly lighter than his old ship, the *Blue Jacket*, and relied much more on exotic materials and clever structural engineering to keep her straight while the stresses of interstellar flight were imparted on her hull. When the mains were brought back up from a cold start all the little burps of the plasma feed smoothing out were felt much more starkly in the lighter ship and always gave Jackson the irrational impression that Tsuyo had sent him out to fight the Phage in a beer can. One could say what they wanted about the low-tech approach to starship construction of a century ago, but they couldn't deny that the *Blue Jacket* had taken a horrific beating at the hands of a Phage Alpha and kept coming back for more. The *Ares* had never really been tested in the same way and as such Jackson just couldn't put the same faith in the new *Starwolf* class that he did in his old command.

"Engine output has stabilized, Captain," Hayashi said after another twenty minutes of powered flight. "ETA to our transition acceleration point is now... thirty-one hours, eighteen minutes."

"Thank you, Ensign," Jackson stood up. "Lieutenant Davis, you have the bridge for the remainder of the watch. Split the duty roster up so that First Watch is back on when we're approaching the jump point. Everyone stay sharp, there is no reason to assume that those three Alphas won't return, nor are we guaranteed that they were the only enemy forces in this system."

"Understood, sir," Davis said to Jackson's departing back.

****

"Another bust. They're getting better at hiding."

"It would appear so."

"Okay," Colonel Robert Blake exhaled in one explosive breath. "Report to the rest of the group that grid tango-one-six is clear of any trace of the enemy. Not even as much as an abandoned nesting site or any remnants of a digestive viscid patch."

"Message sent along with all scan data," the computer said.

This was the fourth suspected star system that Blake had searched and so far he hadn't turned up anything. Not even a far ranging patrol or small exploratory construct. He was quickly becoming concerned. Relatively speaking, the section of space they were searching was quite small. There should have been *some* evidence of the Phage in the outlying systems if they were truly getting close to the core mind.

He slammed his palm into the armrest of his seat and began programming in their next waypoint, not bothering to tell the computer he was ready to depart the system. There were six more systems to search on his board while the other seventeen ships of his group also searched multiple systems.

The procedure had been pretty straightforward and Blake had had high hopes of an early success. His ship would hop into a system, wait and listen for any evidence of the carrier signal the Phage used to employ their networked consciousness, and then investigate further if it was detected to see if it was the system they were looking for.

After the first two goose eggs he altered his mission profile and began flying down further into the system, taking active scans of planets, moons, or asteroids that would have been of interest to any Phage force passing through or trying to establish a node. When he found no signs the enemy had ever been in any of those systems he began to fear that the Vruahn liaisons had been mistaken when they told him that the core had been detected in this region of space.

"How many hops to the next objective?"

"Three hops will be required in order to maintain prescribed low-observability protocols," the computer said.

"Proceed." Blake leaned back and rubbed his eyes. "Stop just before the final hop into the next system and alert me. I'll be down in the galley."

"Acknowledged."

Blake climbed awkwardly out of the low-slung seat and walked stiffly off the flight deck. He had been taking short naps in the pilot's seat since setting out from New Sierra, fully confident that he'd be the one to quickly locate the target. He'd carefully pored over the intelligence report his ship had received from the Vruahn and intentionally picked his search location based on the higher likelihood of the core mind location. Not only had he not found the target, he'd not even located the slightest bit of evidence the Phage were even in this region of space, while over half his group had been reporting positive contact with enemy combat units before slinking back out of the system after determining the core mind wasn't there.

The simple logistics of supporting something as vital as the core mind had to be immense, or so Blake assumed. He'd seen the Phage bring in overwhelming force just to protect one of their production facilities, something that could be recreated within a matter of weeks, so he could not conceive of them leaving the most important single construct of their species without enough defensive firepower to handle anyone they'd pissed off within a two hundred lightyear radius. The fact that he was seeing no sign that they were around told him that they'd been given bad information.

As he sat and mechanically chewed on the grayish lump of whatever the food dispenser had spit out, his thoughts greatly disturbed him. For the first time since waking up after going into hibernation on the *Carl Sagan* he was beginning to have doubts about the Vruahn. Doubts about their honesty and doubts about their true intentions.

He'd observed Jackson Wolfe closely before and after he had gone aboard the cruiser to talk with Setsi. When the starship captain had returned Blake couldn't help but notice how… off… he was, almost angry, despite having successfully negotiated some measure of aid from the reluctant, near-pacifist species.

The more he idly reflected on Wolfe's strange, or at least unexpected, reactions, the more he found that what he was really doing was reexamining his own humanity. Where did he fit in? Humans had kept evolving societally for hundreds of years while he and his crew were dead and then later working for the Vruahn. What struck him as especially strange was that he had worked for the better part of a century for the Vruahn, had maintained his own sense of culture and self, but until recently he'd never felt any real desire to return back to his own people. Now that he had been back among large groups of humans and had breathed in the air of Earth he was overcome with an almost uncontrollable need to be back as soon as possible.

With thoughts of what building a life back on Earth could possibly be like once he'd completed this last and easily his most ambitious mission, Colonel Blake trudged back to his quarters. Although exhausted both physically and mentally, sleep did not come easily for him as strange, conflicting visions swam through his consciousness.

Chapter 14

"Position confirmed, sir. We're just inside the outer boundary of the Zulu System and carrying enough velocity from transition to clear the jump point."

"Very good," Jackson said. "Tactical, begin passive scans of the system. OPS, give Tactical a hand... I specifically want you looking for nearby navigational hazards. This system has a lot of large asteroids that fly right through the jump point's locale."

"Aye, sir."

"Coms, you know the drill. Keep watch for the rest of the squadron and keep any communications directional and short range."

"Yes, sir." Keller didn't look up from the terminal he'd configured to watch the aft thermal imagers for the transition flashes of the other destroyers.

"Any Phage signatures in this system?" Jackson pressed his earpiece further. Why the hell they couldn't come up with a "universal fit" earpiece that actually fit but could move hundreds of thousands of tons worth of starship across billions of miles faster than light was beyond him.

"*Affirmative*," the voice from the Cube said. "*Strong contacts in the inner system; preliminary analysis indicates they are the same units encountered in the previous system.*"

"Good," Jackson said quietly. "You're clear to interface with our main display to provide distance and bearing. No other systems are to be accessed for now."

"*Acknowledged.*"

"Captain!"

"As you were, Mr. Barrett," Jackson said as numbers and targeting brackets began appearing on the main display. "We've interfaced the main display with the telemetry output of the Vruahn device in the hold. Nav! You are to assume that the bracketed contacts on the main are enemy ships. I want a course that takes us downhill with the least chance of being seen."

"Aye, sir." Accari spun and began punching the numbers into his terminal.

"Tactical, these are most likely the three Alphas that we encountered in the X-Ray System and not of the type we're hunting," Jackson said. "We won't know for certain until we're able to get a hard confirmation from our own sensors. I want you to give me the optimum range you'll need to quickly paint them with the active array and still give us enough room to accelerate and attack."

"Aye, sir," Barrett said. "This may take me a moment."

"We're still far out of range. Take your time and make sure you're as accurate as possible," Jackson stood. "OPS, make sure the monitor teams are in place and still keeping a close watch on the Vruahn cargo."

"Yes, sir."

"What's your plan if these are the same three Alphas, Captain?" Davis asked.

"I'm working on that, Lieutenant," Jackson frowned. "Thankfully we have a bit of time before we have to commit to one strategy or another."

The rest of the squadron slipped into the system without incident, their next-generation warp drives making a much smaller visible light flash during transition than any other capital ship in the fleet. After a quick message via short-range com laser from the *Ares,* they all stacked up behind the lead ship to provide a minimal cross-section to any active sensor sweeps and began the slow march down into the inner system.

As the procession moved along at a relative crawl, Jackson ran dozens of scenarios through his head as to what he would do if the ships down in the inner system were just the three basic Alphas they'd already run into. While he'd given a few motivational speeches about not giving up until the mission was complete, there were some stark realities he faced that were cause for serious concern. First and foremost the *Starwolf*-class starship was a destroyer, not an expedition ship. They just didn't have the range to fly out much past the Zulu System and make it back in any sort of realistic timetable with the fuel they had on board. High-warp flight chewed through their deuterium reserves, and they were already nibbling into the safety buffer Jackson liked to keep in reserve when flying a mission with so many unknowns.

The range issue was a bit academic because the space beyond Zulu was largely unexplored. There were no jump points into warp lanes that would take them to the next system that might have Phage ships. So far they were concentrating on systems with planets that were habitable by humans, but there was no indication the Phage needed such specific conditions to survive and thrive. For all he knew they were massing an enormous battle fleet in the next system and they could fly right past it trying to get to another star with Goldilocks planets. So going out past Zulu wasn't an option, but neither was turning back and making the trip back to the DeLonges System empty-handed

For the thousandth time since leaving New Sierra he cursed their new allies for providing aid in the form of a veritable puzzle box he was forced to figure out before they could even begin planning an assault on the Phage core mind.

"Steady as she goes, Lieutenant," he said quietly to Davis. "I'm going down to CIC."

"CIC?" she asked, her voice betraying her surprise.

"I've got less than twenty hours before this mission goes completely sideways," he almost whispered. "I'm going to go through the sensor logs with the analysts and see if there's something obvious we're missing that could get us back on course."

"Of course, sir." Her skepticism was evident even though she did an admirable job of maintaining a neutral expression.

****

"Report."

"According to the Vruahn equipment's feed the Alphas have drifted into a high orbit over the fourth planet and their velocity has been constant," Barrett said. "I don't believe they see us or intend to break orbit and flee, sir."

"How long until we go active?" Jackson sat down, forcing his clenched hands open.

"Five hours, nine minutes."

"Very good, Lieutenant Commander." Jackson leaned back. "OPS, inform Engineering that we will need the *Ares'* full performance available shortly. While you're at it, make sure all applicable departments know that we will be abandoning stealth and charging down into the Alpha formation within the next twelve hours. Coms!"

"Aye, sir," Keller anticipated. "Prepping a tight-beam transmission for the rest of the squadron now."

"Lieutenant Commander Barrett, when you go active you are authorized to bring all tactical systems online," Jackson said.

"Yes, sir!"

"Captain, a word please?" Lieutenant Davis leaned in.

"Speak your mind, Lieutenant." Jackson made no move to get out of his seat. Davis looked a bit unsure of herself at that but pressed on regardless.

"Captain, is it wise to waste the time and munitions to engage three targets that aren't our objective?" she asked. "Not to mention the risk?"

"You feel I'm acting rashly?" Jackson asked conversationally. "Perhaps even foolishly?"

Davis' cheeks burned red and she set her mouth in a thin, hard line. "I would not presume to understand your motivations, Captain," she said. "But my responsibility is to ensure the safety of the ship and the crew. Perhaps if I knew what the plan was I would not be so concerned." She was still keeping her voice low enough to not be overheard, but Jackson could hear the steel behind her words.

"Relax, Lieutenant," he said with a small smile. "I was just pressing you."

"Sir?"

"There may be times when I am either incapacitated or otherwise unavailable, Lieutenant Davis," he continued. "I need to know that you place your responsibilities ahead of anything else, including your trust in your superior officers or conflicts from personal relationships."

"I see." She looked confused and no less concerned.

"Listen up!" Jackson stood up. "We're getting ready for a five-ship attack run on three Phage Alphas sitting in high orbit over a large, rocky planet. On the surface this is fairly routine, but our objective will not be to eliminate the targets.

"Since we don't have one of the Super Alphas here to try and capture and we don't have the time or the resources to continue to hunt blindly, we're going to try and draw one in to us. The plan will be to destroy two of the Alphas and let the one escape while we put on a show of harassing it. Hopefully it will go and tell one of its big brothers that we're here."

"Why not let two go, sir?" Barrett asked. "Double our odds of success."

"Because I can't be certain that our objective won't return with the Alphas we let go," Jackson said. "I'd rather thin out their potential retaliatory force here while we have the slight advantage."

"Understood, sir," Barrett nodded.

"So since you're all old pros at this sort of thing, I want a detailed plan for the attack sent to me within the hour," Jackson sat back down. "Your XO will coordinate your efforts and you will all report to her. Impress me."

Fifty-three minutes later and his crew did just that. Barrett, Accari, and Hayashi worked to put together an impressively workable plan of attack. It was even complete with contingencies and did not ignore the fact that the *Ares* would not be attacking alone. With the amount of time left before they would need to commit to the attack by activating their active sensor arrays,

Jackson had decided it was a perfect time for a little real world training.

He was both relieved and surprised at how tight the plan was his crew had put together. Much of the relief was due to the fact that he was now reasonably confident that, should something happen to him during a battle, one of his bridge officers would be able to assume command and have the instincts to know whether they should continue to press or disengage and withdraw.

"Well," Jackson said neutrally, looking up from his tile at the trio arrayed in front of the command chair. "I suppose this isn't a complete cluster fuck. You've smartly deployed the squadron to maximize our weapons coverage, but you've left the *Ares* too far ahead. Depending on how the target reacts, the *Atlas* or the *Icarus* could end up inadvertently hitting us on the aft quadrant."

"That was my fault, Captain," Hayashi spoke up. "I'm sorry."

"Don't be sorry. Be right," Jackson said. "Lieutenant Commander Barrett should have been the one to catch that oversight as he's intimately aware of the auto-mag's capabilities and limitations."

"Yes, sir," Barrett said. "I—" He trailed off before clamping his mouth shut.

"What?" Jackson demanded.

"I may have assumed a margin of error that was too tight for our flanking ships," Barrett said. "But that's no excuse, sir."

"Not all explanations are excuses, Lieutenant Commander," Jackson said. "Now... let's rework the deployment of the ships during the initial attack run so that we're not putting the other two ships in a position where they could accidentally fire on us. I'd also like you to think a little more three-dimensionally. There's no reason to array the wedge parallel with the ecliptic during the approach, and it actually cuts off some potential escape lanes for the inner three ships. Once the shooting starts this could all fly out the airlock since we have no idea how those Alphas will react, so let's leave ourselves as many options open as possible."

"Yes, sir," they said in ragged unison.

"A little harsher than I expected, sir," Davis remarked after they left.

"I've come to realize that perhaps I've insulated them from making the tough choices, you included," Jackson sipped his coffee. "Their plan wasn't bad, even workable, but they need to be pressed a bit. If this war has taught us anything it's that relying on any single person can lead to lost battles and countless lives lost. Remember the *Dao*?"

"The Asianic Union battleship that was lost during the second battle for Xi'an?" she frowned.

"Yes. Her captain, the one with the politically connected family, panicked and simply tried to flee the area," Jackson said. "He not only killed everyone aboard an irreplaceable battleship, but the gap he left in the line let the Phage swarm and kill even more aboard the smaller support ships trying to clear the area."

"I'm not sure I understand, Captain."

"Just think if the *Dao* had an XO, or even a tactical officer, that would have recognized that the captain was incapacitated and had assumed command," Jackson sighed. "I watched the sensor logs from the *Brooklands*. If someone had simply turned the ship into the onrush of Bravos and let her automated systems fight back the way they were designed to, from the front, they could have held on long enough for us to arrive."

"I understand now, sir," she nodded.

"Then this wasn't a waste of time, Lieutenant," he smiled at her briefly. "I'm going to grab a quick bite in the wardroom and then I'll relieve you before things get exciting around here."

After a sandwich that had been sitting out for far too long to still be considered edible, but offset with a cup of coffee that was outstanding, Jackson was back in his seat and watching the updates from the Vruahn telemetry link. The device was now able to clearly resolve the three Alphas and seven Bravos holding formation over the lifeless hulk of the fourth planet in the system. They were just about to fire up their active sensor systems, including the Link, so soon they'd have five high-power, high-resolution radars painting the target area and sharing the data so he'd be able to verify just how accurate the cube really was.

"Passive sensors confirm that all ships are redeployed into our final attack formation," Barrett said. "Warming up active array transmitters now."

"You are clear to activate the array at your discretion, Lieutenant Commander," Jackson said. "Helm! Stay sharp and keep alert for any snap course changes. We're going to be flying in a tight formation at a group of bunched-up targets. It could get a little hairy."

"Aye, sir." The helmsman was cinching down his restraints tighter and reconfiguring his panels for close quarters combat flying... at least "close quarters" by starship standards.

"Stand by!" Barrett called out. "Going active... Now!" Jackson mentally counted to three in his head.

"Engines to full operational mode," he called. "Helm, all ahead flank!"

"All engines ahead flank, aye!"

"OPS, get the Link active." Jackson leaned into the surge of the main engines shoving the *Ares* forward with more power than the grav generators could compensate for. "Coms! Verify status of the rest of the squadron."

"All ships have responded to our opening maneuver and are reporting all greens across the board," Keller said, referring to the master status board above the main display that gave a quick go/no-go visual indicator for the ship's primary systems.

"Tactical, weapons hot," Jackson said. "Begin calculating a distributed firing solution once we have confirmed returns from our own sensors."

"Weapons hot, aye!"

The radar returns started coming in and, once they were resolved by the computer, Jackson could see that the Vruahn data was quite accurate. There was a slight discrepancy since the data from the cube was instantaneous and their radar returns were hampered by the delay of the RF travelling to the target and then having to come all the way back to be interpreted. He could also see that the Phage were moving as soon as the first pulses from their radar hit them, but not before. It was another nugget of information about his enemy that he catalogued and stored for later.

"Tactical, use the Vruahn telemetry data to calculate your initial firing solutions until we're close enough to negate our own sensor lag," Jackson ordered.

"Yes, sir," Barrett said. "Updating plots now. We'll be firing the first wave of Shrikes in less than two minutes."

One hundred and seven seconds later the two ships on the right side of the formation, the *Icarus* and *Artemis*, fired two Shrikes each for the same Alpha before angling their course out and away from the other ships. Jackson watched them peel off on his tactical display and crossed his fingers that the Phage would react the way he thought they would.

The Shrikes raced ahead of the formation towards their target. Silent and deadly, they were utilizing a broadcast telemetry uplink from the formation and had not activated their own onboard sensors and had shut down their engines after one quick, intense burn. It wasn't long before the Vruahn data told the story: the Alphas had been sitting, waiting, and hadn't detected the four missiles until three slammed into the one that had been trailing behind and below the other two. The fourth missile went ballistic and continued on to the planet's surface, but the other three had solid impacts and fired their engines again to dig into the organic hull as deep as possible before detonating.

"Tango One is in an uncontrolled tumble and falling out of orbit," Barrett said. "High-res radar is showing significant damage to the entire front half. It should impact the planet in less than five minutes."

"*Icarus* reports the Bravos are pursuing them away from the planet," Keller said.

"Tell Captain Wright to allow them to close before taking them out," Jackson said. "What are the other two Alphas doing?"

"Both have turned and are moving towards us," Barrett said. "Their acceleration rate indicates they're coming out cautiously."

"Let's disappear," Jackson said. "Coms! Have the *Atlas* and *Hyperion* light up the sky. Tactical and OPS, go to passive sensors and switch the Link to receive only."

"Aye, sir," Barrett said. "*Atlas* and *Hyperion* have both ignited their auxiliary boosters. They're overtaking us."

"Helm, zero thrust. Steady as she goes."

"Engines answering zero thrust," the helmsman said. "Maintaining course and speed, aye."

"Tactical?"

"Stand by, Captain," Barrett said. "They haven't fully committed—there they go! Both remaining Alphas are swinging out to pursue the *Atlas* and *Hyperion*."

"Coms, inform Captain Walton that he is clear to engage Tango Two at his discretion," Jackson said. "We'll move on him."

Jackson had ordered both of his remaining destroyers to blast their radars at full power while also igniting their auxiliary boosters and pulling out of the formation and away from the planet. Simultaneously the *Ares* went dark and cold-coasted along her original course that would now take them up behind the two pursuing Alphas. It was a calculated gamble since, if they were spotted or the Phage weren't fooled, the *Ares* would be flying dark into the teeth of two waiting Alphas and none of the other ships would be able to come about and offer any assistance in time.

But as he'd anticipated, the sight of two Terran warship flaring brightly and fleeing was simply too much and they were moving out to pursue. If there had been a heavier Phage presence in the system, or even one of the Super Alphas, he wouldn't have tried something so transparent. But with only three Alphas and a handful of Bravos he'd been confident that their collective consciousness hadn't reached a level of sophistication past that of a simple predator.

"The *Hyperion* has locked two Shrikes on Tango Two." Barrett watched the status updates of the squadron over the Link. "*Atlas* is reducing acceleration and drifting to port to provide a backup shot without us being in the line of fire."

"Good, good," Jackson said distractedly. "How long until we can pursue?"

"Three hours, forty minutes until our first course change," Ensign Hayashi said.

Jackson had to force himself to sit still in his seat. The last tussle he'd been in with the Phage had been aboard Colonel Blake's awesome Vruahn strike ship, and it had spoiled him by showing what he was missing. Having to fight his battles once again over the span of hours and days instead of seconds and minutes hardly seemed fair and he once again cursed his new allies.

Thankfully the Phage obliged them by cranking up their acceleration rate once they'd cleared the influence of the planet. It was just over two hours when they crossed the *Ares'* flightpath on their way towards the two fleeing destroyers.

"*Hyperion* is firing," Barrett said. "Time to impact... ninety-seven minutes."

"Helm! Come to course Sierra-Delta," Jackson chose from the list of pre-programmed contingency courses on his display. "Ahead one-third, just enough to get us moving in the right direction."

"Helm answering new course," the helmsman said. "Ahead one-third, aye."

166

The nose of the *Ares* swung around to her new heading and the engines gently began pushing them off their current intercept course with the planet. Since they were still trying to remain unnoticed the ship was in reality still flying sideways faster than she was moving forward, as the engine power wasn't enough to overcome the inertia they were carrying. Spaceflight was a strangely relative thing and it was something the human mind seemed to still struggle with on an instinctual level as there was no "up" and moving "forward" didn't mean what it did when on a planet.

"Targets are now separating," Barrett said. "Tango Three is drifting down relative to the *Hyperion*'s line of fire."

"That's it," Jackson stood. "We can't let it get behind us. Helm, ahead flank."

"Engines ahead flank, aye."

"Tactical, begin updating your targeting pattern and bring the auto-mag online." Jackson began pacing as the rumble of the engines throttling up vibrated the deck plates.

"Auto-mag capacitor bank is at full power," Barrett said. "Updating firing solutions now. When am I allowed to go active sensors, sir?"

"Wait until we've completed our turn and we're actually on a pursuit course," Jackson said. "There's a chance they didn't notice the thermal bloom from the engines, but we know they'll feel the radar pulses. Nav!

Let Tactical know once we begin to close the interval between us and Tango Three."

"Yes, sir!" Accari called out, never looking up from his display.

Jackson watched their interval actually increase slightly on the main display before the roaring engines could get the massive starship turned and moving in the right direction. He watched the helmsman expertly cheat the nose over slightly off-course to direct the engine thrust over just enough to tighten up their turn.

"Tactical, we're now accelerating along our pursuit course."

"Acknowledged," Barrett said. "Going active." They were close enough to the target to not have a long wait before the tactical computer updated the Alpha's orientation, speed, and heading. It was more or less right where the Vruahn cube said it was.

"Computer is now constantly updating our firing solution."

"Weapons free," Jackson said. "You may fire at will once you have the optimal range."

"Aye, sir," Barrett said. "Turning over control of the auto-mag to the tactical computer now... projected time until firing range is three hours, thirty minutes and decreasing."

The frenetic activity on the bridge simmered down to a tense quietness, punctuated only by the muted alerts from the terminals and the hushed conversations of operators talking to their backshops or each other. For his part, Jackson felt the familiar calm that came in knowing that he had made his preparations as best he could and now there was nothing to be done until his target reacted to what was about to happen next.

"*Hyperion* is reporting good impacts on Tango Two," Keller called out.

"Confirmed," Hayashi said. "All missiles detonated on Tango Two; unknown if target was destroyed or disabled."

"Let Captain Walton worry about that," Jackson said. "Any reaction from our target?"

"No reaction," Barrett said. "It's still maintaining course and speed, no longer accelerating."

"Change of plans, Lieutenant Commander," Jackson said. "Fire your full spread now. OPS, reinitialize our Link telemetry feed. Coms! Tell Captain Walton I want his two ships to come about and charge at Tango Three; make sure they're aware of our shot trajectory through the Link."

"Updating firing solution... Assuming attitude control... Firing!" Barrett called out. The deck plates under their feet rumbled as the auto-mag began spitting out ferrous shells at high velocity. The auto-mag was a powerful railgun system hard-mounted to the destroyer's internal structure, so the bang of the initial discharge as well as the transit of the shells shook the entire ship from stem to stern. The fact the weapon couldn't be aimed independently of the ship's bearing also meant the tactical computer had to take control of the attitude jets and actually steer the ship to aim.

Jackson despised the system, but it was a concession he had been forced to make in order to get the weapon on the new class of destroyer in the first place.

"Full volley away," Barrett said. "Trajectories confirmed. Safeing gun and surrendering attitude control back to the helm."

"Helm confirms resumed attitude control," the helmsman said.

"Time until the shells overtake the target?" Jackson asked.

"Seventy-six minutes," Barrett said.

"The *Atlas* and *Hyperion* have completed their course change and are inbound—"

"Target has altered course!" Barrett interrupted Hayashi. "It is now accelerating towards the outer system at seven hundred g's and climbing. It has already evaded all of our shots."

"That's fine," Jackson stood. "Those shots were fired to elicit a specific response, Lieutenant Commander. They can still accomplish that without actually hitting the target." Even as Jackson spoke the cube's targeting bracket on the tactical display disappeared.

"Target has disappeared on radar," Hayashi said. "Suspect that it went to FTL and left the system."

"Stand down from general quarters," Jackson said. "Begin post-combat inspections and maintenance and go to normal watches. Coms, send out a general order to rally the squadron in high orbit over the fourth planet. Nav, that goes for us too so make it happen."

"Aye, sir."

"How long do you think we'll have to wait?" Davis asked.

"If this works? I would expect that we won't have long to wait at all," Jackson said.

Chapter 15

It was the second to last system on his list and Colonel Robert Blake was no closer to finding the core mind than he was when he flew into the first one. The apparent failure of his team to locate the core, the most important part of the overall mission, was eating at him like nothing he'd ever experienced.

"Where in the fuck is it?!" he shouted.

"Unknown," the computer replied unhelpfully.

"Thanks," Blake rubbed at his eyes. Two of his teammates that had search grids that overlapped his own had reported a Phage presence: two Alphas of the type that had been attacking human planets and three of the big ones that had attacked the Vruahn cruiser during their meeting with Setsi. While it was a hopeful sign, they were running out of star systems to search and a few stray combat units wouldn't be enough evidence to mobilize the entire Terran fleet.

There was a blast of an alarm that startled him so bad he jumped out of his seat, ceasing before he'd even been able to sit up and see what it was. "Report."

"There was a brief detection of the underlying carrier frequency we've been searching for," the computer said. "It was detected for less than twenty milliseconds. This could be an anomalous reading. Beginning full internal diagnostics of the passive detection network."

"You do that," Blake said absently. "While you're at it, activate all the passive detection gear... full spectrum."

"The incoming data of a full spectrum recording cannot be interpreted in real time," the computer said. "It will be stored and analyzed as processing resources are available."

"Understood," Blake sighed. "Just do what I said."

"Acknowledged."

He walked the corridors of his warship on his way to the galley and, for the first time in as long as he could remember, he was lonely. Not just lonely as in he'd like someone to chat with. No... this was a deep, depressing, crippling loneliness that tore at his soul. It was almost as if his recent interactions with humans that weren't part of the *Carl Sagan* crew had awakened a deep need for social interaction within him. Once those floodgates opened he found that the effect was cumulative and, all of a sudden, he was feeling the crush of decades of solitude. He chewed his food mechanically as the parade of depressing thoughts weighed him down.

"When did I turn into such a wuss?" he snapped and shoved his tray away, forcing his introspection to the back of his mind. Having never developed the deep-seated love of coffee the rest of his military brethren had, he grabbed a couple of the sickly sweet energy drinks that were kept on hand throughout the ship and stalked back up to the flight deck. They only had a few more chances to get a bead on the core mind if this mission was going to happen at all.

It had occurred to him that they might never find the precise location of the core mind and the Terran fleet would have amassed for nothing, would have torn the political fabric of the Confederacy to shreds for nothing. Without that target there was simply no way Admiral Marcum could risk all of humanity's military might on a wild goose chase. Hell, the trip alone might cost him a sizable chunk of his fleet.

Another, darker thought went through Blake's mind at the same time. What if the Vruahn had intentionally set them onto a path they knew would not bear fruit? Their pacifist nature was well-known to him, and they'd always been reluctant to let him and his crew take the fight to the Phage instead of coming in with well-meaning but ultimately ineffective holding actions. Had they sent them out into this region of space to simply burn up time until the humans' desire for revenge began to wane?

"Anything new?" He poked his head onto the flight deck. He could access the information from anywhere in the ship, of course, but he liked to come up just before turning in for bed to give the indicators and displays a last once-over.

"Two more instances of the anomalous carrier pulse have been detected since you left the flight deck," the computer said. "There were no discernable patterns in the interval or duration of all three pulses."

"Keep running an analysis of that and keep recording at full spectrum in this system," Blake yawned. "This has been the only interesting thing we've found so far and I want to be as thorough as possible."

"Acknowledged."

****

Blake's troubled sleep was harshly interrupted by a strident alarm blaring through the ship that indicated something one step below an actual emergency required his attention. He rolled out of bed and sprinted out the hatch without bothering to dress first. He idly wondered why he had put his quarters so far away from the flight deck when he'd laid out this newest ship.

"Report!"

"The system in which the core mind resides has been identified with a 99.4% degree of certainty," the computer said. "Strike Six is still sending all the pertinent data."

"Six, huh?" Blake climbed into his seat. "Halsey's ship. Bring up her search grid on the forward screen." He was dismayed to see that Halsey had been searching along the perimeter of the AOR and practically on the opposite side from where he was searching.

"Show me what data we have so far." The computer wordlessly complied and the raw stats that scrolled down the screen made Blake's eyes bulge out of his head. The system had the strongest Phage infestation he had ever seen in one place. There were over four thousand Alphas within the almost ten-thousand-strong swarm, with over a thousand Charlies just for good measure.

In all his years fighting the Phage he had never seen anything like the Charlie constructs before he had been called to human space. There hadn't been any at Nuovo Patria, but he'd seen the aftermath from the annihilation of Haven as well as the raw footage a CIS drone had managed to capture and transmit before it was destroyed. As impressive as the swarm was, he didn't see anything that would indicate definitively that the core mind was in that system. For all he knew this could simply be the staging point for a fleet that was meant to wipe out humanity in one fell swoop.

He dismissed that thought even as quickly as it popped into his head. If they were planning on using a force this massive against humanity it made no sense to put it so far away. Even the Phage had to consider logistics when it came to moving their largest constructs into the area. Blake also didn't see any indication that they were forming up for deployment or intended to leave the system anytime soon.

As he continued to stare at the swirling dots on the screen, he thought he could begin to detect a pattern. All of the heavy units seemed to have a definite epicenter to their wide-ranging flightpaths and it seemed to be concentrated around the second planet in the system. Or more specifically, its moon.

"Does Strike Six's preliminary analysis say the core mind is likely located on the largest moon orbiting the second planet in that system?" he asked.

"It does."

"And you agree?"

"My probability isn't as high, but I also have yet to analyze all the data in context," the computer said. "That probability is likely to go up."

"Continue analysis," Blake said. "Make this a priority over the analysis of the full-spectrum data recording of this system. We'll stay here another ten hours and then pull back."

"Shall I continue passive recordings of this system during that time?" the computer asked.

"Affirmative." Blake climbed back out of his seat. "If there are no changes in status by the end of the ten hours we'll issue a general recall order and rally back in the DeLonges System in Terran space."

"Acknowledged."

Blake went to his quarters to shower and dress, not bothering to try and get back to sleep. His mind was racing after all the recent developments and he didn't feel like just lying in his rack and staring at the ceiling. There was something about the massive Phage swarm in that unnamed, unexplored system that bothered him. He couldn't pin down exactly what it was, but he knew that he would be far more comfortable going back to Admiral Marcum with hard evidence that the core mind was on that moon.

He knew that the ships would be sharing their data with the Vruahn analysts, as they always did, so maybe he'd get word from them once Halsey's records were looked over. It was highly likely that the Vruahn had some insight that they'd not bothered to share with their human partners that would add context to the behavior he was seeing in the raw sensor feeds.

****

"Core mind location pinpointed and confirmed. Human strike force returning to Terran space."

The Vruahn cube had sent the message directly to Jackson's comlink. Now that they knew where the core mind location was, there was no backing out of this mission. He would have to fully commit the Ninth to capturing a Super Alpha.

He quickened his pace down the port access tube on his way to the main cargo hold. One of his monitor teams had reported that the larger, second Vruahn cube had become active. Jackson had immediately pulled the teams, had Major Ortiz post his Marines at all the hatches, and made his way to the hold fervently hoping that this was a good surprise.

"What new fresh hell is this?" he asked after the Marine at the main hatchway had let him through. The larger cube had reconfigured itself so that it was now, more or less, a large shipping pallet, its sides having folded down flat on the deck. What was sitting there in the open were six skeletal racks, each cradling twelve shimmering spheres that were no more than half a meter in diameter. The spheres were an inky black with purple swirls moving through them, giving them an almost liquid appearance.

"So what are these?" Jackson asked aloud.

"Configurable gravitational munitions," the smaller cube answered.

"Elaborate," Jackson rolled his eyes.

"Each sphere is a programmable weapon that is capable of causing gravitational distortions at a specific yield."

"Could they be programmed with enough force to shred a Phage Alpha?" Jackson walked closer to the racks.

"Affirmative, though that would be counter-productive to stated mission goals," the cube said.

"Understood," Jackson said. "I just want to get a feel for how much force we're talking about here. What would be the optimal deployment for such a weapon?"

"The distortions generated are capable of disrupting or even negating the enemy's reactionless propulsion system," the cube answered.

"Would this need to be a necessarily powerful blast?" Jackson asked. "That's all well and good, but if it creates enough force that our ships can't survive then it's more or less useless. What sort of effective area are we talking about?"

"Area of influence can be predetermined," the cube explained. "The force necessary to disrupt an enemy ship's reactionless drive should not significantly damage this vessel."

"Not exactly the reassurance I was looking for," Jackson muttered. "Okay, new protocols... I need you to speak to my chief engineer and tactical officer and work out a plan for using these weapons. It probably would have been better if you'd revealed what these were long before now."

"Mission directives dictated that the existence and function of the weapon was to remain a secret until the core mind was located and the secondary objective of capturing an Alpha ship was achievable with a probability of success over seventy percent," the cube said.

"Of course," Jackson sighed. "Stand by while I call my officers down so you can brief them and then we can get on with trying to figure out how a Vruahn weapon will be fired from a Terran warship."

****

"It's really quite ingenious," Daya Singh said as he sniffed suspiciously at the soup he'd grabbed from the quick-line before dumping in an alarming amount of hot sauce. "The funny thing is... we could have built something like this ourselves. Not as slick or compact, but we have the fundamental understanding of the principles involved to pull it off."

"So why didn't we?" Jackson asked idly, wrinkling his nose at Singh's now-inedible soup.

"Same reason all of our stuff is two-hundred-year-old tech," Singh shrugged. "No need. A low yield charge won't do much to our ships since we're still pushing them with raw thrust. A big charge would tear a ship to pieces, but so will a nuclear-tipped Shrike."

"And on an Alpha?"

"The best way I can describe it is agitating the water enough around a surface vessel that it significantly reduces the surface tension," Singh launched into another of his overly simplistic, astonishingly insulting explanations, again forgetting that Jackson held advanced degrees in engineering. "These grav charges are more than just tossing a rock in a pond and causing ripples. They create random variances and eddies in local space that will make it nearly impossible for a reactionless drive to operate."

"I understood that much," Jackson bit back his sarcastic retort while they were in the crowded Officers' Mess. "Let's leave the theory of operation aside for the moment and talk about how we deploy them."

"Working on that now," Singh incredibly dumped more hot sauce into what must have been an almost toxic soup after his taste test. "Apparently they can navigate themselves somewhat, so my first inclination is to load them into the launch tubes and tell the cube to toss them out."

"If they can self-navigate I want them loaded into launch tubes eight and ten," Jackson said.

"Both of those are aft-facing tubes," Singh frowned.

"Do you really think that we'll be the ones pursuing in this fight?" Jackson snorted.

"Point taken," Singh said. "So, what are your thoughts on the cube itself? Knowing you, I'm sure you were livid once you realized that the Vruahn had put a sentient, self-aware weapon aboard your ship without telling you."

"I wasn't pleased," Jackson said, "but I don't believe it's actually sentient. I believe it gives the appearance of a self-aware personality for our sake. I had a similar experience with the Vruahn computer aboard Colonel Blake's ship. It seems the Vruahn are able to give their AIs varying levels of intelligence depending on use and function. What I find more interesting is whether these interfaces are something they developed for our benefit or if they prefer to relate to their tech on a more personal level."

"Interesting," Singh said in a tone that indicated he thought it was anything but before draining his water glass. "I better get back down there. I'm not really sure how much work this will require and I don't want some ambitious lieutenant modifying my ship while I'm up here eating."

"Always a pleasure." Jackson raised his own glass in mock salute. He concentrated on trying to force the rest of his meal down past the icy lump that had formed in his stomach over the last day. Colonel Blake had come through and found the Phage core mind, and with that the mission was no longer an academic exercise. There was an entire armada waiting in Terran space for the Ninth to come through and actually capture a living Alpha.

Chapter 16

"G eneral quarters! General quarters! All hands to battlestations. Set condition 2SS."

Jackson had rolled out of bed before Lieutenant Davis had finished her announcement calling the crew to action. It had been nearly eleven days since the frenzied work that had integrated the Vruahn weaponry and prepped the squadron for the coming battle. Eleven long days that had frayed nerves and worn tempers thin, but it looked like that might all be coming to an end.

Once they had finalized their strategy, Jackson had gone down to the main cargo hold and had one more conversation with the cube before they actually began implementing their plan. Now that it was more or less general knowledge aboard the ship that the cube was much more than just a packing crate he had loosened the restrictions he'd placed on the device regarding its interfacing with the *Ares*. The cube was able to detect the Phage almost instantaneously once they entered a system, so he had made sure that it would issue a warning no matter who was on the bridge.

"Report!"

"Possible contact, sir," Davis frowned. "The Vruahn device issued a warning with a general distance that would put it near the edge of the system and a heading that had an accuracy of seventy degrees."

"That's not very accurate, Lieutenant," Jackson said. "Why isn't the tracking data updating?"

"Enemy signal lost. Attempting to reacquire."

"So that answers that," Jackson said as the words scrolled across the main display. "Or maybe not."

"Sir?" Davis asked.

"If this is a Phage Super Alpha, and it's the only Phage ship in the system, will it still be broadcasting their carrier frequency?" Jackson held up a hand to silence Davis. "Go ahead and answer audibly through the bridge speakers."

"Probability is high that you are correct, Captain," the cube said. "Adjusting search parameters to compensate for a single advanced forward unit."

"Just think how much easier it would have been if the Vruahn had just given us a few sets of their active sensors that are capable of picking a Bravo out of an asteroid field," Barrett groused.

"I asked for them, Lieutenant Commander," Jackson said. "Apparently with our metal alloy ships the system couldn't be adapted. Vruahn ships use a type of ceramic composite material for their hulls. No metal."

"Sorry, Captain," Barrett said. "Just complaining out loud."

"Coms! Send the order to the *Artemis* and *Atlas* to get started," Jackson ordered. "We are operating under the assumption a Super Alpha has arrived in-system, sent out a query message to any potential Phage left, and will now be coming downhill to investigate. Tactical, how're we looking?"

"All perimeter Spheres have been successfully deployed, as have their associated Shrikes," Barrett said. "The Spheres are operating autonomously, but I have an override command that the Vruahn cube has put on one of my terminals."

"I have to say, handing over control of so many nuclear penetrators isn't my favorite part of this plan, sir," Davis said softly.

"Nor mine," Jackson agreed, "but the risk is minimal and our technology is simply too slow to make proper use of them anyway. You have to look at it as a calculated risk… why would the cube bother firing our own missiles at us when it has seventy-two gravity bombs already at its disposal?"

"Of course, sir," Davis nodded.

"Coms?"

"Orders confirmed, Captain," Keller said. "*Artemis* just answered via tight beam laser."

"We are now running silent," Jackson said. "Full emission security protocols are in effect. Tell your backshops that I do not want a single radiation source active that has a path to an antenna on the hull."

There were two more pulses on the frequency that they were assuming was the Phage network carrier upon which they built their "hive minds." Jackson wondered how accurate the term frequency was, since the signal was not at all related to the EM spectrum and, as it had been explained to him, utilized a quantum effect that humans had barely begun to look at in theory, much less any sort of practical application. As such, they were wholly committed to trusting the Vruahn when they said that not only did this carrier signal exist, but that they had the means to detect it.

Thankfully the second Alpha they had killed of the three they'd found in the system was intact enough for him to implement his strategy. He had the *Atlas* and *Artemis* fly up next to the burnt-out hulk and match its velocity, rotation, and heading. After that it had been just a matter of waiting for evidence that a Super Alpha had made an appearance before ordering his two ships to begin lancing into the dead Alpha's hull with pinpointed laser fire in what he hoped looked like an effort to dissect and recover pieces from the ship.

"Still nothing on passives," Barrett reported. "But our range isn't so great that I'm expecting to detect anything until the shooting starts."

"I hope you're wrong about that, Lieutenant Commander," Jackson said. "We have two ships sitting down there with their asses hanging out in the breeze. Even with their active sensors running the Link won't update in time at this distance for us to provide any meaningful support."

"Understood, sir," Barrett said tightly.

This was the part of the plan that Jackson was least happy about, but he felt there wasn't much he could do to mitigate the risk. With the entire squadron flitting around the dead Alpha the target wasn't likely to risk its own safety by getting close enough for them to fire on it. But with only two destroyers performing what was hopefully an obvious salvage operation Jackson hoped that the Super Alpha would be much more brazen in its approach. He knew that this particular breed of Phage had the ability to hide from their sensors, so the danger to his two ships was significant, but he also knew that if they ran silent and became a dark hole in space that the Phage had an equally tough time detecting them.

Under normal circumstances the risk of losing forty percent of his total force would be completely unacceptable, but they had been tasked with the success of this mission no matter the cost. Admiral Marcum had even gone so far as to intimate that he fully expected the Ninth to take significant losses. The part of that conversation that had galled Jackson so badly was that the admiral made it clear that he expected Jackson to make it back even if not everyone else did. Even as angry as he'd been when he had departed the *Amsterdam*, he had to concede that the ability to put his emotions aside and think purely strategically was a lot of what made Marcum fit to wear his stars and, conversely, Jackson's own inability to do the same made him a questionable starship captain at best.

"One more pulse detected by the Vruahn sensor," Barrett said. "Signal strength was good, but still no actionable information. Indeterminate—"

"Whoa!"

Jackson's head snapped up at the outburst from the helmsman just in time to see the fading light of a massive explosion on the main display. They'd been sitting with the optical sensors trained on the *Atlas* and *Artemis*, and while they couldn't make out exact details there was no doubt about the magnitude of the explosion they'd seen on the display. Explosions in space were an odd thing to watch, or at least not what one would normally expect. Once the oxidizers were gone it disappeared as quickly as it appeared.

"Rep—"

"Telemetry from the *Artemis* has dropped!" Hayashi shouted.

"*Atlas* is declaring an emergency!" Keller had to shout overtop of everyone else. "I can't make it all out... too much shouting on the bridge."

"Coms! Try to raise the *Artemis*!" Jackson was gripping the armrests so hard that his hands hurt. "Tactical, full active scans! Get me a fucking location on the target! OPS, I want the *Ares* at full power within the next five minutes."

"Formation is going active," Barrett said tightly as all three ships that were loitering in a loose triangle around the target area began bombarding it with high-power radar energy. They were at a close enough range that they didn't have to wait long for valid returns.

"Got the bastard!" Barrett called out. "It's moving on the *Atlas*. *Artemis* does not appear in the area."

"Helm! Put our nose on the target and drop the hammer." Jackson leapt to his feet. "All ahead flank, emergency acceleration."

"Aye aye, sir!" The helmsman shoved the throttles all the way up and disengaged the safety interlocks to allow the engines to run up past their accepted maximum operational output. The *Ares* surged forward with the helmsman manually piloting the ship down towards an enemy that had seemingly appeared out of nowhere. From what they'd learned the Phage were unable to mask themselves from detection after firing their primary weapon, but the effect only lasted for around twenty minutes. Jackson hoped to close the gap to the point that it would be unable to hide from him no matter what it tried.

"Coms, have the rest of the squadron stand by," Jackson said. "I don't want them accelerating towards the target until we're certain what it's going to do. Tell the *Atlas* to do whatever it can to clear the area. OPS, is there any evidence the *Artemis* is still intact?"

"Negative, sir," Hayashi's voice sounded very small. "Radar is detecting a debris field that is consistent with the mass and composition of a destroyer. No lifeboat signals." Jackson had to swallow three times in quick succession to make sure he didn't vomit on the deck.

"Tactical, begin plotting a firing solution," he said once he trusted himself to speak. "Targeting pattern Echo-Three-Three. Helm, come starboard seven degrees, four degrees declination and reduce engine output to one hundred percent."

"Coming onto new course. Engines ahead flank, aye."

"All offensive systems are online, sir," Hayashi said. "Engineering is reporting all primary flight systems are good to go."

"Prep the auxiliary boosters and deploy the nozzles." Jackson could still feel his heartbeat in his ears after the loss of the *Artemis*. "Prime the fuel lines and stand by for ignition. We cannot let this bastard slink back off into the outer system."

"Target is underway, sir," Barrett said. "It's accelerating slowly on a course that will almost perfectly bisect us and the *Icarus*."

"Coms, tell Captain Wright to be ready for it to try and rush by her," Jackson said. "She's clear to engage as per our original targeting plan, and if she doesn't have a shot she is to withdraw."

"Target is approaching one of the gravity mines," Barrett said, referring to the Vruahn gravity bombs they'd peppered the system with as a contingency. "Range of three hundred and forty thousand kilometers and closing, but it's not on a direct intercept. It will cut across the outer range."

"Can we catch it before it clears the weapon's maximum range?" Jackson asked.

"Negative, sir," Specialist Accari spoke up from the nav station. "Even with the auxiliary booster we won't close within weapons range until we're both within the gravity mine's effective radius."

"Shit." Jackson looked at the graph the tactical computer was updating on the main display. The Super Alpha would cut across the influence of the gravity bomb at such an extreme range he'd have to order a full-yield detonation. That also meant that if he continued his headlong pursuit he would put the *Ares* at significant risk when the bomb went off.

"Is that bomb's corresponding Shrike in position for a shot if the Alpha continues along this course?"

"No, sir," Barrett said. "The missile will be far out of position even if the bomb succeeds in slowing it down or stopping the Alpha. We'd deployed it with the intent of detonating when the target was inbound from the outer system."

"Understood," Jackson said. "Helm! Zero thrust. We'll continue along this pursuit course on momentum. Nav, I assume you're tracking our progress and will alert the helm to any potential hazards?"

"Affirmative, Captain," Accari said.

"Tactical, give the order to the Vruahn cube to detonate that gravity bomb when the Alpha passes at its closest projected point," Jackson said. "Coms! Tell the *Icarus* and *Hyperion* to hold position."

"Orders sent," Keller said.

Jackson looked back at his com officer, and then around at the rest of his bridge crew. The shock and dismay they felt at the loss of the *Artemis* was written plainly on all of their faces. For the duration of the war the spacers of the Ninth had walked around with a cocky strut, secure in the knowledge that their squadron commander and their fast, powerful ships would see them through every conflict without a scratch. And why not? Every engagement the *Starwolf* class ships had participated in to date had been won with hardly a scorched hull plate to show for it. But they'd never stared down an enemy like this: so much like the powerful Alpha constructs but so much more devious and cunning. Only the original crew members left from the *Blue Jacket* remembered what it was like to go up against a Phage ship like this.

Now, in the very first shot of the engagement, the *Artemis* was completely destroyed with all hands aboard, and the *Atlas* was damaged to the point she was out of the fight. If he didn't address this soon he would lose his crew to fear and doubt. The only problem was that he hardly felt qualified to comfort them; he was concerned that they would see right through his hollow words and look at the truth of the matter: his orders had directly led to the deaths of thousands of their fellow spacers. What right did he have to offer them comfort?

"Sir?" Davis said quietly from beside him, nudging him with her elbow. "Are you okay?"

"Hardly," he mumbled before raising his voice. "Coms, patch me through on the shipwide and establish a com link to the rest of the squadron."

"Channel established, sir," Keller said.

"This is Captain Wolfe aboard the *Ares*," he said without preamble. "As you've already heard or seen, we lost the *Artemis* in the opening salvo of this battle. Captain Forrest and her crew were brave, skilled, and performed their duty without question. Let's not dishonor them by doing any different than they.

"Word has come back that the Phage core mind has been located by Colonel Blake's strike force. The entire Terran Starfleet is now relying on the Ninth Squadron to once again complete its mission so that the safety of all human worlds can be assured. We will mourn our comrades after we execute the capture of this bastard... and then we will take our vengeance out on the core mind that sent it. *Ares* out."

"You heard the captain," Chief Green shouted to shake everyone out of their stupor. "Let's get to work!"

The *Ares* continued her unpowered flight pursuing the Alpha, which appeared completely unconcerned about their presence. It undoubtedly had the positions of the three remaining combat-capable ships left in the system but seemed content to keep just ahead of the *Ares* with no overt move to evade or escape. Even across the vast distance and across the species-lines Jackson could almost feel the arrogance the thing exuded. It had already taken out two ships with a single shot, destroying one, and now glided away in an almost taunting manner.

Jackson hoped he was about to kick the smugness right out of the son of a bitch. Never in his life had he hated something so completely as he did the Phage, an intelligent species with inexplicable motivations that seemed only bent on killing as many as possible with no warning or explanation. The loss of the *Artemis* had stoked the flames so that now his hatred burned white hot within his chest like a mini-supernova. He wanted to not only eliminate them… he wanted them to suffer for what they'd done.

"Target has not significantly altered course," Barrett interrupted his thoughts. "The gravity mine's internal sensors have a lock and the Vruahn cube is updating the countdown. Detonation in ninety-eight minutes."

"Nav! How far will that put us out of the affected area?" Jackson called.

"We will be two hundred and seven thousand kilometers out of the sphere of influence and just over four hundred kilometers behind the target," Accari anticipated his captain's next question.

The next hour and a half passed at an interminable crawl and it played hell with Jackson's nerves. He was anxious to swing back at the Alpha and let it know that it wasn't going to have an easy time of it, but he also wanted to get the mission back on track and get Barrett into a position where he could target the specific regions the Vruahn had indicated would disable the marauder. The biggest challenge now became keeping the Alpha engaged without taking any more casualties but also not allowing it to escape.

"Stand by," Barrett said unnecessarily as everyone with a free eye had it turned towards the countdown timer on the main display. "Detonation!"

Jackson had no idea what to expect from a Vruahn gravity weapon, but at such a close range he'd sort of expected there to be some visible light phenomena given the forces that were at work. There was no discernible effect that was visible from the bridge of the ship, but the sensors told an entirely different story. The cube had warned him that the weapons were somewhat unpredictable at full yield, but he'd not bothered to ask just *how* unpredictable they were.

"Alpha has been... *thrown*... nearly seventy thousand kilometers off course." Barrett shook his head. "It was sucked in towards the epicenter of the detonation. High-Res radar is showing that it's tumbling in an uncontrolled flight roughly parallel to its original course and streaming something dense into space."

"The opposing forces of the weapon must have ruptured the hull." Jackson was suitably awed. The hide of a Super Alpha was nothing to sneer at, and at the edge of its effective range the Vruahn weapon had managed to split it enough that it was spewing that viscous glop that ran through it into space. "Is the blast area clear?"

"Our own accelerometers are picking up some residual eddies and ripples, sir," Hayashi reported. "But there's nothing that should cause more than a few bumps."

"Very well." Jackson stood. "Helm, direct pursuit course, all ahead flank. Coms, I want the *Icarus* and the *Hyperion* turning in and running ahead of the target but not to pursue. I want to box it in, not give it an avenue to escape from. The Vruahn weapon knocked the piss out of it, but it'll be coming around soon and when it does it won't be nearly so overconfident. Expect something new and horrible from this thing as well as a few ploys to try and get us within range of that plasma weapon."

The *Ares* rumbled to life as the engines were reengaged, and the helmsman corrected their course so that they were once again rushing after the target at full speed. Jackson had seen how tough these things were first-hand and he knew there was no way that a single blast, even one like he'd just seen, was going to put it out of commission for long. By the time they closed the gap it was likely that the hull breaches would be healed up and it would be hauling ass out of the area to rethink its next move.

"What's our range?" he asked.

"Five hundred and thirty thousand kilometers and closing," Hayashi answered. "The blast also knocked it further out relative to our position."

"Make sure the *Icarus* and *Hyperion* are angling out to compensate," Jackson said. "Coms! Any word from the *Atlas*?"

"Just automated responses, sir," Keller replied. "Any transmission that includes the name or registry number of the ship triggers the automated mayday."

"Understood," Jackson said. "Keep trying." He was almost tempted to have the *Hyperion* peel off the pursuit and go render aid or at least investigate, but he couldn't afford to try and corral the Alpha with only two destroyers on the line.

"OPS, prep a Jacobson drone for launch," he ordered instead. "I want it to fly back and confirm the status of the *Atlas* and verify the loss of the *Artemis*."

"Aye, sir," Hayashi said. "Sending mission parameters down to flight ops now."

It flew in the face of all Jackson's training to leave a potentially stranded group of spacers aboard a stricken starship when he had resources available to effect a rescue, but this wasn't training and he couldn't reduce his force by another third when he was already outgunned. The likelihood that anyone on the *Artemis* survived the plasma burst was so slim that he dared not pull another ship from his formation just to verify that, especially not when he had a hangar full of drones that could accomplish the same thing.

"If Colonel Blake was successful in his mission, why is his group returning to Terran space instead of flying out here as fast as they can to help us?" Davis asked him. "From what I understand, their FTL technology could put their strike ships out here well before this battle is over."

"That's a good question, Lieutenant," Jackson frowned. "But since I have no direct way to contact New Sierra or Colonel Blake it'll have to be pondered another time. The cube has been very specific about what it will and won't do… and apparently talking to the human strike group is on the 'won't do' list."

Davis didn't offer a rebuttal, but Jackson was more than a little disturbed at the obviousness of her observation. Why were the Vruahn leaving the Ninth flapping in the breeze against such an overmatched enemy when Blake's ships could easily and more precisely subdue the monster they were chasing? Even more puzzling, why was the cube restricting such an obvious asset as the instantaneous interstellar com capability to talk to Blake or at least simply relay a message? The more he thought about it the more he again felt the gentle tug of the strings, being made to dance to the Vruahn's tune. What left him seething was the fact that he had little choice for the foreseeable future but to continue letting them call the shots until he had more information.

The Super Alpha recovered from the gravity bomb much quicker than Jackson would have expected, much quicker than the first one he'd encountered would have been able. This made him approach the target with a bit more respect, a feeling that was apparently mutual as the Alpha abruptly changed course to take it away from the two closing destroyers ahead of it while still keeping ahead of the *Ares*. Jackson allowed himself a small, tight grin as he thought about the surprise the bastard must have had when they'd lit off a weapon that was generations ahead of anything it thought humans were capable of building.

"Captain, we're approaching delta-V roll off," Ensign Hayashi said over the muted rumble of the engines. "Target is still maintaining its interval and is matching all velocity changes."

"Understood," Jackson said. "Stand by for course change." A ship like the *Ares*, which was pushed through space via the brute force method of direct thrust, would eventually come to a point at which the thrust of the engines were only able to give them a negligible bump in velocity. The roll off was just before they would reach their maximum velocity and it was an area in a ship's performance band captains preferred to stay out of for a couple of reasons. The first was that the ship had to expend an incredible amount of propellant for not a lot of gain, and the other was that it didn't allow for maneuvers that required them to accelerate ahead.

He could ignite the auxiliary boosters, but that wouldn't give him a significant boost at their current velocity, and he had no doubt that the Alpha could just match their increase and keep ahead of them. The problem with this breed of Alpha was that they weren't so easily fooled into taking rash action and tended to be much more cautious once their nose had been bloodied. Jackson didn't think there was anything he could do to try and goad the Phage ship into coming about and charging him.

"Helm, come to port forty-six degrees relative, eleven degrees inclination," Jackson ordered after staring at the tactical plots for a moment. "Reduce engine power: ahead one-half."

"Coming onto new course and reducing engine output, aye." The helmsman shot a questioning look over his shoulder.

"Specialist Accari, I am not relieving you of your task," Jackson caught the look. "I'm just playing a hunch here and flying by feel."

"Of course, Captain," Accari said, his voice giving no indication he'd been insulted by his captain assuming the job of navigating the ship.

"Coms, tell Captain Wright I want her formation to continue along their current course and mirror any move made by the Phage," Jackson said. "She is to maintain her interval to it unless it turns away and makes for the outer system, then she is authorized to assume the lead position and disable it before it can escape."

"Yes, sir." Keller slid his headset fully back onto his ears.

"Another hunch?" Davis asked.

"More like another blind stab into the dark," Jackson muttered. "I just want to get a feel for how this one reacts to changes before we close the range and get into a running gun fight."

The Alpha continued on as the *Ares* ceased accelerating and began to gently push off course towards the inner system. After three hours of steadily coming onto their new course, the Phage ship began to respond, but not in any way Jackson had assumed it would.

"Alpha has come to a full stop," Barrett said.

"What?" Jackson nearly shouted in disbelief.

"Confirmed, sir," Hayashi said. "Vruahn telemetry and our own Link updates show the target sitting stationary in space relative to the primary." Jackson looked at the tactical plots in disgust as he realized he'd put all of his ships out of position. The *Ares* was travelling entirely in the wrong direction and the *Icarus* and *Hyperion* were bunched up and on a course that would make it almost impossible for them to come about onto a direct intercept without the Alpha having limitless options to easily evade them.

"Clever bastard," Jackson ground out. "It wasn't sure what we were doing, so it's just not going to play. It's completely taken the initiative away from us."

"Orders, sir?" Davis asked.

"Helm, steady as she goes," Jackson said. "Coms! Tell Captain Wright I need her to accelerate and angle out… get between the target and the outer system."

"A blockade with two destroyers?" Davis asked.

"Watch and learn, Lieutenant," Jackson smiled with a confidence he didn't feel.

Once Celesta Wright had ordered her two-ship formation to an obvious course to cut the Alpha off from the outer system the Phage ship stopped again. Jackson watched the twenty-minute-old data on his tactical display with narrowed eyes. Redeploying Celesta's ships had been an obvious move, but it was also the only logical ploy left to him given the fact that the *Ares* was so badly out of position. He thought the Phage must be confused as to why the *Ares* was still slowly drifting out of the area and wasn't willing to blindly run into another trap.

"Coms! Get me a direct channel to Commander Singh," Jackson barked.

"*Go for Engineering,*" Singh's calm voice came over the bridge speakers.

"Commander, I have a series of unusual requests to make of your equipment and I don't have a lot of time to explain the why of it." Jackson sat back in his seat, heart racing.

"*We aim to please, Captain,*" Singh said. "*What can we do for you?*"

"I want Reactor Two vented to space," Jackson said. "At the same time I want the appearance of a plasma breach on Engine One. Open the constrictors so that the chamber evacuates in an uncontrolled burst... obviously not enough to damage the engine but enough that it looks like we've lost containment."

"*All simple enough requests, sir,*" Singh said. "*I think I know where you're going with this. Just so you know, once we purge and restart Reactor Two it will be up to an hour before it's generating power again. Reactor One can handle both main engines, but you're going to be limited to whatever charge the weapons have currently until the powerplant is back up to one hundred percent.*"

"Understood," Jackson said. "Get to it."

"*Will do, sir,*" Singh said. "*Engineering out.*"

It wasn't even ten minutes later when alarms began blaring on the bridge and the output of Reactor Two dropped to nothing. Along the ventral surface of the ship a pair of baffles snapped open and the superheated helium byproduct of the fusion reaction was vented into space. As the blast of ionized gas began to taper off, brilliant flashes of uncontrolled plasma billowed out of the forward and aft thrust nozzles of Engine One. The *Ares* began to list to port slightly and even rolled into a forward tumble, a nice touch suggested by an enthusiastic helmsman and approved by Jackson.

"Vents are sealed and Reactor Two is being purged and prepped for restart," Hayashi reported. "Engine One's magnetic constriction system is back to normal operation and the propellant injectors are coming back online. Engineering says the plasma chamber will be hot within the next fifteen minutes."

"Thank you, Ensign," Jackson said. "Helm, reassert attitude control on the *Ares*. Bring us back to stable flight along our same course. Zero thrust until Engine One is back to normal ops."

"Aye aye, sir."

"Now we wait," Davis said tightly.

"Now we wait," Jackson nodded.

The sensor lag was especially excruciating as Jackson felt particularly vulnerable with his ship literally at half-power. He didn't think he'd need the laser batteries or the auto-mag in the anticipated action, but experience told him that if they were unavailable then it would be those systems needed most. He resisted the urge to send a transmission to the *Icarus*. Celesta knew what she was doing and there was nothing to be decided until they found out what the Phage ship was doing.

"Target has come about and is accelerating on a direct intercept vector!" Barrett called out twenty-three minutes after they'd put on their lightshow.

"I don't think it's fully committed yet," Jackson frowned. "It should be capable of acceleration rates four times that. Coms! Order our two remaining ships onto a pursuit course. Tell Captain Wright to make it look like they're coming to our aid."

"Aye, sir."

"It's still cautious," Davis said. "That Vruahn weapon must have really shaken it."

"Agreed," Jackson said. "But it's still coming. No matter how much smarter it is than a normal Alpha, it's still a predator. Its prey instinct is just too strong. It'll chase us."

"And we want that?"

"What we want is for it not to flee the system," Jackson said. "If we have to use ourselves as bait to make that happen… so be it."

"Yes, sir."

****

"It's still closing, sir… but it certainly isn't in any hurry to catch us." Davis stifled a yawn as Jackson walked back onto the bridge. The Alpha had made it clear that it had no intention of blindly running into close range with the *Ares*, but it didn't seem inclined to pass up the opportunity of a wounded Terran starship either.

"Thank you, Lieutenant." Jackson sat down and rubbed his eyes. "You're dismissed. Try and get some sleep."

"Yes, sir."

They had been flying under the ruse of only one operable engine for nearly two days. When the Alpha had halted its advance and began to pace them Jackson had little choice but to stand down half his crew and go to two watches. There was a certain symmetry to being doggedly pursued by a Super Alpha. He'd nearly forgotten how unnerving it was to have a silent enemy trail along behind them for days… just waiting for them to make that critical mistake.

"Do you think we could try another ruse with the flight equipment?" Barrett asked. "Draw it in closer?"

"I doubt it would work." Jackson shook his head. "It's closed in as much as it's going to until some new, unknown conditions are met and then it'll press the attack. I think we may need to force the issue. It's not going to be fooled by the *Icarus* and *Hyperion* lagging behind like they are. Any word back from the Jacobsen drone?"

"Uh… yes, sir," Barrett blinked at the change of topic. "Stand by." He swung around at his terminal and brought up another window that contained all the raw data from the drone sweep.

"Intel just sent up the report from CIC. As suspected, the *Artemis* is a total loss, sir. No beacons or lifeboats; there actually wasn't much debris that was recognizable as parts of the ship."

"Understood." Jackson swallowed hard. "And the *Atlas*?"

"The drone hasn't sent an updated packet yet; the preliminary report shows the *Atlas* in a slowly decaying orbit over the planet, but she appears to be mostly intact. She looks to be streaming atmosphere and does not seem to be under power."

"Thank you, Lieutenant Commander," Jackson said. "Make the information available on the Link. Tell flight ops I want the drone continually hailing the *Atlas* until they respond or we order it to stop."

"Aye, sir."

"Nice of you to join us, Lieutenant," Jackson said without turning around.

"Yes, sir," Lieutenant Keller said. "I'm sorry, sir."

"Open a direct command level channel to the *Icarus*, if you would," Jackson sat down and slipped in his earpiece. It wasn't long before the channel was established on the other end.

"*Captain Wright*," the familiar voice said, causing Jackson to smile in spite of himself.

"Captain," he said. "I feel like our little charade here has run its course."

"*Agreed, sir,*" Celesta said, the com lag just barely noticeable. "*I assume you're contacting me with a plan?*"

"You assume correctly," Jackson said. "I don't want to give this bastard time to collect its thoughts, and I sure as hell don't want to allow any reinforcements to get here and ruin the party. Here's what I had in mind."

Over the next forty minutes he and his former XO hammered out their strategy, planned for contingencies, and then set about trying to pick holes in both. Once they had both agreed on a course of action and a timetable Jackson terminated the link and looked at his mission clock. He wanted Davis back on duty once the fun started, but he could allow her a few more hours of sleep. It would take Celesta some time to brief her crew and wingman and then get her ships redeployed. The *Ares* was as ready as she could be. They were still feigning a failed engine, but at least had the powerplant back to full capacity. If their plan worked they'd need it soon.

****

"Targeting scans from the *Icarus* and *Hyperion* detected, Captain," Barrett called over the other conversations on the bridge. "No reaction yet from the target."

"They've begun accelerating," Hayashi reported. "Both ships are following their predesignated course."

"Track them through the Link on the main display," Jacksons said. "I don't want the lag of watching our own radar tracks."

"Aye, sir." The other two destroyers were broadcasting their positions over the Link, so simply using that data to populate the tactical display would cut the reporting time at least in half.

The Alpha was still pacing behind the *Ares* as the other two ships bore down on it, and Jackson knew it would have to make a decision soon. He hoped it would be a hasty decision that would work out in their favor. All they knew about the Super Alphas was that they were significantly smarter than their similar cousins, but nobody Jackson had talked to had been willing to quantify exactly what that meant. They had no frame of reference for judging the Super Alpha's intelligence other than the fact they were the only Phage ships that were able to operate alone.

Watching the responses of this one, and taking into account his experience with the first Phage ship that had attacked human space, he was inclined to look at these units as more instinctual than cerebral. They lashed out when wounded, pounced on damaged or weaker ships no matter if it exposed them to risk, and although they appeared to be able to reason out basic tactics they also seemed unwilling or unable to disengage from a skirmish once they'd locked horns.

If one were to believe the Vruahn and there really was one central, massive intellect controlling all of the Phage, then it made sense that even the Super Alphas wouldn't be as intelligent as some believed. There was a loose consensus among Terran scientists that seemed to correlate the large amount of neural mass to an equally large intellect. When Jackson pointed out contradictory observations to this theory he was patronizingly told that perhaps the subject was a bit outside of his field of expertise.

"Sir! The Alpha is now accelerating towards us!" Hayashi's voice was bordering on shrill. "Four hundred Gs and holding."

"Steady, Lieutenant," Jackson said. "This is what we wanted. Helm, Engine Two ahead full and stand by on Engine One."

"Engine Two ahead full, aye," the helmsman said. The *Ares* surged ahead on the power of her starboard engine, but they had no chance of staying ahead of the Alpha without their other main. Jackson hoped the Alpha realized that as well and would move in just a little closer for the kill.

"Target is still closing," Barrett said. "Range… three hundred and twenty thousand kilometers."

"We need to get it in just under twenty-five thousand kilometers," Jackson said. "Helm! What's the status of Engine One?"

"Engine One is in standby and ready to engage, sir!" the helmsman called.

"Very good." Jackson sat and took a deep breath. "Let's stay calm and continue playing the wounded prey. We cannot flinch or the *Icarus* and *Hyperion* will be flying right into the monster's teeth."

The *Ares* continued to limp across the system under a straining single main engine, while an ever more brazen Alpha began to eat up the distance between them, throwing caution to the wind and accelerating. Behind the drama between the hunter and hunted, two destroyers were still roaring in under full power and letting the Alpha know they were still there with constant tracking and targeting radar scans. All in all, it was a nice bit of chaos that Jackson hoped would keep the Alpha fixated on rushing in to kill the *Ares* first and then try to get separation from the other two Terran warships.

"Alpha has crossed the one-hundred-thousand-kilometer mark," Barrett said after another six hours of flight. The enemy ship was still closing but had once again decreased its rate of acceleration.

"Thank you, Lieutenant Commander," Jackson said. "Did it set off the threshold trigger in the tactical computer?"

"Affirmative, sir," Barrett nodded. "Aft, starboard launch tube is in launch countdown. Weapon deployment in… thirteen seconds."

"Update our weapons status through the Link," Jackson said. "No outbound com traffic until further notice."

"Weapon away!" Barrett called. "Status updating on the main."

"Helm! Bring Engine One online," Jackson said. "All ahead flank!"

"All engines ahead flank, aye!" The rumble felt through the deck plates doubled in intensity as the *Ares* surged away from the Alpha on the tactical display.

"Thermal buildup on the enemy ship's prow," Barrett said. "Still no—"

"Detonation!" Hayashi yelled.

"Helm! Zero thrust—" Jackson never finished his sentence as the *Ares* was hit by something so violently that anybody not sitting down and holding on was sent flying. Jackson rolled up on to his knees, not trusting his prosthetic leg while the deck was still heaving, and tried to figure out what the hell had happened.

"Report!"

"Gravitational distortion was more than we—"

"Aft pylon sheared on Engine Two," Hayashi interrupted Barrett. "Plasma containment is failing."

"Jettison Engine Two! Now!" Jackson shouted.

"Engine Two is jettisoned! Only one of the separation rockets fired!"

"Helm, get us—" Another blast hit the *Ares*, this time sounding like something had physically struck the ship. Alarms blared, red strobes flashed, and all over the ship pressure hatches were slamming shut.

"Engine Two exploded before it was clear," Hayashi wiped the blood out of his eyes from the heavy gash over his forehead. "Multiple hull breaches… containment protocols are enacted."

"Tactical! Report!"

"Aft scan radar is out." Barrett shook his head, trying to focus on his displays. "Link telemetry shows that the *Icarus* and the *Hyperion* both fired on the target. *Hyperion* is reporting minor thermal damage to her prow."

"Coms!"

"Keller is down, sir," Davis said, pulling the com officer down to the floor before slipping the headset on. "Contacting the *Icarus* now."

"OPS, I want a concise damage report and I want it now!" Jackson barked. He grabbed the nearest console and hauled himself up, tentatively putting weight on his artificial leg before walking back over to his seat. "Helm! Are we under power?"

"Yes, sir," the helmsman said. "Engine One is responsive."

"Zero thrust and bring us about." Jackson sat down. "Get us pointing back towards the engagement and let her drift until we know what's going on. Tactical, get sensors on the target ASAP… I need to know what's happening."

"The *Icarus* is reporting that the target is down!" Davis called.

"Is it still alive?" Jackson asked.

"Thermal scans indicate there is still activity aboard," Davis said. "But it is no longer maneuvering."

"*Status confirmed*," the words came over the bridge speaker. "*Enemy ship is alive and disabled.*"

"Nice of you to suddenly become helpful again," Jackson snapped. "Lieutenant Davis, make the call to Sick Bay and get a team up here to see to Lieutenant Keller. After that, send word to the *Icarus* that they're to begin the grappling procedure and we'll join them as soon as we can."

Chapter 17

"It was a hell of a thing to see." Celesta leaned back in her seat. She was in her office aboard the *Icarus* and Jackson could just make out the picture in the background over the video channel. It was of the two of them along with Davis, Singh, and Pike standing in front of the *Ares'* main entry hatch just before the ship was christened and launched.

"We didn't get to enjoy the show," Jackson said sourly. "We've taken a serious beating. When the main exploded it opened up the hull along the aft quadrant in a dozen places. So you actually have optical sensor data of the incident to go with the radar and accelerometer records?"

"We do," she nodded. "I'd ordered the sensors trained on the spot in space we knew the Alpha was, and we were able to just make it out on the thermal optics at the time of the incident. When the gravity bomb went off it jerked, spun around twice, and then just floundered around a bit before our missiles impacted."

"Amazing," Jackson shook his head. "The bomb must have modulated its output for a sustained effect. One big ripple to slow it down and then just enough disruption of local space to make sure its drive was effectively nullified."

"I suppose we're lucky the Phage don't have any sort of backup propulsion that isn't based on gravity manipulation," Celesta yawned. "Were there any casualties on the *Ares*?"

"Six dead, over twenty injured," Jackson said quietly. "Not to mention the loss of the *Artemis*."

"Yes," she said sadly. "This operation had better pay off considering the price we've paid for it so far."

"I couldn't agree more, Captain," Jackson said. "I'm ordering the *Hyperion* back to the planet to recover the *Atlas* or at least confirm her condition. The probe hasn't been able to send back anything conclusive on the condition of the crew. We're limping back to you now; it took a while to come to a full stop and then accelerate back the way we came on one main engine."

"Will you be able to achieve transition velocity?" Celesta asked.

"Singh says yes," Jackson shrugged. "I'll worry about that when the time comes. For now, maintain your position and we'll hopefully hear from the Vruahn cube soon about what the next step is. Obviously we can't take the thing back to Terran space intact."

"Understood, sir," she said. "*Icarus* out."

Jackson terminated his own connection and leaned back. Despite the horrors around him like losing an

216

entire ship under his command and the deaths aboard his own vessel, he couldn't help but smile as he thought about how much Celesta Wright had matured as a commanding officer. She'd grown much from the unsure executive officer who had boarded the *Blue Jacket* to someone he now considered one of the most solid, dependable captains in the Fleet. He expected big things for her… assuming their next campaign was a success and that they actually survived it.

He hauled himself out of his seat with a groan, wincing as his leg straightened out. He'd landed pretty hard both times he'd been tossed about the bridge and cursed himself for not ordering everyone into restraints before setting off another of those accursed gravity bombs. They knew so little about the capabilities and limitations of the weapon that he should have exercised greater caution when lobbing them out into space and hoping for the best. Even though they had given some instruction to the cube before deploying them, and had even received a confirmation from the damn thing, he suspected that it had set the weapon's output based on its own calculations with little regard for the safety of the humans aboard the ship.

Jackson walked quickly from his office back to the bridge, intent on getting his orders to Captain Walton on the *Hyperion* before checking in with Singh about how the repairs were going. He also intended to have another discussion with the cube even though he knew it was likely a wasted effort. The device had shown that it had its own motivations and seemed to be operating on protocols that were not made available to Jackson. Either way it was clear that when it came to the alien tech aboard his ship he was *not* the one in charge. The best he could hope for at this point was that it didn't cost him any more of his crew before he could get it out of his hold.

****

"I'd like a few straight answers from you," Jackson bluntly shouted across the hold. He'd already ordered Major Ortiz's Marines to take up position outside as well as his own monitoring teams.

"To the best of my ability, Captain," the cube said.

"That would be a nice change of pace," Jackson snorted. "Let's start with the most pressing: you're aware your gravity bomb severely damaged my ship and cost six of my crew their lives?"

"Unavoidable," the cube said matter-of-factly. "The output of the weapon had to be set so as to be certain the enemy ship was disabled long enough for your escort ships to fire upon it. At the time you ejected the gravity modifier they were too far away for the effect to be reduced enough to ensure the safety of this vessel."

Jackson had to clench his fists and count to ten before continuing. "Okay," he said through clenched teeth. "Why did you not inform me of this issue? We could have easily adjusted our intervals before the Alpha could have caught up."

"Your reactions, Jackson Wolfe, are far too unpredictable for me to make calculations based upon them and still stay within my allotted margin of error," the cube said. "While there are tertiary protocols in my programming to ensure your safety, they do not supersede my primary role of securing vital mission material from the disabled enemy ship."

"How in the hell did you intend to—" Jackson trailed off as he realized the truth of the matter. "You would survive the destruction of the *Ares*, wouldn't you?"

"Affirmative," said that same emotionless voice. "If this vessel were to be disabled or destroyed, my secondary protocols would be to make contact with Captain Celesta Wright should that be necessary to complete the mission. If the enemy was already disabled then I would await contact from Colonel Robert Blake."

"Interesting." Jackson was beginning to lose his grip on his temper. "And could you survive a one-way trip into the corona of the primary star in this system?"

"Irrelevant."

"How about this one: why are you not willing to let me communicate with Colonel Blake?" Jackson asked. "You have that ability, do you not?"

"I do; however, for reasons I do not know that ability is blocked unless secondary protocols are activated," the cube said. Jackson took a slight pause from his fantasies of hurling the cube into a star and thought about that for a moment. Despite the appearance of personality and sentience the thing was just a computer programmed with prearranged responses to certain triggers. The Vruahn handlers had made sure that no amount of human bungling was going to risk the success of this mission, even if nobody survived the effort.

"Are you in constant contact with Vruahn handlers?" he asked. If he'd taken the time to think about his interactions with the cube as simply queries to a computer rather than questions to an actual intelligence he might have made better progress before it had cost him six lives, possibly two ships, and an engine.

"My telemetry output is being monitored."

"Is there any chance of direct communication from me to them?" Jackson asked. "Or possibly a relay from me to Setsi?"

The display on the cube went dark for a moment.

"Direct communication is neither necessary nor desired, human," the cube said, this time with genuine emotion. "Accomplish the task to which you agreed and this unsavory alliance can be dissolved."

Jackson was taken aback for a moment before he realized what had just happened.

"Were your questions answered satisfactorily, Captain?" the cube's normally dispassionate voice asked.

"Oh yes," Jackson said, staring right into the display. "More than you know."

****

"Captain, this is as close as we can approach until the *Icarus* stabilizes the spin of the Alpha," Hayashi said. "In addition to missing one of the main engines, our stability and maneuvering systems have been degraded by nearly forty percent on the starboard side as well as significant damage to the dorsal and ventral thrusters."

"Let's take it slow and safe," Jackson said. "Anything else?"

"The *Hyperion* is seven hours from intercepting the *Atlas*," Davis told him. "So far Captain Walton hasn't seen anything to be hopeful about."

"Let's hope he's wrong, Lieutenant." Jackson sat down. "How are Major Ortiz and Commander Owens coming along?"

"EVA teams are prepped and standing by," Hayashi said.

"Good," Jackson said. "Tell them that they will need to prep for one more team member. I'll be accompanying the EVA crews."

"Yes, sir," Hayashi said with an uncertain glance to Davis that Jackson pretended not to see.

"You disagree, Lieutenant?"

"Yes, sir," Davis said. "There are multiple reasons why you should not be going over to a still living Alpha."

"Such as?"

"Ignoring the dozen or so regulations it would break, you know that your prosthetic leg disqualifies you from EVA operations," she said.

"True," Jackson nodded. "But there is also one very good reason why I need to go over there."

"Oh?"

"I'll just say that we're more likely to get better proactive help from the Vruahn equipment aboard this ship if I'm on that team," Jackson said. "Trust me, Lieutenant… that's the last place I want to be, but I also don't want to send any more people needlessly to their deaths. I don't trust that cube to not consider anyone else as expendable."

"I'm afraid you've completely lost me, sir," she said.

"I'll explain the whole thing to you someday, Lieutenant," Jackson promised. "But for now I need to get ready."

Jackson had ordered his EVA crews to assemble in the main cargo hold so that the cube could directly observe their preparations and make any adjustments necessary. As it turned out, they didn't need a whole Alpha for their purposes, just a small piece of it that needed to be carefully put into stasis. While this was good news in that they didn't have to figure out how in the hell they would have transported the entire Alpha back to the DeLonges System, it did present other challenges.

The obvious problem of needing a piece of a living Alpha was that it wasn't likely to be handed over willingly. The Vruahn had provided the clever gravity bombs, a wildly inaccurate term that had already been embedded into the lexicon aboard the *Ares*, which allowed them to immobilize the target without inflicting any collateral damage. After that the cube had given very specific targeting instructions to them as well as the precise yield their weapons would need to be at in order to keep the Alpha disabled. Jackson was assured that not only would the Alpha never be able to repair its propulsion system, but that its long-range beacon had also been knocked out. Given some of his recent interactions with the cube and its handlers, however, he wasn't inclined to just blindly trust what he was told.

"Captain on deck!"

"As you were," Jackson waved to the assembled group of Marines and spacers. "What's our status?"

"We're good to go, sir," Major Ortiz said. "Gear check is complete and now we're just waiting on a go-signal." The words had no sooner left the major's mouth when the display on the cube lit up, beckoning them all closer.

"There are four pieces of equipment you will need before proceeding," the cube said, its voice startling everyone in the hold but Jackson. "Three are in a container next to the munitions racks."

"And the fourth?" Jackson asked.

"This housing is the fourth," the cube said. "I have been integrated into the stasis chamber in order to directly monitor and manipulate the apparatus that you will be removing from the enemy ship."

"This would have been nice to know before now," Commander Owens said. The chief medical officer was still in his utilities since he was only there supervising the preparations of the science team.

"You get used to this, Commander," Jackson said. "Apparently we're only given information when we need it and sometimes after. Major Ortiz, would you have a detail grab the gear from the other cube? It will be fairly obvious what they're supposed to take."

"Yes, sir." Ortiz turned and walked off.

"You," Jackson pointed at a spacer that seemed to not have any specific tasks at that moment. "Call flight ops and tell them we'll need this cube moved down to the hangar bay ASAP."

"Aye aye, sir."

"Is there any chance of you telling me exactly what we're after over there?" Jackson asked the cube.

"The structure you will retrieve is fairly close to the surface, or the 'hull' as you've referred to it," the cube said. "It is the primary communications node, specific to this type of construct, and it not only allows the Alpha to access their networked consciousness but identifies it to others of its kind. If properly secured and integrated into the stasis housing it will allow us to gather intelligence over their communications network and also give us the ability to pass unchallenged into their space."

Jackson squinted at the cube's display, unsure if he'd been talking to the cube itself or the handlers on the other side again.

"Very well," he said finally. "I assume this is the part in which detailed instructions are given as to how we'll accomplish this."

"Correct."

The briefing that followed was as straightforward as Jackson had hoped it would be given that they would have no time for a dress rehearsal. The equipment they had been given included some type of injector that would soften the outer hull enough that they could cut through it with a standard laser, a handheld holographic projector that would guide them in and walk them through the process of removing the node, and a kit with all the needed tools to keep the node viable until they could get it out and stuff it into the stasis cube.

Jackson watched his EVA team nod as the instructions were provided and they went over the tools which had been thoughtfully designed for human hands, but he still had grave misgivings. The lack of prep time and the fact that they only had one set of the crucial tools meant that they would only have one shot for a successful outcome. In his experience that rarely happened with such a delicate operation, even with a well-trained crew. Had he known that they would be dissecting an Alpha he would have requested a specialized team from Fleet Research and Science, but then he ran the risk of losing a group of irreplaceable scientists if something went sideways during the operation.

"Okay! Let's get buttoned up and get this show on the road," Jackson called loudly over the half-dozen side conversations as the rigging crew from flight ops arrived to transport the cube over to the main hangar bay. "The sooner we get this done, the sooner we can get this ship back to New Sierra. Let's move!"

The process of getting the cube into the assault shuttle was absurdly simple: it began to collapse in on itself until it was no bigger than one and a half meters on each side. The hangar crews lowered the gravity and then they just lifted it into the shuttle for the short ride over to the disabled Alpha. Jackson had begun to get a case of nerves at the thought that the thing was still alive... feeling, thinking, and wanting nothing more than to kill every last human in the system.

"Captain! We're going to keep the shuttle's cargo bay evacuated of atmosphere once we get underway," the pilot was shouting so Jackson could hear him, not bothering to mess around with patching into his EVA suit's intercom. "The flight deck will be pressurized and sealed, but you and your team can move in and out of the bay without having to pump down or purge." Jackson simply gave him a thumbs up and a pat on the back, motioning the rest of the EVA team to start loading into the shuttle through the airlock hatch.

Like most Terran starships, the *Ares* didn't have a pressurized hangar deck. The shuttles and other support craft entered the bay and docked to an airlock to allow access to and from the ship. The system was a simple yet elegant solution to the problem of quickly getting smaller craft loaded and unloaded from the capital ship without wasting tons of precious air or time to pump down enormous transfer chambers.

Jackson swallowed a few times as his stomach did a backflip when the shuttle slid out of the bay doors and away from the influence of the *Ares'* artificial gravity. The flight was short and uneventful as the cube projected their target LZ on the pilot's heads-up display.

"Contact!" the pilot said over the open channel. "Stand by while we anchor down." There were a few heavy *clunks* as six heavy spikes were fired down into the hull of the Alpha and the winches pulled the shuttle down tight against the surface. Jackson looked out of the small slit of a window in the passenger compartment, a cold chill running up his spine as the shuttle lights showed the convoluted and utterly alien landscape of the massive ship. He'd seen plenty of Phage remains up close during the course of the war, but up this close and personal to one that was still alive was enough to cause his breath to catch in his chest.

"We're ready to begin operations, Captain," the pilot said again. "We can't extend the cofferdam for you since the laser would damage it, but the crew chief will anchor two safety lines on either side of the work area that your team can tie off on."

"Understood, Lieutenant Commander," Jackson said. "We're ready to begin back here." As the rear ramp lowered Jackson saw a private com channel request light up on his helmet display. He moved aside and waved his crew past, allowing them to begin unloading and securing the equipment while he grabbed a handhold and tried to stay out of the way.

"Wolfe," he keyed his mic.

"*Captain,*" Davis's voice sounded in his headset. "*We've heard back from the Hyperion. The crew of the Atlas is alive, but not for long. Main power was knocked out and their emergency power failed to initialize; the batteries on the ship are the only thing keeping the CO2 scrubbers running and they're about spent. They've been communicating with the Hyperion by flashing a light out one of the portholes. The ship is in a rapidly decaying orbit.*"

"Understood." Relief flooded through Jackson. "Tell Captain Walton to take the *Hyperion* closer and get a power umbilical down to that ship so that they can at least get their life support systems running again. After that I want him to grapple on and pull the *Atlas* up to a stable orbit so they can begin effecting repairs without worrying about tumbling to the surface. I want you to handle this, Lieutenant. I'll be tied up over here and unable to coordinate both efforts."

"*Understood, sir,*" Davis said. "*Ares out.*"

By the time Jackson made his way to the edge of the hatch he saw that his crews were already cutting into the Alpha's hull, the laser easily slicing through the compromised material after it had been injected with whatever was in the device the Vruahn had supplied. The cube had also claimed the inhibitor would keep the hull from closing back up once they were in.

It took almost an hour to cut away a section large enough for them to safely get in with their bulky EVA suits and the necessary equipment. Two members of the science team were there only to record every aspect of the operation since every other Alpha that had ever been examined had been dead and usually massively damaged from the preceding battle. Once the last chunk of hull/hide had been pulled off and tossed away, Jackson grabbed Major Ortiz's shoulder just before the big Marine officer went to climb in.

"I'll go first, Major," Jackson said over a private channel.

"Of course, Captain," Ortiz replied. If he was miffed about being moved aside he was too professional to let it show.

Jackson wasn't sure what he had expected the inside of a living Alpha to be like, but it certainly wasn't what he was seeing. They had made entry in what appeared to be a large, irregularly shaped duct that ran along the inner surface of the hull. What was interesting was that the walls of the structure were translucent and he was able to see through them into the bowels of the Alpha with surprising clarity.

He was shocked to see that much of the interior was open space. There were supports as thick as the *Ares* at her widest point that soared out of the interior to brace against the outer hull, each festooned with what appeared to be a haphazard placement of organic structures.

"What is the light source in here?" Major Ortiz asked on the open channel from beside him.

"I'm not sure, Major," Jackson admitted. "It's coming from too far below us for me to tell for certain."

"Well, I guess I'll leave that for Owens's geeks." The shoulders of Ortiz's EVA suit shrugged slightly before he lifted the Vruahn holographic projector and activated it. "It looks like we take this access tube aft from here."

"Lead on, Major."

"Swanson! Ellett!" Ortiz barked over the channel. "Get up here! You two are on point. You keep ahead fifteen meters and you call out anything that looks unusual."

"Unusual, sir?" Sergeant Swanson asked. "Here?"

"You know what I mean, smartass," Ortiz said. "If you think it's dangerous, call a halt and wait for us."

"Yes, sir," Swanson said without much enthusiasm and pushed off to float ahead with Ellett.

The ten-person group traveled quickly down the duct, using their arms to keep from bouncing off the walls, until the Vruahn projector indicated that they needed to stop and began displaying on the wall itself where to begin cutting.

"Careful with that laser," Ortiz said. "This indicates that the... thing... we want is just under the surface here. Cut too deep and this was all for nothing."

After a chorus of confirmations two Marines came forward with the laser cutter and set the power down to thirty percent, while members of the science team used their own instruments to monitor the progress. Even with the inhibitor the Vruahn had provided the hull material had still been very tough and resistant to the laser, but the inner walls of the duct split apart instantly and retreated away from the beam of concentrated light.

"What the hell is this anyway?" Ortiz asked over the open channel. "It looks like an artery or something."

"Not far from accurate, Major," Jackson answered. "I'm told this is a fluid channel that helps pipe that viscous sludge these things have to wherever it's needed. The fluid is then able to adapt and become whatever type of material it needs for repairs."

"Clever," Ortiz nodded.

"We're through, sir," one of the science team said, peeling back the duct wall so that they could peer through. The holographic projector scanned the area beyond the cut and then highlighted a hard nodule hanging from three supports that anchored it to the inner surface of the hull. There were four more flexible conduits that were connected to it, one of which pulsed with a dull reddish glow.

The team began to pull out the rest of the equipment provided by the Vruahn and apply them where the projector indicated, the instructions being simple enough that a troop of monkeys could have come in and accomplished the task. Jackson realized that was probably the exact analogy used by the Vruahn when designing the gear.

Four identical devices that looked like plastic donuts were clamped around the four flexible conduits coming into the device. Once attached, the devices climbed on their own to some predetermined length and then began to glow orange as they sliced through the lines, cauterizing them as they went. The severed conduits retreated quickly out of sight and the walls of the duct they were in began to quiver.

"What the—"

"*Captain! The Alpha is beginning to show signs of life,*" the shuttle pilot radioed through the remote link they'd established on the surface of the hull. "*The Ares is telling me it's twitching in space. You'd better hurry.*"

"Understood," Jackson answered before turning to his team. "You heard her. Let's finish up and get the hell out of here."

The team quickly took the cutting laser and began slicing through the three anchoring supports, two cutting while three reached through the hole and steadied their prize. By the time they cut through the heavy, dense supports the interior of the duct was really starting to rock and roll. The three Marines quickly hauled in the nodule while the others began to pack up their gear.

"Leave it!" Jackson ordered. "Let's go! Back to the shuttle as quickly as you can."

After a bit of floundering about they all got purchase on some piece of the duct wall and got themselves moving in the right direction. Jackson hadn't realized how far they'd come since he'd been so focused on watching the Vruahn map projection, but he guessed they had to be at least half a kilometer from the opening they'd cut into the hull.

Once they reached their breach point two Marines wordlessly hauled themselves up out of the hole and hooked their tethers onto the safety lines before reaching down and offering assistance to the others.

"No!" Ortiz shouted. "The objective first! Get it in the shuttle." After some clumsy shifting about the nodule was pushed up and out to the waiting Marines.

"Major! We have a problem out here!" Jackson accepted the proffered hand and allowed himself to be pulled up out of the Alpha's interior to see what the Marines were referring to. The first thing he saw was that the crew chief was floating at the end of his tether, clearly unconscious but thankfully tied off like he was supposed to be. When he looked into the interior of the shuttle he was confused momentarily until he realized that the cube had expanded while they'd been gone, filling the entire space. The Vruahn projector was shrilly ordering them to place the nodule into the cube's now-gaping maw.

"Captain, there won't be enough space for us in there," Ortiz said calmly. "I'm guessing when it expanded it whacked the crew chief pretty good."

Before Jackson could answer the hull of the Alpha shook under them, pushing them off the surface and making them all grab for their own safety lines.

"Get that thing into the cube," Jackson ordered. "Without it this whole mission was a waste."

The Marines wasted no time shuffling the nodule over to the opening where six long, black tendrils shot out and grabbed it, pulling it into the cube before it closed itself back up. Jackson watched, expecting it to contract back down enough for them to board, but that didn't happen. Instead the hatch of the shuttle swung up and locked and the maneuvering thrusters angled down to blast the ship off the surface.

"Unhook from the safety lines! NOW!" Jackson bellowed into his helmet, making his own ears ring. "Hook onto each other, as many as can be reached!" He hooked his own line to Major Ortiz even as the other Marines hooked in, creating a cluster of bouncing EVA suits. Two from the science team also made it before the thrusters fired and hauled the shuttle up and away from the Alpha, the safety lines snapping taut before breaking. Jackson watched helplessly as two more of Commander Owens's people were blown off the hull from the downwash and the crew chief was yanked away so violently that it was doubtful he'd survived.

"*Ares*, this is Wolfe," Jackson keyed his external com. "What's your status?" His call was met with only silence. He tried a few more times before he realized that the ship was either not receiving him or his hails were being blocked somehow.

"*Icarus*, this is Captain Wolfe. What is the status of the *Ares*?"

"*Captain?*" Celesta Wright's voice came back after a moment. "*They're just about to pull your shuttle into the hangar bay. What's going on?*"

"We're not on that shuttle!" Jackson said. "Tell Davis to lock down the hangar deck. That shuttle is not to be allowed to dock with the *Ares*. I want every Marine left on the ship to get their asses down there immediately."

"*Captain, that Alpha is beginning to stir,*" Celesta said. "*Are you telling me you're still on it?*"

"That is affirmative," Jackson said. "We'll activate our beacons and push off. Try to recover us, but your priority is that this Alpha *does not leave this system*. Am I clear, Lieutenant?"

"*Clear, sir.*"

"Now what, Captain?" Major Ortiz asked. He was privy to the command channel so he'd heard the entire exchange.

"Listen up, everyone," Jackson addressed the whole group. "I have no idea what's happening, but our immediate concern is clearing off this fucking alien ship before it takes off. I've ordered the *Icarus* to destroy it before it can get far and Captain Wright will do that whether we're still on it or not.

"The *Ares* is non-responsive and we have to assume she's been compromised. We'll use our maneuvering thrusters to get as far clear of this thing as possible and then wait for the *Icarus* to send someone to get us. Is everyone clear?"

"Clear, sir!" The chorus of affirmatives came from the usual source. Jackson had a strong affinity for the Marines that served aboard his ships. They didn't quibble about the details. Tell them it's time to go and they go. Give them an enemy, point them in the right direction and turn 'em loose. Fleet spacers, on the other hand, seemed to think most orders were open to debate if they didn't agree or understand them.

"Okay, there are eight of us, so we'll fire two suits at a time to conserve propellant and maximize our potential distance," Jackson said. "Everyone activate their emergency locators and then the major and I will fire first."

The leap-frog technique worked well and each blast from the compressed-gas thrusters added to their total velocity as they shot away from the Alpha. One thing about deep space, even just the gaps between the planets, is that there is far less light than people expect. It wasn't long before the Alpha was swallowed up by the blackness and even the faint flare of starship engines and winking navigation lights blended in with the countless stars. Jackson thought about ordering their suit lights on just for the psychological comfort it would provide to be able to see each other, but the battery power was better spent on keeping their locator beacons squawking.

He was debating on contacting the *Icarus* again for another status update when a light source from behind him illuminated Major Ortiz and one of his Marines. He turned his head but all he could see was a blinding point of light that seemed to be coming closer.

"*Stand by, Senior Captain,*" a voice came over the open channel. "*I have all of you on thermals. I'm going to slide up above your cluster and the rescue crew will begin to reel you in. We'll have you back aboard the Ares in time for dinner, sir.*"

The rescue operation was executed completely by the book, and by the time the shuttle crew was pulling the last spacer in and securing him to a jump seat barely fifteen minutes had elapsed. The crew chief closed and secured the aft hatch while the rescue team efficiently checked the health of their charges and made sure all of the EVA suits were still providing heat and atmosphere.

"Word just came in from the *Icarus!*" the call came over the shuttle's open channel. "Stand by for a nuclear detonation!" Protective covers slammed into place over all the portholes and all side chatter stopped, everyone holding their collective breath as they waited on additional information from the *Icarus.*

"Senior Captain Wolfe, Captain Wright has asked me to inform you that the target Alpha has been completely destroyed," the pilot said after another ten minutes. "We'll be taking you back to the *Ares* now."

"Thank you, Pilot," Jackson keyed his mic. "Let's not spare any fuel on the way back, shall we?"

"Of course not, sir," the pilot chuckled.

****

"We've made contact with the flight crew," Davis said as Jackson rushed onto the bridge like a madman, parts of his EVA suit still hanging off his thin frame. "They're alive in their own suits, but they can't reassert control over the shuttle."

"Where is it?" Jackson demanded.

"Stationary relative to our position, five hundred meters off the bow and ten degrees to starboard," Davis said. "The Vruahn cube is not answering any of our hails but it must be receiving. I threatened to open fire if it continued its approach and it stopped there."

"Coms! Patch me through."

"You're on a live channel, sir." Jackson noticed in passing that Lieutenant Keller was back at his station with a large bandage on the left side of his head.

"This is Captain Wolfe back aboard the *Ares*," he said, trying to reign in his rage. "You have ten seconds to convince me not to turn you to slag."

"Primary protocols dictated the protection of the communication node," the cube's voice came over the bridge speakers.

"At the cost of more lives?" Jackson seethed. "You'll have to do better. I am not allowing you back on this ship while you're operating under unknown protocols that are a clear danger to my ship and my crew."

"If you do not allow the cube back aboard your vessel, Captain, your mission will have been for nothing," the cube said. "Is that really what you want?"

"Ah… the handlers," Jackson recognized the shift in the cube's speech patterns. "Now we're getting somewhere. My ultimatum stands. Get someone on the channel that can offer assurances or I vaporize the cube with the node in it."

"Your officers are also inside the shuttle," the cube pointed out.

"You're wasting time," Jackson ignored the barb. The channel fell silent for a few minutes before he felt they needed another prod.

"Tactical, lock forward battery onto the shuttle," he said. "Maximum power."

"Aye, sir," Barrett said without hesitation. "Forward laser battery coming online. Targeting sweep initiated."

"Captain, there's a private com channel request coming in for you from the shuttle," Keller said. "The header tag says it's from a 'Setsi?' Am I saying that right?"

"Send it to my office, Mr. Keller," Jackson turned to walk off the bridge. "And it's good to see you back on duty."

"Yes, sir. Thank you, sir."

****

"Captain, I thought we were past all this needless posturing." Setsi's expressionless face appeared on Jackson's terminal screen.

"Your animated stasis pod just fucking killed another three of my crew!" Jackson raged, not caring that the hatch wasn't soundproof. "What kind of bullshit alliance is this? We are not expendable beasts of burden and I am not posturing. I *will* destroy that cube."

"That *cube* was designed, built, and delivered at your request." Setsi actually seemed exasperated. "Did you think that you would win your little war without any more bloodshed?"

"I did not," Jackson said. "But I also didn't expect said blood to be spilled because of Vruahn arrogance or incompetence… I haven't decided which."

"You dare to accuse *us* of such things?" Setsi's face morphed through a few unreadable expressions before settling back down again. "Captain… we have worked with humans for nearly two of your centuries and never had we come up against such inexplicable hostility or obtuseness."

"You've kept human pets that you've trained to be attack dogs," Jackson shot back. "Don't bullshit me, Setsi… you had no intention of helping us until your own little corner of the galaxy was threatened. There is so much about this that stinks to high heaven, but right now I only care about one thing: are you going to give me *all* of the information on this machine that's been carving a bloody swath through my crew? Or am I going to give the order to fire and end this ridiculous one-sided alliance?"

Setsi stared blankly at him through the monitor in what could have been interpreted as an attempt at intimidation, but Jackson knew to mean that whoever was controlling the avatar had stepped away for something.

"We will be sending the entire technical specifications for both the stasis pod and the proposed mission parameters as well as updating the primary protocols to make the machine more... forthcoming and flexible," Setsi said. "We regret the deaths of your crewmembers, Captain. We hope they will not have been in vain. Stand by for data transmission."

"I wasn't expecting that," Jackson said to a blank screen as the channel had been terminated remotely from the other side.

"Captain, we have an incoming channel request from the cube," Davis broke in over the intercom. *"Data only."*

"Let it through," Jackson said. "Tell Barrett to power down the forward batteries and then get me a channel to Captain Wright. I need to be briefed on the particulars of the Alpha."

"Aye, sir."

During Celesta's debrief about how she had made the call to fire two Shrikes into the hole they'd cut through the Alpha's hull, Jackson was preoccupied with the odd shift in their arrangement with the Vruahn. He wasn't sure if the sudden acquiescence made him feel any more secure about his allies or not.

"I ordered Jillian to have the *Ares* ready to move but to stand fast," Celesta was saying. "Your standing order to kill the Alpha had technically been to me, and I didn't want her taking any heat if somehow it had been the wrong move while you were out of contact."

"Hmm?" Jackson murmured. "Oh, yes. You did exactly as you should have, Captain. Thank you for confirming we were aboard the shuttle before firing.

Two months of radiation treatment isn't my idea of a good time."

"Of course, sir," Celesta said. "Will there be anything else?"

"No, Captain, this mission is concluded," Jackson sighed. "At great cost we managed to pull it off and now it's time to get back to New Sierra. I'll bet the political powers that be have shaken off their initial shock and are coming at the admiral in full force. Be ready to depart the system within the day. If the *Ares* isn't ready to make the transition then the stasis cube will be transferred to the *Icarus* and you will fly the flag back to Terran space."

"Yes, sir," Celesta nodded. "*Icarus* out."

Jackson stayed in his office a bit longer, not wanting to go out on the bridge just yet after the debacle that was the EVA mission. He swung his chair around, pulled his utility pant leg up, and detached his prosthetic to allow the skin around the socket a chance to breathe a bit while he read the latest report that had come in from the *Hyperion*.

From what Captain Walton was implying it was good that they arrived when they did. There was almost a full-blown mutiny ready to erupt on the *Atlas* when they made contact, two separate factions fighting over whether to abandon ship or not. Disaster was barely averted there, and the *Hyperion* was able to drag the powerless *Atlas* up to a higher orbit so that engineering teams could get the stricken ship's powerplant back up and running. As of the timestamp on the report they had fully charged the batteries and starter banks on the *Atlas* and were ready to begin priming Reactor One for a restart. The emergency backup fuel cells still would not engage, and they couldn't figure out why, so for the time being they were ignoring that problem.

With a grunt of pain Jackson reattached his leg with a snap, waiting as the nerve sensations evened out from the prosthetic, and then fixed his uniform. He desperately wanted to sit down and enjoy a hot meal and he would seriously consider doing great bodily harm to someone if it meant he could lie down and sleep uninterrupted for at least five hours, but that wasn't in the cards. The *Ares* was in a bad way and the crew had been beaten up plenty. He had to see to them and he wouldn't be able to rest until the shuttle was back aboard and he talked to the cube again to see just what changes had been made when the Vruahn shifted the protocols around.

****

"All of the hull breaches are repaired to the point that Commander Singh feels comfortable clearing the ship for warp transition," Hayashi was saying as the rest of first watch filtered onto the bridge, all of them holding some sort of liquid stimulant in their hands. "The cube has been secured and the shuttle crew has been cleared to return to duty."

"Good, good," Jackson said. "Any word on if they were able to locate the bodies that were missing from the EVA mission?"

"I'm sorry, sir, but no." Hayashi looked down at the floor. "There was simply too much debris from the destroyed Alpha and our own engine to pick out the small profiles of the EVA suits on radar."

"Very well," Jackson said. "Tell the crew that we will have a memorial service for our crewmembers directly preceding the planned service for the *Artemis*. Inform Engineering that I intend to begin accelerating for the jump point as soon as the *Atlas* and *Hyperion* join the formation; the other ships will follow two days later. Given that we'll be limping to transition on a single main we'll all arrive in the X-Ray system more or less together that way."

"Yes, sir." Hayashi bowed his head again. "I will prepare a brief and inform the crew." Jackson watched as he hustled away, and he made a mental note to make sure the young officer was taken care of if they survived the upcoming fight. He had no illusions about his own future; he had no chance of ever advancing past captaining a destroyer and he was just fine with that. He would retire with a collective sigh of relief from the Fleet brass, but he had a talented crop of junior officers that he wanted to see given every chance to go as far as they could. Barrett and Davis in particular had command written all over them, and Hayashi needed to be given experience past the OPS station. There were also some hard-charging enlisted spacers like Accari whom he would like to see given the option to attend the Academy's accelerated officer training program.

He shook his head to clear out all the fluff. What the hell? He had to be completely focused on the task at hand and put all the administrative crap on hold until they were in a position to worry about such things. The damnable, unfair misery of it was that the whole thing was just a form of mental masturbation meant to accomplish one thing: distract him from the fact that he was leading these men and women to almost certain death. It wasn't just the numerical superiority that had him concerned; he was still quite shaken at how the *Ares* had responded in her first real bare-knuckle fight with a Phage heavy. While the gravity bombs were a unique and unpredictable element to the fight, it hadn't taken much and she was now missing an engine and streaming atmosphere from a dozen temporary hull patches.

The *Blue Jacket* had taken harder hits on the chin during her engagement with a Phage Super Alpha and wouldn't lay down, kept coming back for one more round. The *Starwolf*-class was maybe too clever, too dependent on the exotic materials and cutting-edge structural engineering methodologies. There was something to be said for the old iron. His previous ship had a hull that was three meters thick of solid alloy in most places. But maybe the problem was him. He was given a new ship that was faster, nimbler, and loaded with tech that he hadn't even dreamed of years ago and he still tried to fight her like she was a drunken bar brawler instead of playing to her strengths.

"Are you okay, sir?" Davis asked.

"Yes, Lieutenant," Jackson smiled absently. "Just thinking."

"Yes, sir," Davis looked unconvinced. "We'll be ready to get underway shortly. Engineering is just making some final inspections of the drive."

"Very good," Jackson stood. "You have the ship, Lieutenant. Make sure everyone knows that it's dress blacks for the service unless they're working in an area that precludes it."

"Yes, sir," she said somberly.

Chapter 18

"Transition successful," Hayashi announced.

"Position verified, sir," Accari said. "We're right on target and in the X-Ray system."

"Tactical, full passive scans of the system," Jackson said. "This is still contested space. Use the cube's detection equipment if you need to. Helm, push us out of the jump point on thrusters, maintain our carried-over velocity from transition."

"Aye, sir," the helmsman said. "Pushing off to starboard."

"OPS, have Engineering perform a full set of checks on the warp drive and on Engine One before we fire it up," Jackson said. "Let's not take any unnecessary risks with our only MPD pod."

The *Ares* slid into the system with the momentum she carried from the warp transition, while Commander Singh's crews worked feverishly to make sure she was ready for the next short warp flight to the Xi'an System before the long burn all the way to New Sierra. Jackson spent his time reviewing the new technical data the Vruahn had transmitted over, specifically the rough mission parameters they'd set for the attack on the Phage core mind. The plan was pretty cut and dry, which was good in some ways. They were fielding the largest armada in the history of human spaceflight and there were a lot of moving parts. Command and control would be an issue no matter what, so Jackson did lean towards the elegance of a simple plan that everyone could understand.

The bad part was that the Vruahn weren't exactly tactical geniuses. A good strategy didn't have to be overly complex to be workable, but it also shouldn't be too obvious. The idea of using a Phage transponder to allow them a close approach was a good one, if it worked, but he had no illusions that they would be so easily fooled for long. A species that was able to communicate across such vast distances almost instantaneously would be aware when one of their big boys had dropped off the map without a trace. Having it just pop back up next to one of their most strategically important installations was sure to put them on the defensive almost immediately.

As he read the synopsis provided with the Vruahn battle plan he started to recognize certain themes. The Phage were vicious and instinctual, but they were not unthinking beasts. While they certainly reacted to stimuli in a way that gave the appearance that they were mostly animalistic in nature, Jackson had observed them employing increasingly complex tactics against Fleet forces based on their limited experience with humans, even to the point of dabbling in the nuances of psychological warfare, tiring the easily stressed humans to the point of rash action. The Vruahn seemed to think that the Phage were just advanced constructs that, in spite of the core mind's influence, were incapable of higher reasoning and that the simple, blunt methods they'd laid out would secure a victory.

Or... they knew that it wouldn't but the battle would effectively eliminate humanity's military strength while weakening the Phage to the point that they wouldn't threaten the Vruahn for many years to come. Could their new allies, a species of avowed pacifists, really be so coldly calculating with the fates of entire species? The answer he had for that question sent a cold chill up his spine.

"Captain, we have a standard Fleet hail coming in from the inner system," Keller said. "No registry or callsign attached."

"I see," Jackson rolled his eyes. "Please transmit our greeting to Agent Pike and ask him if we have clear skies back to Xi'an."

"Yes, sir."

While still going through the Vruahn data dump Jackson kept an eye on the mission clock above the main display that had started an elapsed time count the moment the ship had shuddered her way back into real space in the X-Ray System.

"Sir, a reply came back with a generic CIS transponder code requesting a private channel with you," Keller said eventually. Jackson looked at the clock again: thirty-three minutes. Pike must be on the near side of the system, likely watching the jump point and waiting for them to pop out.

"Send it to my office, Lieutenant." Jackson pushed himself up out of his seat with a certain amount of dread. If Pike was waiting for him to come back from the Zulu System it probably wasn't for a congratulatory cheer; the CIS agent was much too valuable to his superiors to waste time sitting in an empty star system waiting for a few ships to straggle through.

"How did you know it was me?" Pike grinned widely on the display.

"Who else skulks around in the dark, harassing me at every turn?" Jackson settled into his seat. "What brings you all the way out here, Pike?"

"I'm mildly insulted by that," Pike sniffed. "I see you're not bringing all your ship back with you."

"No, I'm not," Jackson said. "I'm also not bringing back all of my squadron."

"The *Icarus?*" Pike sat up quickly, causing Jackson to narrow his eyes suspiciously.

"No… the *Artemis* was lost with all hands in the opening shots of the battle," Jackson said slowly. "But we were successful in our mission. Thanks for asking."

"Yes, of course," Pike composed himself. "Well done, Captain, and the loss of the *Artemis* is a huge price to pay. So is the Alpha still in the Zulu System?"

"I'll fill you in later as well as send you a private copy of the report I'm filing with Admiral Marcum," Jackson said. "It's not so simple as bringing back a crippled Alpha, but to answer your question, we were successful and we didn't leave anything alive in the Zulu System. So, not to be rude… but what the hell are you doing out here?"

"The usual," Pike said. "Things have become a bit more complicated in the DeLonges System since you've left. The sky has been polluted with com drones as all the political wrangling has started up again. President McKellar has tried to reassert his authority from the Ark and, believe it or not, Earth has now entered the fray claiming that they are the de facto seat of power now that Haven is gone."

"Funny, since Earth has no military power with which to exert their political will," Jackson snorted. "I assume there's much more going on behind the scenes within the enclaves to cause them to make such an absurd statement."

"You betcha," Pike said. "Anyway… Marcum asked me to come out here and give you warning that your name has been tossed around quite a bit in all the posturing."

"He could have done that with a com drone," Jackson said.

"I was also supposed to look for your remains if you were gone for too long," Pike said.

"I'm flattered," Jackson deadpanned. "Are you going to escort us all the way back?"

"You should be able to beat me back," Pike reminded him.

"The whole squadron is pretty banged up," Jackson shook his head. "We won't be setting any records this flight. How about I forward you some files for the admiral and you get back to New Sierra and warn them that we'll need at least two full-service berths."

"Aye aye, Cap'n," Pike said with a crooked salute. "Anything else?"

"Just tell me we're clear all the way back to Terran space and that will be enough."

"Nothing simpler," Pike shrugged. "You'll have a nice boring flight all the way back. See you there." The channel closed abruptly and Jackson couldn't help the chuckle that escaped his lips. Under any normal circumstances a personality like Pike's would have grated on his nerves like a nuclear-powered belt sander, but after all their interactions he had to admit that he considered the quirky agent a friend.

The rest of the Ninth made it through the jump point and out to the Xi'an jump point in a sad, battered procession without incident. Jackson was just happy they were able to make it in a straight shot and the *Ares* was able to simply maintain velocity and not limp along ahead of the rest of the formation.

It was with a great sigh of relief from almost everyone aboard that they transitioned out of the Xi'an System and onto the last leg, albeit the longest one, before they would find safe harbor and be able to lick their wounds and properly mourn their comrades. Jackson stared at a live video feed of the stasis cube as the warp drive engaged, hoping the cost they had paid so far was worth the price of admission when the time came to use it.

****

"*Ares*, departing!"

Jackson walked down the gangway that had been attached to his ship after she'd been dragged into a fully enclosed maintenance dock by the harbor tugs. He felt much older than his forty-two years and a strong sense of dread as the reality of the coming campaign stretched out in front of him. The location of the core mind had been discovered, and it would take the Terran fleet nearly six months of hard flying to get there. It was so much further than their longest reaching exploration efforts had gone, and this wasn't some tireless automated probe. This would be an entire armada made up of dissimilar warships, supply vessels, and over a hundred thousand spacers that would be exhausted from the journey before the fight even started.

"Senior Captain," Admiral Marcum returned Jackson's salute and stuck out his hand. "Welcome back and well done."

"Thank you, Admiral," Jackson shook the proffered hand. "It's certainly good to be back. You got the data I sent ahead?"

"I did," Marcum nodded. "Along with your report. A terrible tragedy, losing the *Artemis* like that, but it wasn't your fault. The strategy was sound."

"Yes, sir."

"I'm serious, Wolfe," Marcum said as the pair turned to talk along the docking arm and out of earshot of the others filing off the destroyer. "Forrest knew the risks when she went along with the plan. I need you to move past this and be completely focused on what's ahead of us."

"I am, Admiral," Jackson said. "But I must admit to having some misgivings about this. The simple logistics of it are—" He trailed off, trying to couch it as least offensively as possible.

"Impossible?" Marcum provided. "Absurd? Suicidal? Trust me, Captain… I've been hearing it from my advisory staff since you came back from Vruahn space. However, time is not on our side with this one. Yes, we could simply amass our fleet facing the direction of the Phage core mind and deploy a detection grid along the Frontier.

"Then we could wait. And wait. And wait. Now how long do you think we'd be able to maintain wartime footing like that? A year? Ten? Twenty? What does time mean to a species like the Phage? They'll sit and watch, and wait, and when we let our guard down they'll hit us so hard there won't be any coming back from it. You know I'm right."

"I do," Jackson spit out. He wanted desperately to disagree with the admiral's assessment, but the proof was in orbit right over his head. Complacency had led to a human martial force that was a military in name only. Black Fleet was supposed to be exactly what Marcum was referring to, and in the span of two generations it had turned into a dumping ground for worn-out people and equipment.

"I'm onboard, sir. It's just been a long mission."

"Understood," Marcum nodded. "Let the crews here on facility get the *Ares* ready to fight again. I want your crew to take as much time off as they need."

"Thank you, Admiral," Jackson said. "I'll see that they're well-rested, but I also don't want them sitting around reflecting too much on what's happened. I need to keep them busy and focused."

"They're your people. Do what you need to do, but make sure you're all ready when the time comes. The Ninth will be the pointy end of the stick on this one... that means *you* will be the very tip of the spear. I need you at your best."

Jackson watched the admiral walk away and felt sick to his stomach all over again. That there wasn't anyone else far more qualified than he for the job in all of humanity scared the shit out of him. How many more times could he possibly get lucky and manage not to fail as completely as he knew he inevitably must? He felt that the admiral was rolling the dice one too many times by tossing him out in front and hoping that it would work out again.

****

The repairs to the *Ares* were accomplished at an astonishing speed. A lot of that had to do with Tsuyo having a large technical staff stationed permanently at the New Sierra Shipyards which included a group of engineers familiar with the particulars of the *Starwolf*-class ships. The main engines were actually fairly simple pieces of equipment, and a replacement had been manufactured and tested by the time the aft pylon had been repaired and the intricate, layered material of the hull had been fabricated to patch up the breaches caused by the original engine exploding.

What chewed up most of Jackson's days in the beginning of the process were the Tsuyo reps wanting to rehash every detail of the engine failure that caused all the hull breaches. This was the first engagement that had really tested the new ships and there were mountains of data to pore through. Jackson appreciated that they at least pretended to be as concerned as he that the ship seemed have a glass jaw. They explained to him, again, that the hull was built to be able to absorb and dissipate the incredible heat of a Phage plasma blast, not shrug off kinetic strikes like the old *Raptor*-class destroyers. Jackson told them, again, that he fully understood that but a warship had to be able to handle debris impacts as well. It was the same conversation he'd had with them when the *Starwolf*-class was first coming out of development and into production, and in the end he was given the same patronizing nods and empty promises that they'd "look into it."

"Fucking idiots," he mumbled as he walked out of the last meeting, not caring a bit if the Tsuyo and Fleet bureaucrats heard him.

After realizing that he was neither needed nor wanted in the area while the crews were fitting the new engine to the pylons and shipyard personnel crawled through every part of his ship with abandon, Jackson sequestered himself in the plush visiting dignitaries' quarters in the upper part of the orbital platform. There he called up a secure connection and began going through the entire list of ships in the formations flying past the small porthole in his room. He cataloged the class, type, and origin of each ship and went so far as to pull up the service records of their commanding officers. The results of his research were not encouraging.

For all their bluster it seemed First and Fourth Fleet had let their ships fall into the same state of disrepair that Black Fleet had, and their crews displayed the same lack of readiness. The ships that had filtered in from the Warsaw Alliance were an utter disaster, six of which Jackson seriously considered recommending for decommission, and the Asianic Union had a lot of ships, but none that packed much of a punch.

It was these particular ships that Jackson was most concerned about. They were small, lacked any serious armor, and had short legs so they would need replenishing from the supply convoys much more often. Their lack of any serious armament also made them more of a liability than a help. He knew Marcum was looking at the raw numbers, but he recognized these ships for what they were: cannon fodder. Without anything to offer other than the ability to fill out their ranks, Marcum would have little choice but to either order these ships to stay back out of the way or advance them into the line of fire and get thousands of brave AU spacers needlessly killed.

After he compared their raw numbers to what the Phage were just suspected to have in the system they had dubbed the "Hive" Jackson had to suppress the urge to vomit.

"There is no way we can win," he said to the empty room. "I'm going to get them all killed." He shut down his tile and tossed it on the table, leaning back to rub his temples. What was he missing?"

Chapter 19

"Come in!"

"Do you have a moment, Captain?"

"Colonel, come on in and grab a seat." Jackson waved Blake into the room. "I didn't know you were aboard."

"I just docked about twenty minutes ago," Blake said. "After convincing the Tsuyo techs that they would be killed if they attempted to force their way onto my ship I came looking for you."

"Something important?" Jackson frowned.

"Maybe." Blake was evasive. "Let's just call it a curiosity for now. I don't want to taint your interpretation of what I'm about to show you."

"Let's see it." Jackson slid his drink on the desk with a slightly embarrassed look on his face.

For the next five hours straight the two looked over the raw sensor feeds from Blake's ship, discussed it, argued over it, and tried to pick apart each other's analysis just as an intellectual exercise. Even after the marathon session, however, Jackson was more certain of what he was seeing than he had been about anything else in his life. The elegance of the solution made complete sense, and once the initial shock of it wore off he was convinced that this was the *only* answer that made sense.

"Grab your shit," Jackson stood up. "We need to see the admiral."

"It's 0330 ship's time," Blake pointed out.

"Then grab your shit. We're going to hit the mess deck for coffee and some decent food and then wake his ass up."

"Right behind you, sir," Blake said with enthusiasm.

****

"We have the wrong target," Jackson said without preamble when Marcum's bleary-eyed face appeared at the door.

"Wolfe," he growled. "Have you been fucking drinking?"

"A little, sir," Jackson admitted. "But that's not the point."

"I see you have the colonel with you." Marcum stepped aside and let them in. "Let's hope for your sake that this isn't a waste of my time. I'm trying to keep myself on *Amsterdam*'s time and I just got to sleep. Now what in the hell are you babbling about."

"Admiral," Blake stepped in smoothly, "I'd like to show you some sensor footage from my ship I recorded while we were searching for the core mind. At the time the significance of the anomaly I was seeing didn't quite sink in, but now, combined with the collated data from my ship, I believe we've stumbled upon the actual location of the target."

"Whoa, whoa, whoa!" Marcum waved his hands in front of his face as if waving off something rancid. "*Your* goddamn people gave us a target package that your Vruahn handlers have assured us is the core mind. They gave us a ninety-nine percent probability. What the hell could you have found that disputes that?"

"Let me show you." Blake spun a strange-looking device around to show the admiral. It looked like a tile display that had a mechanical keyboard attached to it by a hinge. The more Jackson saw the colonel using it the more he liked the idea.

"When I was sitting in this system there was nothing of note, but I kept receiving a blip on what we've identified as the carrier signal for the Phage networked consciousness."

"Go on." Marcum assumed a defensive posture while looking at the display.

"At first they didn't mean anything," Blake continued. "As I said: anomalies. But the longer I observed, the more of them were detected. I had the ship run a full spectrum passive scan, which is a massive amount of raw information, and then process it as resources became available. To get to the point, each time there were one of these blips, look at what showed up at the edge of the system." Blake hit the long, thin key at the bottom of his device and a grainy thermal image showed up that made Marcum suck in his breath.

"An Alpha," he said.

"A Super Alpha," Jackson corrected. "The Vruahn have the ability to differentiate between the two even on passives. The point is that the signal originated from somewhere in the system, and each time there was a Super Alpha lurking along the perimeter to receive it. On two occasions there were burst broadcasts from the Alpha back into the system."

"You're not exactly blowing my dress up, Wolfe," Marcum said.

"Think about it, sir," Blake stepped back in. "The core mind sits isolated in a system that holds zero strategic or logistic value. Why would anyone search there? It can sit silently and pass specific instructions out to the Alphas via these burst transmissions and allow them to propagate the orders out to the rest of the Phage."

"I still think this is a steaming load, Colonel." Marcum's jaw set. "Let's be objective about this, boys. You've captured something... interesting, yes. But you expect me to divert the entire fleet to this bit of nowhere on something so thin? Wolfe, I expected better of you."

"Not the whole fleet, sir," Jackson shook his head. "Just the *Ares* and—"

"Absolutely not!" Marcum said. "That destroyer will be leading the charge, along with the giblets you yanked out of that other Alpha, flying the flag for all the rest of the fleet to see. This attack falls apart without at least some measure of blind faith, Senior Captain, and that is you. For some reason God has decided that you need to survive every desperate situation you get into and I want my other COs thinking that some of that can rub off on them."

"Sir, if we could just—"

"We're done discussing this, gentlemen," Marcum said. "While I am dutifully impressed with your enthusiasm, I cannot ignore the mountain of evidence provided by Colonel Blake's people that the core mind is sitting behind an impenetrable wall of Phage ships. The attack goes on as planned, and if you try to pull any of your usual shit when you don't get your way, Wolfe, so help me God I will have you keelhauled. I'm not even sure how the hell that will work on a starship but I *will* find a way. Dismissed."

"Well that could have gone better," Blake said in the corridor after Marcum had slammed the door to his quarters.

"It actually went about as I expected," Jackson said. "The admiral has an obligation to pick the course that has the greatest chance of success, and all the information he has is pointing big flashing arrows at the system your wingman found. I can't say I'd have made a different call if I was in his position."

"Then why the hell did we bother coming down here?" Blake asked.

"Due diligence," Jackson said. "We had to at least give him the chance to make the call before we struck out on our own."

"You can't be serious," Blake whispered. "You heard him, didn't you?"

"Loud and clear," Jackson said confidently. "I also know how to read between the lines."

"Oh, shit."

****

"Have you ever had real Kentucky bourbon before, Specialist?" Jackson asked, pouring the amber liquid into a glass.

"N-n-no, sir," Accari said, his eyes as big as the glass bottom.

"You nervous?" Pike asked him. "You get used to it after the first sip."

"It's not that—"

"Just Pike."

"It's not that, Pike," Accari said. "I'm just wondering why I'm in the captain's office being offered a drink along with the XO and a CIS agent. Is this about—"

"No," Jackson held up his hand. "And I'm certain I don't want to know what you were about to confess to. Here's the thing, Specialist… I need your help with something. It's something big, something that could have vast implications for the war and whether we win or lose, but if I'm wrong it could cost you your career and probably your freedom. If you want to leave right now, I'll understand."

"I trust you, sir," Accari said after taking a deep breath and accepting the glass from Pike. "I'll at least stay and listen."

"Good man," Pike nodded.

Over the next ninety minutes Jackson made his case to the young enlisted spacer and explained to him how vital his role would be. Accari agreed almost immediately, despite the three officers warning him how much trouble he would be in if they were wrong, and possibly even if they were right. Jackson was more than a little disturbed by the shining hero worship evident in Accari's eyes, and he hated himself for using that to get what he needed, but he'd done far worse for much less.

After stressing to the young spacer the need for absolute and utter secrecy, Jackson and his cohorts got down to the business of working out the details of the rest of their plan and whom they would have to bring on board to make it happen.

"So what about that Phage swarm in the other system?" Davis asked as they were wrapping things up. "What is that for if not to protect the core mind?"

"My gut tells me it's being staged for something," Jackson said. "Maybe even one huge push into Terran space given the composition of the swarm. Either way, one destroyer won't make a difference one way or the other if we're wrong. But if I'm right—" He left it hanging as the other two shared a meaningful look.

"I better get back to my ship," Blake stood up. "I've got a lot to do."

"We all do," Jackson nodded. "Let's get to it."

****

"Thank you for indulging me, Captain," Jackson said. "I appreciated the tour."

"It was our honor to have you aboard the *Icarus*, Senior Captain," Celesta nodded, laying it on thick in front of her staff officers. "I wish you could stay for Captain's Mess."

"As do I," Jackson smiled. "But the *Ares* is still not quite one hundred percent and Admiral Marcum has been quite clear that the Ninth will be mobilizing with the rest of the fleet."

"I understand, sir," Celesta said. "I trust you can find your way back to your shuttle?"

"I can," Jackson shook her hand. "Thanks again."

Jackson turned and walked quickly back down the corridor, his prosthetic starting that annoying squeak again that Daya swore he'd taken care of. He wanted to make sure he was back aboard the *Ares* and ready for power testing on the main engines now that she was out of the dock and being prepped for powered flight. There was also the fact that he'd like to get the overly large cargo shuttle back aboard his own ship before the *Amsterdam* came back around the planet and uncomfortable questions were raised about why he hadn't just taken a tender out on his unannounced inspection of the *Icarus*.

****

"Engineering reports that the primary flight systems have passed all tests with flying colors, Captain," Hayashi read off his terminal. "Commander Singh says he is clearing the *Ares* for full duty."

"Give Engineering my compliments, Lieutenant," Jackson stood. "And then inform the rest of the crew that we are now at full operational status and normal watches are to resume immediately."

"Aye, sir."

"XO, prepare the *Ares* for departure," Jackson ordered. "We will be moving into the lead of the formation ahead of the *Icarus*."

"Aye, sir," Davis said.

"Let's look alive everyone!" Jackson said as he walked off the bridge. "Admiral Marcum wants to depart the DeLonges System in fifteen hours and there will be no excuses accepted for being late for the battle."

He worried that maybe he and Davis were laying it on a little thick, but he couldn't help it. For some reason there was a bubbling exuberance in him that he could not explain nor contain. Maybe it was because, for the first time since the war had been brought to them, they were getting ready to take the offensive and punch back. It could be that the thing he thought he would never see, the end of the war in his lifetime, was now just on the horizon. Or maybe it was just true what most of his superiors said about him: he was at his happiest when he was bucking the chain of command regardless of justification. Either way, they were now committed and by the end of the voyage they would either be victors, criminals, or both.

Despite Singh clearing the *Ares* for duty there was still a ton of work to do before she transitioned out of the system with the rest of the fleet. The work crews from New Sierra, most of whom were civilian contractors, had left the ship an utter wreck by Fleet standards. Trash littered the corridors, greasy handprints adorned polished surfaces, and a fine sheen of grime coated most of the decks that had seen heavy repairs.

There was one person who was ecstatic about this: Master Chief Green. He walked through the filthy corridors with a childlike glee as he shouted strings of obscenities about civilians, to and about the spacers trying to clean it up, and to the universe itself. He declared in booming tones that the "party was fucking over" and that "you lazy shitbirds have had it too easy with a brand new ship." Jackson tried not to crack a smile as miserable faces turned up to him in mute appeal as he walked down the corridors, checking on the rest of his own little side projects.

When all was made as ready as it could be, and he was able to convince Chief Green that the rest of the field day could wait until they were in warp, Jackson went back up to the bridge to wait pensively as Admiral Marcum deployed the rest of the fleet out in the order they would leave the DeLonges System. Soon on the tactical display it looked as if an enormous, pointed comet was streaking through the system as over two thousand Terran starships formed up with the *Ares* at the lead. It was an awesome sight and, for just a second, Jackson had a twinge of doubt about what he was about to do.

"We just received word from the *Amsterdam*," Keller said. "We're clear to begin accelerating to transition velocity and come on course for the Salamis jump point."

"Nav! Enter the new course, if you will." Jackson fidgeted in his seat. "Helm, you're clear to engage when you have it. Ahead full all the way to our transition velocity."

"New course received," the helmsman said. "All engines ahead full, aye."

"The rest of the squadron is moving into transition formation behind us," Hayashi said. "Engineering reports the warp drive is ready."

"Excellent," Jackson said. "Continue monitoring the rest of the squadron and make certain everyone maintains their intervals. Let's try to set a high bar for the rest of the fleet. XO, the ship is yours… go ahead and take her out of the system."

"Aye aye, sir," Davis stood up. "I have the ship."

Jackson sat back and watched as Davis went about the rather mundane routine of prepping the destroyer for faster than light flight mode. Everything had been worked out to the best of their ability, and he was about to take one of the biggest gambles of his life, but it wasn't just his life he was worried about. He was also taking the crew of the *Ares* with him, and a large part of him wondered what right he had to take advantage of their loyalty and order them on what could end up being a suicide run.

On the other hand... damn near every mission they'd had for the last five years could be considered a suicide run.

Chapter 20

"Incoming transmission for you, Admiral. Text only, it's marked as originating from the *Ares*."

"Send it to my comlink," Marcum said as he paced the bridge of the *Amsterdam*.

"Yes, Admiral."

Icarus failed to make the rendezvous. Com drone arrived stating they had powerplant problems and were returning to New Sierra. - Senior Captain Wolfe

Marcum read the short message a few times before walking over to a terminal and brining up a command-level interface to check on something. To his mild surprise the message seemed to be legit. The *Ares'* transponder was squawking at the lead of the now three-ship formation of the Ninth, and the *Icarus* wasn't showing up on the display anywhere. He also back-tracked the message and saw that it had originated from Wolfe's command codes and had been sent from his terminal on the bridge.

Satisfied that Wolfe was still playing it straight, he punched in a quick response and walked back over to the middle of the two-tiered bridge of the *Amsterdam*, a chaotic hub of activity where Fleet spacers were managing both the operations aboard the mighty battleship as well as tracking all other ships in the armada as they filtered into the first rendezvous point. There were twenty-nine more of them to go on this mission and he had no doubt that the *Icarus* wouldn't be the first ship to not make it to the final staging point. He cursed the bad luck of one of his fastest ships and best captains falling out so early. But Celesta Wright was a resourceful young commander. She might yet find a way to get there in time.

****

Understood. Press on for now with your remaining ships. Send a com drone back for the Icarus and have Wright try to catch up if they can get their power issues sorted in time. - Admiral Marcum

Celesta closed the message on her comlink, her stomach tied in knots. She was now fully committed to the plan that Jackson Wolfe had set into motion earlier in the DeLonges System. Her faith in the senior captain, a man she considered a mentor, was unshakable, but that still didn't prevent her from getting a case of the nerves from lying to a flag officer, falsifying official records, flying under a false registration, knowingly assisting in the stealing of a Fleet vessel... the list of transgressions at her court martial would be as long as it was impressive. Yet below that roiling layer of semi-panic was a calm, resolute feeling that things would work out exactly as they were supposed to, and she knew that her faith would not be misplaced.

Wolfe would not fail. The man had the uncanny ability to see through the fog and quickly latch onto a decisive, sometimes shocking course of action that was eventually proven to be right even when at the time most people were screaming that he was a madman and needed to be removed from command. Her first watch bridge crew and her Marine detachment commander were all aware of what she was attempting and had agreed to humor her, for now. But the understanding was that if shit went sideways and Marcum discovered what was going on she would be the one to take the full brunt when he dropped the hammer.

"Nav, set course for our next jump point and stand by for word from the *Amsterdam* that we're departing the system." She sat down in her seat and shook her head at the proffered mug of tea from her OPS officer. Celesta couldn't seem to get it through the young ensign's head that she didn't actually care much for tea, at least not the variety stocked in the galley, despite her Britannic accent.

"Course set, ma'am," the chief at Nav reported. "Helm standing by when we get word."

"Now the waiting game," Celesta mumbled to herself.

****

"Position confirmed," Accari said. "We're just outside the DeLonges-Xi'an warp lane."

"Contact off the port bow, range ninety thousand kilometers," Barrett said. "Confirmed identity on one Vruahn warship."

"That would be Colonel Blake," Jackson said. "Now we're just waiting for a CIS *Broadhead* to make an appearance."

It was another four hours before the transition flash lit up their optical sensors and the stealthy black ship glided into formation just behind and below the *Ares*. Jackson took a deep breath and looked around the bridge at all the expectant faces.

"This is it, everyone. Last chance for anyone who wants to back out," he said. "Past this point we are all committed and will be forced to accept the responsibility and the blame equally in order to protect those below decks that still think we're heading to meet up with the rest of the fleet. Is anyone having second thoughts to the point that they'd like to be relieved of duty?" Nobody raised their hands, coughed, or even shifted in their seats. They all looked tense, but determined and confident as well.

"Very well," Jackson nodded. "Let's get to work then. Coms, get me a networked connection with the other two ships and have the bridge staff meet in the command deck conference room."

"Aye, sir."

****

"So this could be the last ride," Pike said, leaning back in his seat on the bridge of his ship, feet propped up on the console. "I'd say that either way we won't survive, but the mission could mean complete victory over the Phage or a retaliatory strike that takes out all of humanity."

"Thank you for that cheery assessment," Jackson rolled his eyes. "At least you seem to think that we're on the right track in the first place."

"I've seen the data," Pike shrugged. "I have no doubt that you and Blake are on the right track. But there's a lot that we don't know. I can't imagine that the big brain is just sitting there on an asteroid completely unprotected."

"We also don't know what sort of capabilities this entity might have," Blake added as his video feed stabilized. "I do know that the Vruahn were afraid of it. They were perfectly content to keep as much distance between it and them as possible, so it may be more than just a processing center."

"Great news," Pike snorted. "So did you manage everything on your end, Colonel?"

"I did," Blake nodded. "The rest of my strike force is ranging ahead of the Terran fleet as agreed to with Admiral Marcum. They will sniff out any danger and understand their secondary duties to try and keep the fleet safe for as long as possible. I was also able to safely pick up our guests, thanks to you."

"My pleasure," Pike smiled. "Are they settling in?"

"Let's try to move this along," Jackson said sternly. "Are the Vruahn onboard with you helping us with this? I don't want to get halfway there and have them shut down power to your ship."

"It took some fast talking, but I was able to convince them that it was a small gamble that could lead to a huge payoff," Blake said. "They're still shaken up by the Phage directly attacking them and hitting their power generation facilities. I won't swear to it, but I'm getting the hint that the Vruahn may have some sort of agreement with the Phage that keeps them from directly confronting each other."

"That is truly fascinating… and frightening," Jackson said. "But ultimately *way* outside of our sphere of responsibility. I've had my navigation specialists looking over the proposed course and it looks like we'll get to the target at least a full month before the combined fleet begins trickling into their last staging point. This will be cutting things tight. Ideally I'd like to eliminate the target and have Colonel Blake's strike force intercept Marcum and turn him back before they engage that Phage swarm."

"I'd say we'd better get moving then," Blake said. "Do you want to transfer the NOVA team over to your ship before we get underway, Captain?"

"I think it'd be best to leave them over on your ship for now," Jackson shook his head. "You've got more room and it'll cut down on any friction between them and my Marines."

"Some things never change, I see," Blake smiled. "I'll be departing immediately then. I'll be making short hops along the course you'll be taking to ensure there are no hazards along the way."

"Alright then," Jackson stood slowly. "Let's get to it. Good luck, gentlemen." He terminated the link between the other two ships and made his way back to the bridge. There was an anxious energy coursing through him to get started so he could be finished with the task ahead, and he had to temper that with a reminder that they were still several months of hard flying away from even getting started. They weren't going as far as Marcum's combined fleet, but they also had no supply chain or support ships going with them. Anything that happened that couldn't be handled by a field repair meant that it was a one-way trip for them.

"Captain," Davis nodded and vacated his seat. "How did it go?"

"We're all set," Jackson said. "Everyone managed to pull off their part without raising any obvious suspicions. As long as Captain Wright has managed to fool Marcum into believing the *Icarus* is the ship that dropped out and not the *Ares* then we'll be in good shape, at least for this phase of the operation."

"Shall I go ahead and alert the crew?" she asked.

"Proceed," Jackson said. "Inform Major Ortiz that you're broadcasting and have his men on alert."

"Yes, sir." She walked over the OPS station and began instructing Ensign Hayashi on what to do.

Within the next five minutes a speech that he'd prerecorded in his office began playing all through the ship. He ignored his own likeness on the main display and scrolled through the internal security feeds, trying to gauge the reaction of his crew as they listened to him lay out the case for once again giving CENTCOM the middle finger and flying out on his own, taking them along for the ride whether they wanted to go or not.

This time he spared no detail. He laid out the specifics of his case and why he needed them to follow him just one more time. Inspirational speeches were not his strong suit, nor were they something he particularly enjoyed. It felt too much like a performance piece in which he leveraged the loyalty and patriotism of his people in an effort to get them to act in a manner that was against their own best interests. Despite always feeling grubby afterwards, he also knew it was one of his most effective tools to keep his crew motivated and running towards the same goal. Since he couldn't operate the ship without them, he would once again swallow his distaste and do what he needed to do for the greater good.

One big difference this time around was that he kept his Marine detachment commander firmly in the loop, a lesson he'd learned the hard way during an attempted mutiny on his previous ship. Now Major Jeza Ortiz was a trusted confidant that was part of his inner circle. The major, full of shame and embarrassment that some of his men had participated in the incident aboard the *Blue Jacket*, now kept a watchful eye on his charges and made certain he knew where their loyalty lay.

"Reports are coming in, Captain," Davis said after the video had concluded and section chiefs and department heads were asked to report in. As he usually did, Jackson offered anybody not comfortable with his decision to relieve themselves of duty and they'd be confined to berthing with no consequences. There were always a few that simply were not comfortable with a CO that admitted he was disobeying orders and violating the chain of command.

"What's the damage?" he asked, hoping he didn't lose too many people from key departments.

"Zero objectors, sir," she said with obvious pride in her voice. "All departments report that they have one hundred percent willing participation."

"That's somewhat surprising." Jackson wasn't sure what else to say. The complete and unequivocal support of his crew meant a lot and it turned his resolve to steel. The *Ares* was no longer a starship with a rogue captain, she was now a rogue warship with a crew that would fight together to the end.

"Coms! Report to the *Broadhead* that we will be departing the area immediately. Nav, send the second waypoint to the helm and let's get the hell out of here."

"Aye, sir," Accari said. "Course sent."

"Helm! Come onto new course and accelerate to transition velocity, all engines ahead full!" Davis called out as Jackson sat back in his seat.

"Aye aye, ma'am," the helmsman said. "All ahead full!"

In an unknown and unimportant region of inter-stellar space the Terran destroyer surged forward, winking out of existence in a burst of visible light released by the formation of the warp distortion fields.

****

"Ensign! I want a focused visual scan of the Ninth Squadron." Admiral Marcum stormed onto the bridge of the *Amsterdam*. The fleet had just made its third scheduled stop to regroup and resupply, the three weeks of travel so far having been much more difficult on the older ships in the fleet than had been anticipated.

"The Ninth is currently not within line of—"

"I realize that, Ensign," Marcum ground out. "Send a request through the Link to one of the forward ships."

"Aye, sir."

The *Dreadnought*-class battleships were sitting back in the middle of the long, spread-out formation so Admiral Marcum could minimize the com lags to and from the edges of the fleet. They'd added stops early on so that they could reevaluate how they were deployed and make adjustments with the goal of making longer and longer warp flights without losing too many of the stragglers. Marcum had, naturally, reached out to one of his most experienced deep space captains to solicit his advice, but so far all he'd received were some strangely out-of-context video messages, a few vague text replies, and a slew of excuses from his staff that he was unavailable.

Marcum had first suspected that Jackson had simply not come along on the trip and had turned the ship over to Jillian Davis, a decently talented young officer but certainly not someone he wanted in command of one of his most capable ships in a pitched battle. But then he'd remembered that the *Icarus*, captained by Wolfe acolyte Celesta Wright, had turned back with mechanical trouble and his blood ran cold. Could the man really be so brazen?

"Scans coming in, Admiral," the ensign at one of the support stations said.

"Send it over there," Marcum pointed to one of the generic, configurable stations that dotted the *Amsterdam*'s expansive bridge. He rushed over and allowed the biometric scanner to validate his credentials and log him in just in time for the only slightly blurry images of the Ninth to come scrolling across. As expected there were three ships, all gleaming white and flying in a trailing column towards their next jump point. The images were far too grainy due to the distance and quality of the imager used for him to actually make out the names of the ships painted in two-meter-tall letters along both sides of their prows, but after a few more minutes one detail did stand out and hit him like a punch to the gut.

"Fucking Wolfe!" he roared, slamming his fist down onto the console.

"Admiral?" the concerned officer of the watch hustled over to where Marcum still sat.

"Commander, what do you see in this image?" Marcum stood up.

"Three ships," the commander squinted at the monitor. "*Starwolf*-class… is this the Ninth?"

"It is," Marcum nodded. "Notice how pristine the lead ship is?"

"I do, Admiral," the commander frowned. "The *Ares*, I would assume. I'm afraid I still don't see the problem. There doesn't appear to even be a scratch on the hull finish."

"Very good, Commander," Marcum said. "Except that the *Ares* has had one of her main engines replaced and never went back into dock to have it, or the pylons, coated before we departed. That ship should have at least one bare main engine."

"I don't—"

"That ship isn't the *Ares*. You're looking at the *Icarus* flying the transponder codes from the other ship," Marcum sighed. "Call up Captain Epson and have him find me. Also, send a message to the '*Ares*' and tell Captain Wright she is to fall out of formation and rendezvous with the *Amsterdam* immediately."

"Aye aye, Admiral." The commander retreated, appearing more than happy to escape to a safe distance when Marcum was in a barely contained rage.

****

"I expect this sort of idiotic bullshit from him! But what the fuck is your excuse, *Captain?*" Marcum was barely in control of himself as he gripped the table. Spittle flew from his mouth as he screamed and raved while Celesta, restrained and anchored to the chair across from him in the *Amsterdam*'s brig, sat impassively, almost serene, which only served to piss off Marcum all the more.

"I offer no excuse, Admiral," Celesta said.

"Captain, you are in serious trouble here." Marcum forced himself to calm down. "I'm not sure you appreciate just what you could be facing depending on how I feel this initial questioning goes."

"I actually do, Admiral," Celesta said. "I'm doing what I feel I must. I think we're on the wrong course and that we're about to throw away a lot of lives needlessly. Captain Wolfe and Colonel Blake put together a compelling case and the absence of their ships will not turn the tide of battle one way or another."

"You can't possibly know that!" Marcum slapped the table. "The Battle of Nuovo Patria—"

"Admiral! I am not some wide-eyed Academy cadet that you're giving a pep talk to," Celesta fired back. "Do not treat me like a fool. The Battle of Nuovo Patria was a fluke and you know it. That Phage swarm could have taken out every Terran ship at any time, but that wasn't their goal. They were running a diversionary operation while they destroyed our capital along with some sort of game they were playing with Captain Wolfe. Even then it would have been a resounding defeat had Colonel Blake not shown up when he did."

"So we should just give up?" Marcum spat at her, frustrated because she was right.

"Absolutely not," Celesta said firmly. "I agree with you that we need an offensive response. But I also see the logic in allowing a small expeditionary force to verify the other target just in case."

"Just in case?" Marcum frowned. "Captain... Celesta, level with me here. What exactly are you doing out here? If you truly believed that this was a no-win waste of ships and people, why not just take the entire Ninth off the table and at least have those ships available in case we do fail?"

Celesta looked conflicted, looking at the admiral long and hard before continuing.

"I had my own mission," she said finally. "I was going to take out as much of the swarm as I could before the main fleet arrived."

"With one ship—"

"I have the communication node from the Super Alpha aboard the *Icarus*," she explained. "I also have half of the remaining gravity bombs that the Vruahn gave to Captain Wolfe. My intention was to skip the last staging stop, sneak into the system with the piece of the Phage we killed in the Zulu System, and deploy all of those charges as far down into the system as I could, ideally taking out as many of their heavy units as possible."

Marcum was speechless as she explained her plan to him. He could only gape at her in open-mouthed horror once she'd finished.

"The odds of coming away from that mission alive are quite long," he finally said quietly.

"I have faith that Captain Wolfe is not only correct, but that he will succeed," she said. "My only hope was to save as many ships and lives as possible in the coming battle. We have no idea what will happen when the core mind is destroyed, so it's entirely possible that a battle with this swarm is inevitable. If so, the *Icarus* wasn't going to survive anyway; the numbers just aren't on our side even if every missile, every shot took out a Phage ship."

"At least Wolfe was smart enough to pass on the Alpha fragment and the Vruahn munitions before bolting," Marcum said to the ceiling, rubbing at his temples with the palms of both hands. "So... who else is going along with him? The *Ares* can't make the trip alone."

"Colonel Blake's ship and a CIS *Broadhead* are flying escort," she said after another moment's hesitation.

"That fucking Pike," Marcum almost snarled. "I'd have his ass tossed into the darkest hole I could find if I thought he wouldn't just escape."

A slight smile flashed across Celesta's face as she continued to sit calmly, allowing the admiral to come to the obvious conclusion on his own.

"I can't let this go unpunished, Captain Wright," he said with a sigh. "Wolfe has a long history of insubordinate behavior and now it seems he's passing that legacy on. It has to stop. Now. Rogue captains disappearing with starships over gut feelings and others deciding a Kamikaze-style mission is better than following orders is not good for Starfleet."

"I understand, sir," she said. "I also agree with you."

"Don't patronize me," Marcum sneered. "You know as well as I do that I can't afford to have the *Icarus* out of commission and there isn't anyone else qualified to take your place right now. My hands are tied… you'll be going back to your ship along with an observer, but I think we both know that should we make it out of this alive your days in Starfleet are over."

"A sacrifice I'm ready to make, Admiral," Celesta nodded, her voice catching. "I want you to know that this isn't a reflection on you, sir. I have the utmost respect for you and wish that things had worked out differently."

"But your first loyalty is to Wolfe," Marcum nodded.

"No, sir," she shook her head. "Had he not convinced me with the evidence he had I would have come straight to you. Blindly following orders will never be something I'm able to do, and I will accept the consequences of my actions regardless of outcome. I know that you'll have no choice but to replace me if we ever return to Terran space."

"I wish I had ten more like you, Captain," Marcum sighed before banging on the hatch behind him. "Marine! Release the prisoner from her restraints and escort her back to her shuttle."

Chapter 21

"We're going through expendables at a lot lower rate than I'd anticipated," Singh said as he and Jackson walked through the cargo hold. Once they'd hatched their plan to more or less steal the destroyer they'd loaded her up with as much extra equipment and expendables as they could, even some items to make sure the *Broadhead* would be able to make the extended journey.

"I hadn't realized that Colonel Blake would be able to replenish the *Ares* from his ship when we originally drew up the manifest," Jackson said. "He's pumped over water and air at every stop so far so we've not had to dip into the reserves."

"At this rate we'll have enough to get there, operate for a few weeks, and even make the flight back home," Singh said as he worked the numbers on his tile. Jackson gave him an odd look but said nothing. "I do wish that you'd not given so many of the advanced Vruahn munitions to Celesta before we left."

"We still have fifteen charges," Jackson said. "If we need more than that we're already screwed. She's in a position to use them in a more meaningful way… assuming she isn't discovered before they actually get there."

"I cannot even fathom how Admiral Marcum will react when he finds out," Singh said. "That transponder trick won't fool him long."

"I know," Jackson sighed.

"Regrets, Captain?"

"I do wish we were flying this mission with his blessing," Jackson said. "I don't like having to do it this way."

"But you know that you're right and he's wrong." Singh's voice didn't hold any sarcasm, so Jackson decided to not take the comment as a cheap shot.

"It's not about egos and being right or wrong," Jackson said. "It's about taking every precaution possible in the face of an enemy that could wipe us out within a generation if it had a mind to."

"You don't have to sell me," Singh said. "I'll follow you to the end, Jack… you know that."

"I do."

The three ships of the small strike group were drifting in close formation deep in interstellar space. It was a planned stop just before they would make the last, short flight to just outside the suspected target system. So far the two Terran ships had performed admirably, with only the *Broadhead* giving them a little bit of trouble as the minor support systems were taxed on the long flight.

The *Ares* hummed along like she was built for extended voyages, so much so that Commander Singh began griping that he could have stayed back on New Sierra and saved himself the court martial since the ship apparently didn't need him. Colonel Blake's Vruahn warship, as expected, performed flawlessly and Lieutenant Commander Amiri Essa's NOVA team was living in comparable luxury aboard the advanced vessel. Jackson had no idea what to expect when they arrived, so he had contacted the NOVA team commander right after Blake had come to him with his theory of the core mind's actual location.

Essa and Jackson had developed a cordial relationship during a previous operation on the New Sierra Shipyards and had kept in touch in the years after. When Jackson had discovered the team was actually stationed on the facility during the buildup for Marcum's campaign, he had approached the spec ops officer about taking a chance on an unauthorized mission into unknown space. Surprisingly, Essa had agreed almost immediately and went about sneaking his men, one at a time, into tenders and maintenance shuttles and ferried them over to Pike's *Broadhead* to be transferred to Blake's ship.

There were so many moving parts to the plan, any one of which could have easily broken down and landed them all in a Fleet brig, that Jackson could hardly believe that they were only one more warp flight from beginning the actual mission. Just positioning the force had been no mean feat, as it required the two

Terran ships to fly at maximum warp velocity for weeks on end, stopping only long enough to replenish and do minor maintenance before transitioning out again, chasing Blake's ship to the objective.

Jackson left Singh in Engineering and walked along back up the starboard access tube. He was alone, having shot down Major Ortiz's request to assign a full-time guard to him, the mutiny attempt on the *Blue Jacket* still gnawing at the Marine officer. By the time he got back to the bridge second watch was coming on duty and would continue all the loose tasks left over from first watch that needed to be accomplished before the ship departed the area. Jackson milled around long enough to make sure all his bridge officers were actually going off duty. He resisted the urge to tell them to get themselves fed and into their racks; they didn't need him to be their mother, and once Barrett walked off the bridge towards the lifts Jackson made his own way back to his quarters to try and at least get a few hours of rack time before the *Ares* made her final warp flight before potential enemy contact.

****

"Position confirmed, sir," Specialist Accari said after the *Ares* shuddered back into real space. Like everyone else on the bridge, Accari was speaking at just over a whisper. Jackson would have laughed if he hadn't caught himself doing the exact same thing, their hard-wired instincts causing them to react oddly so close to potential danger despite the illogical fear that they might somehow be overheard.

"Let's just become a hole in space," Jackson said. "Colonel Blake will find us and then we'll wait for the *Broadhead* to make an appearance."

"Pulsed LF-band transmission received," Ensign Hayashi said a mere twenty minutes later. "Coms?"

"Stand by," Keller held up a finger. "Encryption verified. Colonel Blake is sitting eight thousand kilometers dead ahead."

"Send no response," Jackson said unnecessarily. "Let's just wait for Agent Pike and try to not even disturb the interstellar particles around us."

They had to wait another three hours before the flash of a warp transition was picked up forty thousand kilometers off their starboard bow. The *Ares* may have been the faster of the two, but Jackson was stunned at how accurately the *Broadhead* had been able to navigate the uncharted space on their way to the system that was now just ahead of them. Even the warp flash from the *Broadhead*'s drive was muted, a testament to her engineering since the ship was over twenty years old.

"Colonel Blake has verified the *Broadhead* via passive sensors," Keller said. "He's asking for the go-ahead to begin the operation."

"Send it," Jackson leaned forward. "OPS, start the clock as soon as the pulse fires." According to the Vruahn, the Phage didn't closely monitor wavelengths over one thousand meters, a frequency the *Ares*'s com suite was able to produce with an extendable antenna. It was such a low cycle signal that it wasn't suitable for large amounts of data, but for extremely low-power simple communications it was perfect. Colonel Blake had argued for the more traditional com laser, which was an ultraviolet device, but Jackson was worried that there might be an extensive passive detection grid across the entire system.

"Clock started," Hayashi said.

"Passive sensors have lost Colonel Blake's ship," Barrett said. "She's running silent, almost zero emissions."

"Nothing on the accelerometers?" Jackson was surprised. The Vruahn ships utilized a reactionless drive that was similar to what the Phage used in that it distorted local space in order to propel the ship. Even though there weren't byproducts of heat and light like the Terran ships produced, their gravity distortion was usually detectable by their passive sensors.

"Nothing for certain," Barrett said. "He must be running at extremely low power."

"As long as he gets where he needs to be by the correct time I guess the quieter the better," Jackson said. "OPS, notify Engineering that we will be getting underway ourselves soon. Configure main engines to low-observability mode... that goes for attitude jets as well."

"Aye, sir." Hayashi slipped on his headset.

"Nav, let's set our first waypoint," Jackson said. "You know the drill, Specialist. Keep us hidden as much as possible. I want to stick to the big, open patches of sky so don't worry about any gravity assists as we get going downhill."

"Aye aye, sir," Accari said, pulling up one of the plots he'd already been working on and tweaking it to match Jackson's requests.

The moment the mission clock displayed 03:17:11.5 the main engines throttled up, the magnetic constrictors limiting the escaping plasma from the aft nozzles to a trickle. The destroyer slid ahead silently at a steady twelve G's, a paltry acceleration compared to the massive bursts she was capable of at full power. But this steady acceleration down into the system would quickly build velocity, and by the time they passed into the inner system she would be carrying enough speed that Jackson felt comfortable he could maneuver her in combat should the system not be as deserted as it appeared.

The plan had been hammered out in broad strokes and, despite complaints from most of the other officers, he had kept it vague intentionally. They were going to be out of contact for most of the mission and he wanted Pike and Blake comfortable with making decisions as information became available instead of feeling the need to rigidly adhere to a plan that may no longer be valid. In a nutshell, Blake was to use his stealth and speed advantage to fly deeper into the system and scout out the area he felt the core mind was likely located. Pike would come down into the system and use his ship's towed passive array to map out any anomalies along specific parts of the spectrum as he spiraled in, and the *Ares*, the toughest ship to hide, would glide in under minimal power.

The destroyer was the only ship that would be at specific waypoints at specific times as a sort of anchor for the other two smaller ships that were ranging out. The *Broadhead* was so small and had such a minimal energy signature Jackson hadn't been overly worried about Pike being detected and the Vruahn warship's unique powerplant meant that under low power modes she was virtually undetectable. The *Ares*, yet again, was the big question mark as Jackson had to decide if it was worth it to shut down one of his reactors in an attempt to mask his power signature.

In the end he decided to keep them both running. Bringing up even the newer generation fusion reactors from a cold start wasn't something that was done quickly under the best of conditions, much less when under fire and sitting defenseless. The *Starwolf*-class designers at least addressed the exhaust of byproducts from the reactors by routing them through the main engines so that whenever a purge was required under normal conditions it would exit through the plasma nozzles and not as a bright thermal plume from a hull vent.

"Now… where are you hiding, you sneaky, evil bastard," Jackson muttered under his breath as the *Ares* crawled into the suspect star system. Every hair was standing at attention on the back of his neck. He had already been convinced that Blake was onto something with the evidence he'd presented, but the feeling he was getting sitting right inside the heliopause… he felt, *knew* this was the right system.

****

"Helm! All ahead flank! Everything she's got!"

"All engines at maximum output, aye!"

The *Icarus* thundered downhill towards the largest cluster of Phage ships, her active sensors singing and the stasis cube in the cargo hold providing telemetry to Celesta's tactical officer. The Phage communications node had worked perfectly so far and she couldn't help but feel her luck had to run out sometime.

They'd transitioned into the system and saw that it was still clogged with Phage ships, most unidentifiable. Coming in alone, they had flown a normal course all the way down through the outer system without so much as a second glance, metaphorically speaking, from any of the passing Phage. In fact, many of the lesser units had scrambled in an apparent panic to clear the way for what they must have believed to be a Super Alpha.

Celesta had come all the way to just inside the orbit of the fifth planet, and clear of most of the debris that made up the sparse asteroid belt, before she slipped her mask off. She'd ordered the full active sensor suite brought up right outside a large cluster of standard Alphas just after telling the cube to squelch their fake Phage-call. The response had been immediate, as most came about to face the Terran ship that had inexplicably appeared in their midst while a few broke for the inner system.

"Eleven Alphas, locked on!" her tactical officer called. "Shrikes are loaded and ready."

"Fire!" Celesta jumped out of her seat, adrenaline coursing through her body. The *Icarus* might not make it out of the system… but what a way to die!

"All birds away! Tracking hot and clean!"

"Shut down the actives! Helm, zero thrust… stealth protocols in place," Celesta ordered.

"Engines to idle, aye," the helmswoman said. They'd crept in so close and fired their Alpha-killer Shrikes at such a close range the results were almost inevitable. The space in front of them erupted into a hellish nightmare of strobing, painful bursts of light as the powerful nukes hammered into the Alphas and began detonating. The *Icarus* was carrying so much velocity that she shot by the mayhem just as the last three missiles detonated.

"All good detonations, ma'am," the tactical officer said. "Eleven dead Alphas."

"Settle down!" Celesta shouted above the cheering. "OPS, tell the cube I'd like our disguise back in place now."

"Aye, ma'am. Phage transponder signal is broadcasting again."

"Tactical, is that next formation moving to intercept?" Celesta asked.

"Negative, ma'am. Cube telemetry shows that all twenty-eight of them are just milling about."

"Twenty-eight, you say," Celesta mused. "Tactical... load up two of our gravity bombs, maximum yield. Helm! Put our nose right on that cluster and engage the mains, ahead full."

"All engines ahead full, aye."

"Remember everyone, the more we kill now, the less the fleet has to deal with when they arrive." Celesta paced the bridge. "This is your chance! You want payback for Xi'an, for Haven, for your friends on the *Artemis*? Now is the time. Make it count!"

"Yes, ma'am!" several spacers shouted in unison as the *Icarus* bore down on the second group of oblivious Phage ships.

****

"Nothing yet," Hayashi reported. "We're at the edge of the time limit, sir."

"Very well," Jackson rubbed at his bloodshot eyes. "Tell CIC I want double watch on the passive array for another ten hours and then they can stand down until the next waypoint."

"Aye, sir."

"And make sure you call up a relief," Jackson told him. "You sound exhausted." The *Ares* had come to her first listening spot right on schedule, but there was no Vruahn warship and no *Broadhead*, so they continued on. There were two more rendezvous spots in the outer system where they could make contact, so he wasn't overly surprised that they hadn't had success on the first stop.

The two smaller, stealthier ships were ranging out trying to pinpoint where the core mind was actually located. Once it was found they would try to intercept the *Ares* and let the destroyer come in and hammer the location. It was a sound plan on the surface, but one of the big stumbling blocks was that nobody knew what the hell the core mind looked like. It could be enormous, far too large for the *Ares* to destroy, or it could be so small that they'd fly around the system for months and never find it. Worse yet, it could be something so exotic that they wouldn't even recognize it when they saw it. It was that last scenario that made Jackson wake up in his rack covered in a cold sweat. While it was the least likely, it was still a possibility that he had no real way to plan for.

"We're coming to our first course change, sir." Accari stifled a yawn. "I've programmed the turn for the compressed gas jets as you requested."

"Excellent," Jackson stood. "Helm, execute the course correction per Nav's instructions. Look alive, everyone! I know this is mind-numbing but we could find ourselves in deep, deep shit at any moment. I want—"

The *Ares* was yanked hard to port and explosions could be felt thumping through the deck plates before he could finish. Screams of shock and fear filled the bridge from those not violently thrown against the starboard bulkheads. Jackson's prosthetic leg smashed into Barrett's head before the captain was flipped end over end and landed in a heap near the nav station.

"Report!" he vaguely heard Davis shout out before the darkness closed in around him.

****

"Captain! Can you hear me?"

The voice seemed to trickle down from the surface even as he floated up towards it and the bright light that was tantalizingly just out of reach. He felt like he should know who was talking, but all he could focus on was how comfortable he was and that so long as he stayed where he was he wouldn't have to face whatever was behind the voice and light.

"Captain! We need you, sir."

"Davis?" he croaked as the fog cleared from his mind as if before a gale force wind. "Where am I?"

"Sick Bay." Commander Owens pulled the syringe out of his IV drip. "This will clear out the cobwebs, but you'll have a pretty nasty headache for a while."

"What happened?" Jackson asked.

"We actually don't know," Davis admitted. Her face was covered with grime and blood that he assumed wasn't hers. "Our operating theory is that it was a lateral meteorite strike. It punched in through the top of the hull at an angle on the aft, starboard quadrant and exited out the bottom on the opposite side. There wasn't anything left behind to analyze, even if we could spare the manpower to do it."

"A through and through meteorite strike?" Jackson pushed himself up. "That's absurd."

"Nothing else makes sense—"

"Send Daya in here," Jackson cut her off. "I need to know what the hell hit us." He looked up as nobody made a move to carry out his orders. "What?"

"Captain... the strike went directly through aft berthing, including the officer's deck," Owens said somberly. "Commander Singh was asleep in his stateroom when we were hit. I'm afraid—" Owens trailed off as Davis turned away, quietly weeping into her hands. The cold lump of ice that had formed in Jackson's gut as he began to realize that Owens was giving him *the* talk had started to spread through his body, numbing him.

"He wouldn't have felt anything, sir—"

"Get the Second Engineer up here," Jackson sat up, stone-faced. "Lieutenant Davis, please send someone to my quarters for the spare prosthetic I have in my wall locker and then I want a full report on the current status of the *Ares*." It was important not to feel anything right now. Shove it down, bury it, and move on. He had to finish the mission if the *Ares* was still able. Nothing else mattered at that moment.

"The ship is still flying under power," Davis reported after speaking into her comlink to have someone fetch his spare leg. "Whatever hit us missed all the primary flight systems, including the warp drive components, but it destroyed the power system for the auto-mag, took out our primary targeting radar, and the MUX controller for Main Bus A looks to be on the way to irreparable failure."

"Which means no point defense or laser batteries while the mains are running," Jackson nodded. "So, we're flying… but toothless."

"More or less, sir," she said. "Pressure hatches activated and closed in time and closed off most of the ship to space. Damage control teams are in full emergency mode and welding patches over the areas that couldn't be contained."

"How long was I out?"

"Seven hours, sir," she said.

"I have to get to the bridge," Jackson said. "We need to see how to salvage this mission."

"But sir." She looked like she was about to break down again. "Your best friend—"

"Will still be dead when this is all over," Jackson said gently to her, reaching out and grabbing her shoulder. "Daya would not want us too distracted to finish what we started all that time ago on the *Blue Jacket*. We honor him now by finishing the job and then we grieve for him later."

"I understand, sir." She sniffed loudly and straightened her posture. "I'm ready."

"Good." Jackson snatched the ungainly prosthetic from an exceedingly uncomfortable looking orderly. "I'm going to need you."

****

"That's over two hundred and seven, ma'am!" the tactical officer whooped. Celesta's tactics of using the Phage node to sneak up on clusters, drop a few grav bombs or fire some nukes, and then disappear again was wreaking havoc among the Phage in the inner system. It wasn't so much that there was a real risk that the *Icarus* could wipe out the swarm that numbered in the thousands, but the chaos and confusion she was creating within the ranks of the Phage were a sight to behold.

"Focus!" It was at least the tenth time she'd had to remind them to settle down. Killing so many Phage was almost intoxicating, and the bridge crew was very much drunk on the bloodbath she'd unleashed upon their despised enemy.

"Ma'am," the OPS officer spoke up over the din. "Look! Those two clumps of Alphas are turning on each other." The short-range optics that were trained on their next target did seem to show that two large groups of Alphas had opened up on each other. Brilliant plasma blasts streaked back and forth as they hammered away on each other.

"Helm, break off," Celesta ordered.

"Ma'am?"

"They're turning on each other, XO," Celesta breathed. "All of them. They have no idea who the enemy is so they're just firing into whoever is closest. Even with our Phage transponder singing we are now no longer afforded safe passage in this system. Tactical! How many gravity bombs do we have left?"

"Seven, ma'am."

"We may have played this hand as far as it's going to go," Celesta sat down. "We are now assuming a defensive posture, everyone. Nav, plot me a course to the outer system that avoids all the larger clusters. I'd especially like to avoid any Alphas or anything that's big enough to be an Alpha, so confer with OPS for the latest Vruahn telemetry updates."

"Seems a shame to run at this point," the XO said quietly.

"We won't be any more victorious by losing the *Icarus* with all aboard, Lieutenant Commander," Celesta said. "We've bloodied their nose, now let's get back to Admiral Marcum and report on what we've seen before he comes charging into the system while the Phage are busy killing each other for us."

"Of course, Captain."

****

"We're still technically flightworthy, but we're in no condition for a battle," Second Engineer Lieutenant Commander Jace Wu said after giving a point-by-point accounting of the massive damage the *Ares* had suffered.

"Thank you for confirming what we'd already suspected." Jackson leaned back in his seat. "You're dismissed, Lieutenant Commander. Go ahead and begin making what field repairs you can."

"Aye, sir," Wu nodded and walked quickly off the bridge. Everyone knew about Jackson's close relationship with Daya Singh, and they all were trying to avoid him as best they could. Nobody wanted to be in the vicinity when that cool, calm exterior cracked.

"I've got us heading back in the right direction, Captain," Specialist Accari said. "We weren't knocked off course too badly, but we did lose a significant amount of attitude control. Aft jets are completely offline."

"Understood, Specialist," Jackson said as he rotated the views from the external cameras on his tile. The damage was spectacular, and he was not at all convinced that they'd been hit by some random meteorite. The entry point showed that the initial impact had liquefied much of the surrounding hull, and the material was rippled and splattered all around the relatively small hole. It was significantly less than half a meter in diameter despite the dramatic surface damage around it. Where the object exited, however, was a different story. A gaping wound over thirty meters across was mushroomed out where the projectile had ripped tons of material, organic and inorganic, from the ship on the way out.

That the *Ares* was still flying and responding to commands at all was a testament to how well she was designed. But the hit shone a sickly light on his worst fear: the hull armor was too thin and too brittle and should never have been used on a warship. It was likely the object that hit them was quite small and travelling near relativistic speeds. He was certain his old ship would have taken the hit without the amount of damage the *Ares* had just suffered. As he continued to idly look at the images, another certainty hit him, as obvious as daylight now that he was looking at it in the right context.

"Jillian, look at this," he nudged his shocked-looking XO. "Look closely at the entry and exit points of the projectile."

"I'm not sure what I'm looking at, sir," she said.

"We were hit with a kinetic weapon," Jacksons said. "Any meteorite would have broken up on impact, even one of solid iron, and shredded the guts out of this ship. This was a hardened alloy penetrator that was fired at us."

"The Phage?"

"It would appear they have some automated defenses here in the system," Jackson shrugged. "If it was a ship or something mobile that fired the shot I don't think we'd be here having this conversation. It'd have taken a couple follow-up shots until it breached one of the reactors or hit the magazine and then this mission would have come to a full stop."

"So does this mean we're in the right system or not?" Davis asked as she leaned over Jackson's arm and flipped through the images on the tile, causing him to squirm uncomfortably.

"I would have to still say yes," he said. "This is a fairly subtle weapon that, while effective, could easily be dismissed. It's also almost completely undetectable if it's chemically fired. We only recognize it because of our familiarity with large-bore kinetic weapons in space."

"Should we sound a general alert?"

"Don't bother," Jackson shook his head. "We can't do anything about it regardless. Let them keep working without the added pressure of waiting for the next shot."

"Yes, sir."

The realization that they'd been hit with a weapon elicited a lot of mixed feelings in Jackson. On some level he was elated that the system wasn't completely empty, but he also had to admit that the Phage had never employed kinetic weapons in all the battles they'd fought, so he couldn't say for sure exactly who had set the trap they'd just flown through. He also felt that he'd utterly failed his crew. His planning had led to not only a number of KIA that he couldn't face at the moment, but a crippled ship that, should the core mind pop up right in front of them, couldn't fire a single shot at it.

The lack of options took him back to a moment when he'd used his own ship as a weapon, ramming the *Blue Jacket* into a Super Alpha to destroy it and end the incursion. Even as he idly considered the idea, he dismissed it. The *Blue Jacket* had been abandoned, the *Ares* still had most of her crew aboard, and they had not signed on for a suicidal plunge into a planet. Moral issues aside, it was a moot point since the *Ares* had lost so much of her stability and attitude control that he wasn't sure she could hit a target the size of a small planet or moon at speed.

The hours ticked by before the scope of the damage became apparent, and it was worse than initially thought. The ship now had serious structural integrity issues since the projectile had severed two of the six main supports that essentially tied the front of the ship to the aft section. Lieutenant Commander Wu's initial assessment was that despite the warp drive being fully functional the *Ares* wouldn't survive the first transition; the shear forces from the opposing distortion fields would tear her apart.

The bad news didn't stop there, however, as damage control teams discovered that the cooling system for Reactor Two had been streaming water out into space through a smaller hull breach that they hadn't found on the first sweep. The pressurized compartment was leaking air at a high enough rate that it kept the thin water stream blowing out the rupture instead of freezing along the hull and sealing itself off. Even though it wasn't a bad leak, it had diminished cooling capacity on the system by fifteen percent and there wasn't enough coolant left in the reservoirs to refill it.

"Throttle number two back to fifty percent," Jackson said as he read the summary report on his tile. "If we lose any more capacity than that shut it down completely."

"Aye, sir," Lieutenant Commander Wu said before leaving he bridge. The man looked ready to pass out where he stood, but there would be no rest for any of them anytime soon.

"We have something on passives, sir," Barrett said. "Just a small thermal blip and then it was gone."

"Can the computer come up with a probable match based on what you have?" Jackson asked.

"Tac-Two is offline, sir," Barrett referred to one of the four computers that made up the *Ares'* tactical processing avionics. Tac-Two handled the database of known sensor contacts and was able to extrapolate probabilities based on even brief contacts like Barrett's thermal blip.

"Why didn't Tac-Four take over when Two went down?" Jackson demanded.

"Still booting, sir," Hayashi said. "Sorry, sir."

"Just keep with it, Lieutenant Commander," Jackson sighed. "How spotty is our sensor coverage?"

"It would be better if any contacts came at us head-on, sir," Barrett said. "Rear coverage is degraded considerably, but I won't have an exact answer until Engineering gets power restored to some of the affected areas."

"Contact!" Keller shouted from the coms stations. "Weak LF-band signal detected… it's Colonel Blake! He's standing off the starboard bow and requesting permission to dock."

"Permission granted." Jackson breathed a short sigh of relief. "Tell him I'll meet him at the starboard airlock."

"I wish we had more precise data from the Vruahn system," Celesta griped. "A real-time sensor suite would be a game changer right now."

"It looks like the infighting is dying down," the second watch OPS officer said. The tall woman from the Warsaw Alliance was filling in as second in command while the XO was down in CIC trying to manage all the confusion.

"From what we're looking at on our own passive sensors I think the Super Alphas in the system are reestablishing control over the swarm, Lieutenant Baska," Celesta said. "I'm not sure what this means for us, however."

"I don't follow, ma'am."

"We have no way to tell if they suspect us or not," Celesta said. "Or if they even know we're out here. Let's just stay hidden out here for a while longer until we get some kind of indication what's happening."

The *Icarus* had single-handedly delivered a massive blow to the Phage swarm. The ship racked up hundreds of direct kills which then in turn sparked the infighting that claimed thousands more as Phage Alphas turned their powerful plasma weapons on each other. Even the smaller, Bravo-type units had gotten in on the action as they ganged up and tried to take down larger targets like schools of predatory fish.

"We're starting to see the individual clusters reorganizing," her OPS officer said. "If I were to make an educated guess, I'd say that each Super Alpha is exerting its influence on the local clusters to keep them from trying to kill each other. This has profound implications on our understanding of how their networked consciousness works—"

"Thank you, Commander," Celesta said firmly. Her OPS officer, while proficient, had a tendency to want to "educate" her at every turn. Perhaps if he had spent a little more of that energy on introspection he'd have figured out why he was still a bridge station operator on a destroyer as a full commander with over twenty years in service instead of commanding his own ship. "Just keep an eye on them and report on any further changes in behavior."

"Yes, ma'am," he said, clearly miffed.

They went through two full watch changes, twelve hours since Celesta had gone to six-hour shifts during the seemingly non-stop, adrenaline-fueled combat operations, and there still was little movement out of the Phage. During that time she had taken three, hour-long naps, bullying her chief medical officer into giving her an entire array of uppers and downers to chemically control her sleep cycle and allow her to remain alert on the bridge when she was there. She was constantly having to temper the crew, the success of the previous ninety-six hours making them feel invincible. At every turn she reminded them that if they were boxed in by just a couple of those Alphas the *Icarus* would be turned to slag in short order.

Despite her admonishments, however, she had to admit to herself that the mission had been thrilling beyond all measure. Sneaking around behind enemy lines, popping up to fire off a weapon, and then slinking off to do it again while the enemy began to turn on itself… it was the type of mission that made legends of ships.

"We have some movement, ma'am," Lieutenant Baska said before Celesta had even fully walked onto the bridge.

"What are they doing?" she asked, now fully alert.

"Leaving," her OPS officer said simply. "They had finally organized into nine individual groups… there are only four remaining."

"Show me," Celesta waved to the main display. "Compress the time so that I can get an overall picture."

She watched as, one by one, the Phage groups winked out of existence as they left the system. They were all leaving along different vectors and had been spread pretty evenly throughout the outer system.

"Maybe the Super Alphas reached a consensus to separate the mini-swarms to keep them from going back at each other," Celesta mused.

"That was my assessment as well, Captain," the OPS officer beamed.

"We'll wait until they've all departed the system before making it back to the main fleet to report in," Celesta sat down. "Keep tracking all movement in the system. The obvious answer might be the correct one, or there may be something else in play that we're not seeing."

****

"What happened?" Colonel Blake asked before the airlock hatch had even fully opened.

"We were hit with what I suspect was a kinetic weapon deployed in the system somewhere," Jackson said. "Punched clean through the ship. We're no longer combat capable, unfortunately, and the structural damage is bad enough that she'll never leave this system. How about you? Any luck?"

"Yeah," Blake said absently as he looked at the chaos around him. "I found it. Or at least, I'm pretty sure I did."

"Go on," Jackson prompted.

"There's an irregularly shaped moon orbiting the second planet of this system. I was drifting by there when there was a sudden burst of traffic on the target frequency," Blake said. "I'm talking about a lot of back and forth, not just the burst transmissions we were originally tracking. There was so much that I was able to determine a source of origin with the passive detection sensors."

"This is interesting for a few reasons," Jackson waved for Blake to follow him as four Marines took position guarding the hatch to the airlock, hurling good-natured insults down to the NOVA team on the other side. It was only then that Jackson noticed that Lieutenant Commander Essa had come through with

Blake and was walking behind them, all without him even noticing.

"This means that something has changed," Jackson went on. "It also means that it was talking to someone along the system boundary if they hold to their SOP we've observed so far."

"Agreed," Blake said. "I came out and found you before making any closer inspections of the suspected site so we could decide on what to do without potentially tipping our hand too early."

"Good thinking," Jackson nodded as they dodged crewmembers running to and fro with tools or parts in hand. "We may only get one shot at this. If the flurry of com activity was due to our being detected there could be a whole fleet of Phage sitting out beyond detection range waiting for us to pop up."

"So what are we going to do, sir?" Blake asked.

"The first thing we *won't* do is something rash," Jackson said. "We'll give Pike another five hours to make contact and then we'll get down to planning the final assault on this bastard and end this war."

As if on cue, the *Broadhead* sent the LF pulse just before the five-hour mark and was directed to dock onto Blake's ship. Since the port airlock of the *Ares* was too damaged to safely operate, he would have to walk through the Vruahn ship to get to the destroyer. He took the damage to the ship in stride, not bothering to pester Jackson about the details of an obvious kinetic strike, something the captain was grateful for.

"So we have a confirmed target location?" the CIS agent asked, obviously having gotten the broad strokes of recent events from Ortiz as he was escorted through the damaged destroyer and up to the command deck conference room.

"Nothing precise enough for a strike package, but we think we've narrowed it down to a small moon," Jackson said.

"That's not really all that narrow." Pike flounced into one of the seats.

"It's better than an entire system," Jackson shrugged. "Either way it further confirms that we're in the right place. But we have some obvious issues to talk about. The first is that the *Ares* is non-viable. She's keeping the crew alive and has minimal propulsion, but she can't fight and if we have to retreat she can't survive a warp transition."

"That's... not good," Pike said. "The *Broadhead* is a spunky little ship, but it's made to hide and listen, not engage and kill. I don't have the firepower aboard to make a dent if the thing has even a little bit of protection around it."

"Using the *Broadhead* offensively isn't what I had in mind," Jackson shook his head. "Unfortunately, what I'm thinking of isn't going to be easy or pleasant."

"Oh, good," Pike rolled his eyes. "I was beginning to think this mission was a bit too easy."

****

"Once we've departed, begin getting the *Ares* up into the outer system," Jackson said as he rummaged through the safe in his office. "Don't push her too hard. Once you get word from us, success or failure, fire off your com drones for Terran space."

"I don't understand why you have to go on this, sir," Davis said. "You're a starship captain, not spec ops. This isn't something you're trained to do and we could use you here."

"There's not much here for me to do," Jackson shook his head. "I need to be with the strike team to finish this. Don't worry, Lieutenant… I'll stay out of the way and let Essa's men do their jobs."

"That's not exactly my worry." She bit her lip. Jackson pulled out a small bundle of datacards and laid them on the desk.

"Here's all the command codes and security by-passes you'll need to access every part of this ship," he said. "Fleet doesn't know I have those; the Tsuyo design rep gave them to me when the *Ares* first launched. Even if we make it back I suppose I won't need them after this… the ship isn't ever going to leave this system."

He pulled out an exact, working replica of an ancient Colt 1911 .45ACP handgun, meticulously crafted for him as a gift by Daya Singh. As he ran his hand over the oiled slide, he could feel the tidal forces of emotions he'd shoved down threatening to rip the wall down at a time when he could least afford it. He quickly shoved the weapon into the leather holster it had been sitting on top of and slammed it down on the desk too.

"And take care of that," he said gruffly. "It has a loaded magazine but no round in the chamber. You'll probably want to look up what that means before handling it."

"I'll hold it until you get back," Davis said. Jackson turned and looked at her, noticed her red-rimmed eyes, and again was forced to face the conflicting and wildly inappropriate feelings he had for his subordinate.

"I guess that about does it," he said. "You know what to do. Just try to keep everyone safe and maybe we'll find a way to get the crew back to Terran space alive."

"I will." She mirrored his movements so that they met at the side of the desk. "But you stay alive too. We need you." Before he could stick out his hand for the intended handshake, Jillian moved inside his arm, wrapped hers around his neck, and kissed him savagely on the lips. Too shocked to protest, all he could do was put his hands on her hips and let his body respond how it would to her. She broke the kiss with a gasp and pulled away.

"I'm… I'm so sorry, sir," she said. "I didn't intend for that to happen."

"We really did kiss on the bridge of the *Blue Jacket* that time, didn't we?" he asked. "I've always thought I imagined that."

"I suppose I've been acting unprofessionally for some time," she mumbled, looking embarrassed.

"Given the circumstances on both occasions, I think we'll go ahead and forego the court martial," Jackson joked lamely.

"Is there—" she left her question hanging.

"There is," he said softly. "Let's both do what we need to do here… and if we both survive we can talk about it then."

"Even if I'm under your command again?" she joked with a half-smile.

"Jillian, this is the second ship I've lost in less than ten years and my fifth major insubordination incident… I think we can safely say that if we make it back I won't be in command of anything," Jackson said. "I'd actually be thrilled if I just avoided any serious jail time."

****

"All the cargo is transferred to Colonel Blake's ship." Hayashi handed Jackson a tile with all the pertinent information. "Major Ortiz and his entire detachment are loaded up and over there as well. Your gear is stowed in your quarters… Colonel Blake said you'd know where that was."

"Very good." Jackson handed the tile back to his OPS officer. "Now get your ass back up to the bridge and back up Lieutenant Davis as best you can. No heroics… just keep our people safe and try to keep your heads down."

"Understood, Captain." Hayashi actually did bow this time. "It was an honor, sir."

"Hopefully it will be again," Jackson said. "Until then, keep her together."

"*ARES* DEPARTING!" Chief Green's voice thundered across the bay, his bellow triggering hundreds of boot heels to snap together as the throng of assembled spacers popped to attention and saluted. With a lump in his throat, Jackson came to attention and returned the salute before turning and striding through the hatchway and into the waiting Vruahn warship.

"Was that Green?" Pike called when Jackson emerged into the main corridor. "I could hear him all the way up by the flight deck."

"He's very proud of his voice," Jackson nodded. "We ready?"

"Locked and loaded, Captain," Pike said. "One last ride?"

"I wish everyone would quit looking at this as a death march," Jackson quipped. "I do have every intention of walking away from this."

"I've heard that before," Pike said over his shoulder as he walked back up the corridor.

Once the *Broadhead* had disengaged and thrusted away the Vruahn ship unlocked from the *Ares* and slid over and above her. Jackson looked on the thermals and felt a raw, burning rage as the imagers played over his crippled ship, thin jets of gas escaping into space through at least three dozen micro breaches. After Blake had engaged the drive and turned them away from the stricken destroyer, Jackson left the flight deck to go and check on his cargo and men.

The NOVAs had already made the ship their temporary home and were busy idly talking and going through gear checks, most nodding politely to Jackson when he walked into the large bay. He left them to make sure Major Ortiz and his Marine detachment was settling in equally well. While the NOVAs were trained to handle almost any scenario, he was completely confident that his Marines would adapt quickly to the conditions on the small moon. They were mostly trained for shipboard combat but they were all pros.

Lastly he went to check on his cargo: twenty Vruahn gravity bombs and one cylindrical tank that was attached to a sort of oversized loadbearing harness that would fit over a combat EVA suit. The tank also had a long, thin appendage attached to it via a shielded line. The tank had been fabricated by his Engineering crew and filled with a substance that was synthesized by Commander Owens's people. The original sample had come from a cryogenically stored capsule that Pike had been carrying on his *Broadhead*. It was a nasty little something from Fleet Research and Science that had never been weaponized until now… Jackson just hoped it wouldn't come down to that, as it was very much an option of last resort.

"Pike should be over the moon." Blake turned his head as Jackson walked onto the flight deck. "We've got another nine hours until we make orbit so he'll have plenty of time to map out the surface."

"Or find out what sort of orbital defenses there are," Amiri Essa said from the copilot's seat.

"Let's hope not," Jackson said. "I'm going to head down and start getting everything ready. We'll be at the threshold for deployment before we know it."

"I'll walk with you." Essa climbed out of his seat. "I'm just taking up space here and I need to get my men ready."

"Already?" Jackson asked.

"We don't know what might be in place around this moon," Essa said. "I was half-joking about Pike triggering a defensive response, but I would rather my men already be in their EVA rigs and ready to go on internal life support in case there is something there to meet us."

"Not a bad idea," Jackson said. "I'll get Major Ortiz moving along with his people as well."

"So is this really it, Captain?" Essa asked, stopping at the corridor that would lead him down to where his NOVAs were berthed. "The end of the war?"

"That's the idea, Lieutenant Commander," Jackson nodded. "We can put an end to the Phage right here and now with a successful operation. There can be no other considerations except the destruction of whatever is on that moon."

"Understood, sir." Essa nodded and walked off down the side corridor.

Chapter 22

"It's definitely more than one contact, sir," the *Amsterdam*'s XO said quietly to Marcum. "But whatever it is, it's still at the outer edge of our detection range."

"So it isn't the *Icarus*," Marcum said. "Captain Wright would have already announced her arrival over the Link."

"Yes, sir."

"Sound the general alert to the fleet, Commander, and wake your captain up," Marcum said grimly. "The Phage have found us."

"Aye aye, Admiral."

"Fucking Wolfe," Marcum muttered for the hundredth time since leaving New Sierra.

****

"The moon is small enough that we can land, disembark, and then have the ship move back up into low orbit and wait for us," Blake said as he hefted his helmet.

"I still don't understand why you're coming, Colonel," Amiri Essa said pointedly.

"Because without the stasis cube or the controller that's still aboard the *Ares* you can't arm the gravity bombs without me," Blake said. "They're coded to respond to me or my team, but just any ol' human won't do it."

"I can't believe we came all this way and forgot the fucking detonator," Major Ortiz growled. "Definitely a Fleet operation."

"It's not quite that simple, Major," Blake smiled. "The controller was built into the rack and integrated into the *Ares*'s tactical avionics suite. The only way to use it would have been to move the *Ares* into orbit."

"Why can't this ship control them remotely?" Jackson asked.

"That is a good question, Captain," Blake frowned. "But I've tried. I can't even get a status update on the weapons from the flight deck, but if I just walk down and directly interface with them there's no issue."

"Design flaw," Essa shrugged. "Fine. The colonel comes with us. Rat, Samson… you're on protection detail."

The ship flew itself in a slow, lazy arc that would put them in a one-meter hover over the erratically tumbling moon within the next thirty minutes. Jackson was again struck at how much the interior of the ship was very much for appearances only. Blake was more or less a glorified passenger for much of the time, only stepping in to provide the final go-ahead to pull the trigger when the time came for the ship to be used as a weapon.

They had received the data from Pike when they were on final approach, now so close that they were no longer quite so worried about stealth since the odds that they were undetected were almost none. After quickly analyzing the multi-spectrum surface mapping performed by the *Broadhead*, they determined that a shallow crater with a sheer face on one side showed signs of having been disturbed. More to the point, there appeared to be definite drag marks in the settled dust of the airless moon.

"*We are in position,*" the computer announced over the common channel in their helmets. "*Stand by for hatch opening. You will have forty seconds to depart before the ship will need to be moved.*"

"Final gear check!" Ortiz called. "Check yourself, check your buddies!" There was a flurry of activity as they all did one final check on all the joints and fittings of their equipment along with those of the people around them. Jackson reached up and cinched the straps of the canister hooked to his back a bit tighter and made sure the attached cylinder was secured to the bracket on his belt. He sure as hell didn't want that damn thing firing off early.

With no discernable sensation of deceleration or even a change in engine sound the red lights that lined the walls began flashing slowly and, with no further warning from the ship, the hatch popped open and swung down into position. They all quickly moved to the edge and hopped off, the sudden change in gravity making Jackson queasy. He bounced off the surface of the moon and turned in mid-hop to see the Marines sliding the gravity bombs out, the powerful weapons bouncing haphazardly across the surface. Despite Blake's assurances that the weapons didn't actually "explode," the sight of munitions tumbling out of an open hatch still caused Jackson to clench up.

Exactly forty seconds after the hatch opened the ship began to rise from the surface and quickly disappeared into the pitch black sky. Without prompting, everyone activated their suit lights and under radio silence began going about their tasks. Most of the Marines bounced around in the low gravity, gathering up the scattered weapons and rolling them into a loose formation at the bottom of the crater.

Jackson, Blake, and Essa shuffled off to the sheer face of the crater that had caught their eye in the mapping data. The "drag" marks they'd thought they could identify from the orbital imagery were now much less pronounced as they saw them in poor lighting and at ground level. In fact, the more he looked around, the more Jackson thought he was just looking at a natural formation and his confidence that they were in the right place began to fade.

"Well, we're already here," Essa said as they looked around at the base of the wall formation. "May as well make this thorough."

Over the next two hours all seventy members of the assault team poked around at the base of the wall, the mood darkening as it looked like they had gone through a lot of trouble for nothing. Jackson shuffled up close to the wall and put his hand against it, pushing in frustration at the impenetrable rock. The evidence for this mission had always been thin, but his conviction was so strong that he'd taken more than a few leaps of faith to connect the dots that this was the place. It was beginning to look like all he had done was take a ship off the line and get his crew killed in the process. While he wasn't a man obsessed with legacy, he couldn't help but shudder at how history would likely remember him.

"Sir! Here!"

"Who said that?" Ortiz shouted. "Raise your hand, you idiot… we can't tell who's talking over the open channel."

Far down the line a Marine raised his hand and waved frantically. Jackson and Essa bounded over to him to see what he'd found.

"What do you have, Marine?" Ortiz beat them there. "It looks like more rock."

"Look at it through your thermals, sir," the Marine said. "Make sure your IR lights are on."

"What in the hell?" Ortiz murmured just as Jackson got there, already activating his thermal optics.

"Indeed," Jackson said, the thermal imagery showing a faint, roughly semi-circle shape on the rock face. He walked up to it and slapped his glove against it. It just felt like all the other rock. "Blake, any idea what this is?"

"It's similar in makeup to a Phage ship hull." Blake's excitement was evident. "Not an identical match, but it definitely isn't rock. I can't give you a more definite answer with this instrument. I'd have to take a sample."

"Not necessary," Jackson said. "Breaching team!"

Ten Marines hustled over and, after a brief consultation with Blake, began placing charges in a specific pattern in an area near the middle of the surface anomaly. Jackson noted the color and saw that they were using thermite charges, not concussive explosives, and nodded his silent approval. Once ignited, the thermite would burn at 2,500°C and couldn't be put out. The testing they'd done on recovered Phage units confirmed that the thermite could burn through it, but the process took too long for it to be an effective weapon against a moving ship.

"Do it," he said when Ortiz looked to him for confirmation. An instant later their visors auto-dimmed as the thermite charges burst to life. The wall began to slough off almost immediately, burning away in chunks rather than liquefying. Before long, large gaps began appearing but they couldn't see past the brilliant flare of the burning metals.

"Step back!" Ortiz ordered. A ragged opening had been torn into the wall and a large cavern could be made out beyond, their lights failing to pierce the gloom to the far wall.

"Second team! Finish making us an entry," he called as the edges of the ragged hole cooled. "First team! Weapons ready to cover."

Using simple tools, and in some cases their gloved hands, the Marines tore the charred chunks of the wall away until there was a hole big enough for three people to walk through shoulder-to-shoulder.

"We can burn more away if you think we need it, Captain," Ortiz said after they'd cleared all the damaged material away, unable to go any further.

"I think we're fine with this," Jackson said, anxious to get going. "We're not taking more than fifteen people in so we won't need it any bigger if we have to egress quickly. I do want the breaching team constantly monitoring this, though. We know their ship hulls can heal, and I'd rather not get trapped in there if we can help it."

"Of course, sir," Ortiz said. Jackson could tell the major was disappointed that his Marines were being left out to guard the opening, but this sort of mission was more suited to the NOVAs' training and he didn't want to mix and match dissimilar units when the situation was so fluid.

"Lieutenant Commander, shall we?" Jackson asked.

"NOVAs, let's move," Essa barked. "Secure the immediate access point and begin fanning out, two-man teams." Without a word the NOVA team quickly streamed into the cavern through the jagged hole, followed by Jackson and Blake.

Once they were inside and began working their way forward, Jackson realized that they weren't in a cavern, but an enormous, smooth-walled tunnel. It was definitely not a natural formation and Jackson was much surer that they were in the right place. He just hoped they hadn't found some long-abandoned Phage depot.

"It's narrowing down sharply," Essa radioed from up ahead. "It looks like it might split up ahead too."

"That's not good," Jackson said. "Any readings that indicate one way might be more interesting than another?"

There was a short burst of static and then nothing over the radio.

"Lieutenant Commander?" He turned to look at Blake and saw that there was nobody behind him. When he spun around to grab the NOVA in front of him, he was also gone. Jackson spun quickly in a full circle and saw that he was completely alone in the tunnel. Fighting down the panic, he saw that there was a soft, red glow coming from the smaller tunnel up on the left. He hoped it was his team and shuffled off towards it, knowing that it would probably be smarter to head back to the wall opening since his radio had apparently died.

The tunnel spiraled down and to the left, the glow becoming ever brighter as he continued along, now suspecting that whatever was ahead of him was not his team. He couldn't tell what was causing the glow as there appeared to be no obvious light source; it was just something that was always tantalizingly ahead of him, but never there whenever he rounded another corner.

"Com check, com check… this is Wolfe. Does anyone copy?" Jackson continued forward, now feeling that whatever was going to happen was going to happen no matter what he did. The feeling of being "herded" was pronounced as he chased the glowing red light like a simple animal.

He had to check his helmet display to verify that he'd only been walking for less than thirty minutes, the trip down the tunnel feeling like it was taking forever, when it opened up into an vast chamber. The walls of the cavern glowed a soft red and his instruments were measuring a spike in temperature as well as a thick atmosphere. He was in the middle of letting the onboard processor analyze it when the voice came out of nowhere and everywhere all at once.

"You may remove your helmet, Captain," it said. "I require much the same type of atmosphere that you do."

Jackson could feel his heart pounding in his ears and felt his mouth dry out as panic gripped him.

"Are you… it?" he managed to get out.

"It?"

"The core mind?" Jackson said more clearly. "The intelligence that controls the Phage?"

"I've never liked that name... *Phage*," the voice said. "But your question implies a separation that does not exist. I am me."

"A distinction without a difference," Jackson said, now back in control of his reactions. "I think you know exactly what I'm asking. Are you the processing apparatus that has sent Phage ships into Terran space to kill humans, as you have countless other species?"

"Yes," it said simply. "To put it in terms you understand, my physical form here is the neural mass that houses the controlling intelligence of the species you have crudely called the *Phage*."

"And yet you sit here in a dark cave without any protection other than whatever it was you hit my ship with?" Jackson asked, now doubting what he was being told.

"It was the only logical answer to a problem of my own creating," the core said. "So many species wanting to eradicate me in misguided notions of vengeance... there was no amount of combat units I could hide behind that wouldn't eventually be overcome. So here I sit, silent and isolated in a system that is of no importance to anyone. It was a calculated risk, but also a perfectly elegant solution. Had there been any obvious presence at all here the system would have been investigated and I would eventually be found."

"And the swarm amassed in the other system?"

"Is doing exactly what it is supposed to do: be the irresistible target," the core replied. "All the time and energy wasted as species smash themselves into a system they assume must be where this neural mass is located, and all the focus removed from finding an alternative answer."

"You've isolated me and led me down here for a reason," Jackson asked. "What is it?"

"You've come to kill me," the core said. "I've watched you from afar since our first fateful meeting, Captain. You are an interesting collection of contradictions... I had hoped we could communicate further."

"You mean you think you can talk me out of killing you," Jackson said.

"I can stop you at any time," the core corrected.

"Except that you know there's a Vruahn warship sitting in orbit over this moon with orders to open fire if we don't come back soon," Jackson said. That wasn't technically true, but he assumed the core mind didn't have the ability to determine whether or not he was lying or if it knew the Vruahn laser on Blake's ship couldn't penetrate to those depths.

"Yes, I am quite... disappointed... that the Vruahn have not honored our agreement and sent one of their ships to this system," the core said, the revelation shocking Jackson.

"So while we have some time... care to tell me why you're on a genocidal rampage across this part of the galaxy?"

"Your sarcasm masks your fear," the core said. "You're afraid that even if you destroy this neural mass it won't stop me. That I will still keep coming for you."

"There's a bit of that, but I genuinely would like to know the motivation." Jackson ambled forward as the lighting in the chamber began to increase. He was beginning to make out details of what was with him in the chamber. It was, more or less, a dark grey, amorphous mass that seemed to have been shoved into the space so that it inhabited every nook and cranny. The surface had a dull, burnished look and appeared to be a hardened shell. Although he wasn't sure what he had expected, this wasn't it. It almost looked like just another lumpy rock formation.

"Motivation is a complicated concept," the core said. "I do what I do, because it's what I am. For example: your species is all-consumed with the need to procreate. Everything you do, your drive to explore, your technological ingenuity... all of it can trace its roots back to the deep need to propagate your species. You can't help it. So is your only motivation for everything you do simply to exist?"

"Isn't that the base motivation of all life?" Jackson asked.

"Ah!" the core said. "But in all of nature, doesn't every force have an equal and opposite force that creates balance? If your nature is simply to spawn and spawn until you've consumed all natural resources and have begun to spread and begin the destructive cycle all over again, wouldn't logic dictate that there should be some reciprocal force to check this?"

JOSHUA DALZELLE

"So you're claiming to be a force of nature?" Jackson scoffed.

"I'm saying that I fill a void and serve a purpose, the same as you, even if neither of us can really explain just why we do the things we do."

"Forgive me if that doesn't make me feel any better about the millions of human lives you've snuffed out," Jackson said, walking along the edges of the mass. It didn't appear to have any form of locomotion or even a way to move. Experimentally, he pushed on one of the tendrils that was clinging to a wall next to him and noticed it gave under his touch, not a hard shell like he'd thought.

"I am in no way attempting to mollify you," the core said in its infuriatingly calm voice. "You asked for an explanation, I gave one as best I understand it." The voice was being broadcast directly into Jackson's helmet, but he wasn't sure if the thing could see or hear directly. It didn't react at all when he pressed on it.

"So you had an agreement with the Vruahn?" Jackson asked, trying to keep the conversation going long enough for his team to either find him or at least make contact.

"I did. It is an agreement that stretches back many thousands of your years... back to my earliest memories when I was new and clumsy and they were very powerful and old." The core almost sounded wistful. "I was not to attack them directly and in return they would allow me to consume those that were suitable. It has been a mutually beneficial arrangement."

"So why the change?" Jackson asked. "It seems you broke the peace when you went after specific strategic targets."

"I may have acted rashly," the core said. "For a long time I had observed how they gave some of your kind powerful weapons, and when I found that they had wanted to speak with you specifically I thought that they were offering you an expanded alliance. I feared they intended to replace me with you."

The answer completely confused Jackson as it made no sense. Did the Phage and Vruahn have an agreement or a full-blown alliance? If it was the latter, what purpose did the Phage serve for the Vruahn and vice versa?

"I have another question, while we're both being honest." Jackson reached down on his belt and began manipulating a set of controls. "You refer to yourself as singular, and I know that there's a sort of aggregate intelligence at work in your swarms, but what about the units that have the expanded neural mass? They seem to be capable of at least some independent thinking."

"They are simply an extension of my will," the core said. "They do not think... at least not as you understand it. I am still connected to them, even over the vastness of interstellar space, and they execute for me even as your own hands do the bidding of the neural center in your cranium though you do not consciously think of each muscle as it manipulates the appendage.

Even now I am aware that your small fleet of ships has engaged the large massing of combat units."

"Any chance I could convince you to call that off?" Jackson asked tightly.

"You know that I will not," the core said.

"So where does that leave us?" Jackson asked. "You hold the fate of our entire fleet in your hands, and I'm down here with you while you're more or less defenseless."

"You cannot harm me nor will I allow you to leave," the core said. "I have already sensed that you carry no weapons, and I do not think your compatriots will activate the Vruahn weapons on the surface while they think you're still down here. It's one of the great inefficiencies of your species: singular units can hold significant influence, causing the all of you to fail to act when necessary.

"Those that mill about on the surface will wait until their contained atmosphere runs out and then waste precious time discussing the situation back and forth, all the while I will have decimated your entire fleet and then I will move on human worlds in earnest, but not before calling in my most powerful units to kill everything in this system. Your disharmony of thought, your inability to quickly reach consensus... these are the things that will ultimately cause your downfall before me. If your species has any hope of surviving then logic dictates that you must kill me—"

"I just did," Jackson said quietly, holding up the cylinder that was attached to the canister on his back.

Three large-bore penetrators were still deployed from one end, each dripping a greenish-yellow liquid. The silence in the chamber was deafening as Jackson watched the blackened area around the spot he'd shoved the injector into spread rapidly.

"So you have." The voice sounded like a sigh of relief. "Very clever, Captain."

"Not my idea," Jackson said, the bile rising in his throat. "That's one of our advantages as a species: each of us knows something the others don't, each contributing to the whole."

"Nonsense." The voice was becoming difficult to make out as the specialized neurotoxin raced through the core mind, destroying it from the inside.

"Know that I took no pleasure in this," Jackson said. "Maybe it's true that we're both just doing what nature demands of us, but my species can't survive as long as yours lives."

"I hold no malice towards you. It has been a worthy fight. Before you leave, Captain Jackson Wolfe, there are some things that you should know," the core said, now struggling to form words. "Things that will matter when I'm no more."

****

"There!"

"Captain! Where have you been?"

"Stand down!" Jackson called as five NOVAs came bouncing towards him. "It's over."

"Sir?" Amiri Essa asked as he came closer.

"The core mind… it's dead," Jackson said tiredly, tossing the empty canister on the ground where it bounced back up in the light gravity. "I'll explain later, but for now let's get everyone together and back outside."

It took nearly two hours to get everyone rounded up and back in the middle of the crater. They'd split into separate search teams once they'd discovered that Jackson was missing, and most of them were deep into the tunnel complex. Three of the NOVAs were sent back down to record the evidence that the core mind was dead and cold before rejoining everyone else.

"We still need to destroy this place," Jackson said over the team channel once they were all reassembled. "There's so much we don't know about this species that I'd rather not take the chance that the toxin simply put it into hibernation or that there's some way it can come back. We're going to cluster up all the gravity bombs and set them off at full yield. Would that do it, Colonel?"

"If by 'do it' you mean create a momentary singularity that will consume all matter within a one-hundred-thousand-kilometer radius then yeah, that'll do it," Blake said, causing a few chuckles from the group.

"Let's make it happen then," Jackson said, shuffling away from the group. Once at the edge of the crater he muted his radio and just stood there, looking out at the stars but not really seeing them as the enormity of what had just happened sank in.

****

"They've stopped, Admiral," the captain of the *Amsterdam* said.

"Stopped?" Marcum demanded.

"Stopped advancing," the captain corrected. "It's as if they were all set adrift simultaneously. Thermal signatures are still consistent with live units, but they're now ignoring our individual formations and one group is now heading off at a perpendicular course... they never completed their turn that would have put them on course to intercept our leading units."

"Have the *Hyperion* and the *Atlas* move in closer and confirm," Marcum frowned. It had been over a week since they'd parked in an empty system to reconfigure the convoy into a battle fleet and he'd agreed to allow the *Icarus* to range ahead. Celesta Wright had yet to reappear, but the Phage had apparently found them and had begun streaming into the system, massing up along the edge of the outer system before beginning their slow march towards the Terran ships.

With the *Icarus* still missing Marcum didn't think it was just some wild coincidence that Phage units were arriving in the system by the hundreds: they'd backtracked Wright and now they were in perfect position to hammer the Terran fleet before it could be organized and prepped for battle. So what the hell were they doing? If it was some sort of ruse Marcum couldn't see the point of it. The Phage knew that humans preferred standoff weapons when outgunned, so coming in with a vast numerical advantage and then playing some game to lure them in closer wasn't likely to work.

As his two remaining *Starwolf*-class destroyers accelerated away from the formation at full burn, he had a bad feeling that the *Icarus* was likely lost and he struggled to remain confident that the *Ares* would make it home. His blood burned as he thought of Wolfe, maybe beginning to believe in his own legend just a bit too much, taking it upon himself to take that ship and her crew and attempt such a long trip unescorted and unsupported.

"Maybe it's good that you aren't here, Wolfe," Marcum muttered to himself. "No point in all of us dying out here in one unsuccessful, and maybe misguided, last stand."

Chapter 23

"The ship is coming back down to the surface," Blake said as they took a final headcount once they exited the cave.

"Everyone is ready," Jackson confirmed. "The charges are fine placed where they are?"

"Yes," Blake nodded. "This is such overkill that they won't need to be precisely placed to work. It's a shame we can't take the time to study the core mind more... or at least get a few samples."

"My choice," Jackson said firmly. "It is such an unknown that I won't risk any part of this thing being taken off this moon."

They stood in silence as the ship descended slowly to the surface, stopping precisely one meter above the dusty landscape before opening the main hatch. Jackson watched as the oddly subdued Blake leapt up into the ship without a word and began having a conversation with what he assumed was the ship's computer. He could see the colonel's lips moving, but his words weren't being broadcast over the team channel.

Jackson stood at the hatchway, waving his men aboard while performing one last count. After they'd all piled in, looking exhausted, he watched as Blake's conversation became more and more animated.

"Is everything okay?" Jackson asked him on a private channel once Blake appeared to have stopped talking.

"Would you care to check on something outside with me, Captain." Blake hopped down out of the hatchway without waiting for an answer. Jackson scrambled to follow him as the former Air Force officer made some show of checking one of the closest gravity bombs.

"Is something wrong?"

"I've just concluded some rather hasty negotiations with the Vruahn in order to secure the safety of your crew," Blake said.

"The what?" Jackson frowned.

"Please just listen," Blake said. "My ship will take you back to the *Ares* and dock. Once there you will be given three hours to evacuate the destroyer. You'll then be taken directly back to Earth, where you will be deposited and the ship will then depart. Any attempts to interfere with the operation of the ship or capture it afterwards will result in immediate retaliation."

"And where will you be during all of this?" Jackson asked.

"The gravity bombs cannot be remotely detonated from my ship, or from yours," Blake said. "The weapons were coded to the AI that was installed on the stasis cube; not even the processor in the racks that kept them stable will allow them to be detonated."

"Why would they be designed so specifically?" Jackson asked.

"These are very powerful munitions that were just handed over to what would be considered a lesser species by the Vruahn government," Blake said. "In order to secure them Setsi had to make guarantees that they would never be able to be repurposed."

"That makes a loopy sort of sense," Jackson shook his head. "So we can't use them here on the moon?"

"We can, but they will need to be activated at the device themselves in order to arm properly," Blake said. "To do that, I'll have to stay behind."

"You know I can't let you do that," Jackson said.

"You have no choice, Captain," Blake answered. "You have a responsibility to your crew, you are not able to perform the modifications yourself, and the procedure leaves the weapons in a state of instability… I cannot make the change and then hope to escape. The distortion from my ship's drive would likely cause them to activate prematurely and then we would all die.

"For this to mean anything, you need to get in that ship and get clear before I activate these here on the surface. It's the only solution that makes sense. I don't belong in your time and I have no place in your society as anything other than an oddity to be poked and prodded."

"You could still live a long, fulfilling life," Jackson argued carefully.

"It's okay, Captain. I already know that I'm not the real Robert Blake."

"How did you know?" Jackson said after waffling for a moment whether or not to confirm Blake's suspicions.

"It was the only logical conclusion available," Blake said. "From the fact that I've lived far too long to the emergence of strange feelings and memories since first coming into contact with modern humans I realized that the story of being rescued was likely not entirely true. Setsi told you of this?"

"Yes," Jackson said sadly. "A lot of what they said was true except that they had the ability to restore the lives to the original crew when they found the *Carl Sagan*. What they are adept at, however, is cloning. They were able to get enough of a brain scan from Colonel Blake and the others to imprint on a new body cloned from their DNA. They also modified behavior and responses in order for you to be better used as they intended."

"Do the others know?" Blake asked.

"No," Jackson said. "You and your team are the fifth generation of clones created from the original members of the *Carl Sagan* crew. I think that Setsi only told me because they had begun to notice anomalous behavior and reactions once you had begun interacting with modern humans."

"Anomalous behavior," Blake snorted. "This is truly a depressing line of thought. I'm nothing more than a biological machine... just like the Phage."

The comment startled Jackson and he peered closely into Blake's faceplate, wondering just how much he knew or if it was just an off-the-cuff comment.

"You still don't have to do this," Jackson said.

"I do," Blake said. "Just like you have to do whatever it takes to save the lives of your crew. Get moving, Captain... let's finish this."

"Colonel, it was an honor," Jackson said before turning and moving back to the waiting Vruahn ship.

"Colonel Blake is still out there!" Amiri Essa shouted as the hatch closed behind Jackson.

"He's not coming," Jackson said simply. "Get your men squared away, Lieutenant Commander. We're departing immediately."

"Sir—"

"That's an order," Jackson said sternly. "I will explain everything to you later, but right now I need you to do your job."

"Aye aye, sir," Essa said stiffly before moving back over to where his men were policing their equipment.

Jackson made his way to the flight deck just as the ship was lifting off the surface of the moon and turning towards where the *Ares* was still adrift. He slid into the copilot's seat, feeling that it would be inappropriate to sit in Blake's seat, and watched on the displays as the ship raced away from the moon back towards the

stricken Terran destroyer. The computer did not speak
to him the entire flight, not even as it began to slow
dramatically and rotate its orientation to snug up
alongside the *Ares* and started the docking procedure.

It took less than two hours to get back aboard his
ship, instruct his crew to begin an orderly disembarka-
tion, and watch from the hatchway as they made their
way across the gangway and followed the arrows back
to the three large cargo bays that would be their temporary home on the way back to Earth. The Vruahn ship
was capable of making the trip in the blink of an eye
compared to *Ares,* so he wasn't overly concerned about
how comfortable they'd be sleeping on the hard deck.

The last bit of business was to take aboard an un-
characteristically somber Pike so that he could ride back
with them and allow the *Broadhead* to make its own way
back to Terran space. With one last look at the interior
of his ship, the last he would ever command, he ordered the hatch closed so the ship could depart the
system. They flew out just to the edge of the system
and the ship obeyed Jackson's request to bring up the
aft-facing sensors in time to see the massive explosion
that occurred after the gravity bombs had shattered the
fabric of local spacetime, crushing all the matter down
to a pinpoint before the effect had run its course and an
opposite reaction blew the matter outward in a brilliant
burst of released energy.

He said a final farewell in his mind to the man that
had, at one time, been Colonel Robert Blake and
thanked him for his help. The dissipating light from the

reaction was not only a memorial to him and his team, but a marking post that signaled the end of the war. In the end it was not won through sheer military might, nor was it won by any particular feat of human ingenuity. The more Jackson thought about it, the more he wasn't sure the war was actually 'won' in the sense that they were the victors; it was more of a case that the conflict was simply over by virtue of one side no longer existing.

As he leaned back in his seat he suddenly felt very, very tired and more than ready to hang up his spurs. He just wanted to find a quiet corner somewhere and let the next generation worry about what humanity's direction would be among the stars.

****

"Captain."

The voice startled Jackson to full wakefulness and he saw that he was once again in a sterile, white room with the unwelcome sight of the impassive Setsi staring down at him.

"Another abduction?" he asked.

"You are still on our ship, almost to your homeworld," Setsi said. "The appearance of the interior is easily changed. As you've guessed, any resemblance to a human ship was done strictly for the comfort of Robert Blake."

"You mean the thing that you built that looked like Blake." Jackson sat up. "I have a feeling you're not appearing like this for a congratulatory pat on the back."

"There are grave concerns among our leadership about your species," Setsi said. "You have—"

"What we've done is to correct a problem you created," Jackson said, already weary of the condescending attitude that radiated off the avatar in waves. "Let's just call Blake and his crew what they were: the next iteration of a bad idea that led to the Phage being loosed upon the innocent species in this region of space."

"A strong assertion," Setsi said. "One that could possibly be construed as an accusation."

"I had an interesting talk with the Phage core mind before the neurotoxin my people developed rendered it incapable of communicating," Jackson said. "Its claim makes such perfect sense that I can see no other explanation: you created the Phage. You created them in an attempt to harness a living weapon that could keep you safe yet allow you to not actually fight yourselves.

"But then something happened... the Phage became self-aware, didn't it? It had become a conscious, free-thinking being but could not overcome the instinctual compulsions you had programmed into it. The mandate you had imprinted on it became distorted until it came to the conclusion that the only way to protect was to eradicate all competition."

"You are speaking of something that you don't fully understand," Setsi said. "Such talk in my society would lead to swift punishment."

"I don't doubt it," Jackson shrugged. "You un-leased one of the most destructive forces imaginable onto species that had no ability to defend themselves. Then, in an effort to mitigate the damage, you found the corpses of Colonel Blake and his crew and felt that you could take another try at it and create something to keep the Phage in check. Possibly on some level you even came to appreciate the Phage and their actions that kept any other species from developing to a point of being able to challenge your supremacy. Why else not destroy it outright when it became obvious you'd lost control?"

"Captain, I must warn you that this conversation may have profound ramifications," Setsi said.

"There won't be any retaliation attempts," Jackson waved him off. "As I said, no matter who created it the Phage was still a free-thinking being. It had a choice to try to overcome its nature and instead decided to revel in it. All we want from you is to be left alone, and that includes resurrecting grotesque copies of people long dead and programming them like little automatons. Once you drop us off, just fly away and don't come back. Maybe in a few thousand years or so we'll be ready to open lines of communications, but I think if all this has proven anything it's that we're not ready and you're not willing."

"A fair, if crude assessment of the situation," Setsi admitted. "I will take your proposal to those I report to. I feel I can say with confidence that your wishes align with our own." The avatar seemed to hesitate for a moment before going on.

"We regret our actions, Captain. Not just the mistakes that led to our creation getting away from us, but the slew of half-measures that followed after. We do owe you a debt of gratitude, but it may be some time before we are able to come to terms with what had to be done and repay that debt. Many among us believe you to be as dangerously unpredictable as the threat you eliminated."

"Fair, if a bit naïve," Jackson mocked Setsi's earlier words. "Just answer me one question: you don't have another of these things waiting out there, do you?"

"It was the only one," Setsi said. "Once we realized how completely we had miscalculated, the approach was abandoned for a more controlled methodology that eventually culminated in Robert Blake and his team."

"Good." Jackson chose to believe him. "Then all I'll say is thank you for the support when it mattered and let's agree to end our collaboration with a grudging mutual respect for each other's wishes."

"It is so agreed, Captain," Setsi nodded. "I wish your species luck for a peaceful and prosperous future."

The room darkened, and when the lighting came back up Setsi was gone and Jackson was looking at the drab, steel interior of what the designers assumed humans liked in their ship interiors.

Jackson rolled back onto the bunk and stared up at the ceiling, sleep a futile goal after the strange conversation. He knew he really had no authority to negotiate on behalf of all humanity like he had, but he felt like they were on shaky ground with the Vruahn. They'd just wiped out an entire species, albeit a species of one intelligence, based on the loss of less than a percent of their entire population. While from a human perspective that seemed completely justified, it must have bewildered and terrified the Vruahn that their response was so immediate and violent. He just couldn't see anything good coming from direct interaction with a powerful, ancient species that looked at them with utter distrust and revulsion.

Given the list of charges he was likely facing when they got home, he figured he'd just keep this last little interaction to himself.

Chapter 24

After the return to Earth there was the expected litany of demands for explanations; later there were accusations, and the memorials for fallen members of his crew. Jackson attended each and every one of them personally, each one like a stab in his heart. Daya Singh's service was especially difficult as he finally had to come to terms with the loss of one of the most important people in his life.

Earth had become a bustling hub of political activity as the enclaves seemed to derive some sense of security by coming back to humanity's birthplace and reconnecting with their origins. After the second debriefing in which Jackson explained his actions and the results, complete with all the recordings compiled from the *Ares*, their EVA suits, and even some sensor recordings taken from Blake's ship before it departed, the Council of Nations as well as CENTCOM were having trouble making the more serious charges stick to him. The public outcry put pressure on the politicians who then leaned on CENTCOM brass to give him a symbolic slap on the wrist, maybe even convince him to retire early, but Wolfe was not to be seriously punished for what he'd done.

Given everything that had happened up to that point, Jackson was more or less numb to the entire thing. He'd never had very lofty career aspirations once he'd been given a ship, and he felt that his days of command were now firmly behind him. He was very thankful when com drones began filtering into the system with news that the main body of the fleet had begun arriving in the DeLonges System. He had to smile at the thought of Marcum coming back, ready to drop the hammer on him only to find out the politicians had beat him to it and given him little more than a stern talking to.

"So you're really going to walk away?" Davis asked him as they walked along the lake shore, now back in Geneva.

"In spite of what's been put out in the public, I'm not really being given a choice," Jackson said. "It's better this way. I'll never be promoted to admiral given my record, and they sure as hell aren't giving me another ship after losing the *Blue Jacket* and the *Ares*. No… I think all things considered it would be best for everyone if I simply requested early retirement. Hopefully it will all end with me, and the rest of you won't have any marks on your records."

"Will you stay on Earth?" she asked. Jackson knew what she was getting at, and he was purposefully avoiding it. While he wasn't sure of what they had together, there was part of him that feared it might be no more than an infatuation based on something that was culturally taboo while he was her commanding officer. He would never insult her by suggesting that, however, so for now he was prepared to just let things progress as they would.

"I'm not certain yet," he said evasively. "There have been some interesting offers from Tsuyo, and Earth's government is interested in possibly having me as a liaison as the individual enclaves are indicating they're not sure they want to reform the Confederacy."

"I wonder what that will mean for CENTCOM and Fleet," Davis said. "With Haven gone and Marcum commanding most of the military power that's now above New Sierra there could be a serious shift in the works that would favor New America."

"Above my paygrade," Jackson laughed. "It's actually the bigger picture I'm more worried about. The Vruahn are still an unknown, and I can't imagine after the elimination of a species as powerful as the Phage that someone else won't step in to fill the void."

"That's a terrifying thought." She shuddered and moved closer to him.

"It is," he agreed. "But I think we have to accept the fact that we've been violently shoved into the next great age of humanity. The centuries of isolation have ended and the Vruahn won't be the only ones that we'll brush up against in the coming years. Blake hinted that there were many others out there, some a lot closer than we might be comfortable with."

"And yet you still think it's a good idea to step down?"

"I do," Jackson nodded. "My time is over. It will be the next generation of officers coming up that will have to face these challenges, hopefully in a much more thoughtful manner than I have."

She didn't answer, but just gave a small, sad smile before looking back out over the still waters of the lake. He took that as a hopeful sign that she realized her place was back on a starship and not worrying about some broken-down captain at the end of his career.

His smile mirrored hers in its sadness, not only for the short time they would likely have together, but for the realization that it was really over. Never again would he walk onto the bridge of a starship as the CO. He would miss it, but he knew in his heart that this was the right decision, not only for him but for Fleet. His greatest hope for the next generation was that they begin positive relationships with their stellar neighbors. The nature of the Phage aside, having the man that was directly responsible for the extermination of an entire species still on a starship bridge might send the wrong message.

****

"I can't believe he's gone," Celesta said, making an effort to keep her face neutral.

"He didn't suffer," Jackson said. "From what we pieced together afterwards we triggered an automated defense system. Apparently our kinetic weapons had left quite an impression and the Phage copied us."

"You didn't scuttle the *Ares*?" she said quietly, changing the subject. They were on the New Sierra Shipyards and Jackson felt like crap for having to tell Celesta about Singh when they were supposed to be celebrating the *Icarus*'s stunning victory over the Phage swarm.

"No," Jackson said. "And that was probably a mistake. We purged all the servers and navigation data, but the powerplant had been shut down while we were on that moon and the Vruahn ship wasn't going to wait around for us to rig her to blow."

"You should have seen Marcum's face when we docked and he found out that you'd already been exonerated by CENTCOM and they'd accepted your retirement," she laughed shortly. "He had some rather unpleasant plans for you."

"None of that is going to splatter over on you, is it?" Jackson asked.

"Not likely," she said. "Had we not been able to pull off such a high kill rate then it would have probably been a different story, but thanks to political pressure we're more or less untouchable right now."

"That's something at least." Jackson looked out over the crowd. He was still wearing his uniform as his retirement wasn't official for another two weeks, but he already felt the separation from the community starting. "Not to mention your reckless charge into the system was what caused the flurry of communication from the core that allowed us to pinpoint it."

"So it's really over," she said after a moment, turning the opposite way from Jackson to look out the large window at the *Icarus*, now docked.

"It is," Jackson said. "There are still some Phage units sitting out there, but without the core they're just idle lumps of material, no will or motivation of their own. They'll die off fairly quick and no more will be produced. I can't believe I was around long enough to see it through."

"It's not going to be the same without you, sir." She turned to him.

"That's not a bad thing, Captain Wright," Jackson said. "You're the future here. If you've learned from my mistakes then it will have not been for nothing."

He reached out and squeezed her shoulder before setting his drink down on a table and walking out of the crowded room. Aimlessly, he walked along a large, sweeping promenade, stopping at a large porthole to watch as no less than a dozen tugs pulled one of the *Dreadnought*-class battleships stern first into the dock. Beyond that he could see three more hulls already being laid for more new generation warships.

As he continued on and felt the thrum of activity break around him like water, the gloom he'd been carrying since returning to Earth began to lift. Singh was dead. His career was over. But regardless of that, thousands of people carried on, building new ships, prepping for new missions. He actually smiled as he thought about all those that would come after him, long after he was dead and gone, each adding to the history and legacy that he'd been a part of for such a short time. He had been struggling to know where he fit in for most of his life. It took talking to an alien intelligence in its dying moments, but he'd finally realized, maybe for the first time, what it truly meant to be human.

Thank you for reading *Counterstrike*,
the conclusion of the Black Fleet Trilogy.
Subscribe to my newsletter for the latest updates on
new releases, exclusive content, and special offers and
connect with me on Facebook and Twitter:
www.facebook.com/Joshua.Dalzelle
@JoshuaDalzelle
Also, check out my Amazon page to see other works
including the bestselling
Omega Force Series:
www.amazon.com/author/joshuadalzelle

From the Author

And there we have it... the conclusion of the Black Fleet Trilogy. This is a story that, from my perspective, was many, many years in the making since I penned the first rough draft in 1998. It has evolved and taken some unexpected turns in this new, final iteration, but I'm overall quite pleased with the end result... maybe more so this third book than anything else I've published thus far.

After sending this book to the editor I sat and really thought hard on what I wanted to do with this universe. Putting it aside as just a trilogy seems to leave a lot of potential stories untold but dragging it out without clear direction just for the hell of it also seems like a mistake. All I'll say is that as of right now I do plan on continuing to write in the Black Fleet universe. In fact, I changed the original ending and kept Jackson alive just for that reason. That being said, Jackson Wolfe's story is concluded and the Phage War is over. I have no intention of trying to figure out some way to string the same story arc along and any future books in this series will likely center around Celesta Wright with the exception of a possible Agent Pike spinoff book.

It's bittersweet to finally have this story complete and out in the world. I've carried this around for a long time and have tweaked and adjusted it over and over while almost never believing that it would actually ever be published. Now I'll need to find some other project to continually fret over.

As always, I can't thank the readers enough. As the number of people who reach out to me grows I find it difficult to keep up and reply to everyone, but I do read all the feedback sent on social media and greatly appreciate it. There are only so many hours of free time we get and the fact that you've chosen to share some of that with me and invest the hours to read one of my books is something I do not take for granted.

Cheers!

Josh

Made in the USA
San Bernardino, CA
15 January 2016